JACKS ARE WILD

A DETECTIVE JACK STRATTON NOVEL

CHRISTOPHER GREYSON

GREYSON MEDIA

Novels featuring Jack Stratton in order:

AND THEN SHE WAS GONE
GIRL JACKED
JACK KNIFED
JACKS ARE WILD
JACK AND THE GIANT KILLER
DATA JACK
JACK OF HEARTS
JACK FROST

Also by Christopher Greyson:

PURE OF HEART

THE GIRL WHO LIVED

Jacks Are Wild
Copyright © Greyson Media April 2, 2014

Find out more about the author and upcoming books online at www.ChristopherGreyson.com.

ISBN: 1-68399-040-4
ISBN-13: 978-1-68399-040-6

CONTENTS

1

BECAUSE OF WHO I AM

TEN YEARS AGO

As she looked across the schoolyard at the sea of boys in identical black pants, white shirts, and black ties, Angelica spotted her little brother's curly mop top of dark hair. Ilario was talking to a group of boys outside the cafeteria. Dodging and weaving, she rushed up to him and skidded to a stop.

"You told Paolo we're staying after school, right?" She grabbed his shoulders.

He rolled his eyes. She couldn't tell if it was from embarrassment or because she shook him. He pulled her hands off and walked a few feet away from the boys. "Yeah, I told him. But I don't like this. Paolo's still freaked because of everything that's gone down."

"I know. But you'll cover for me, right?"

"I'm worried he still has someone keeping an eye on us." Ilario looked around nervously. "You have to be back before the driver gets here to pick us up."

Angelica's big brown eyes lit up with excitement. "I will."

"Don't cut it close. You know how mad he gets."

She leaned in and whispered, "We're only going behind the parking lot. I just want to talk to him." She pressed her elbows to her sides and tried to contain her giddiness.

"Yeah, you want to *talk* to him." Ilario puckered his lips. "Talk to his *mouth*."

She blushed and teasingly whacked him on the arm.

He laughed.

Angelica kissed her brother on the cheek, flung her backpack across her shoulders, and took off back into the school. Heading upstream like a salmon, she fought her way against the flow of kids who poured out the door. As soon as she broke free, she sprinted down the hallway toward the rear parking lot. Her new, shiny black shoes clicked on the tiled floor as her black hair streamed behind her.

Every day, one of her father's drivers took her and her brother to and from school, but today was different. The ruse of staying after school gave her a little over an hour to spend with Anthony, and she didn't want to waste any of it.

As she approached the rear exit of the private school, she stopped, whipped off her backpack, and looked down at her starched white school uniform. She frowned. *Men must make these.* Using her fingers, she fanned out her hair and smoothed down her shirt, then straightened up and pushed the door open.

And there he was, waiting beside his car. Suddenly she couldn't breathe. To Angelica, Anthony Marinetti was everything she'd ever hoped for in a boyfriend. He was tall, sweet, and most importantly to her, he loved art.

A huge smile spread across his face when he saw her.

"Hey, Anthony." She gave him an awkward little wave. They both knew they couldn't risk an open hug in the middle of the parking lot, but their bodies still pulled toward each other like magnets.

"Hi."

They had been secretly dating for a while now, and Angelica had completely fallen for him. But this was the first time they'd seen each other outside of school hours. Anthony had never asked her why, at seventeen, she couldn't tell her parents she was dating, and she'd never explained. She didn't want to scare him away, which was why she'd never told him her real last name either.

She smiled as she opened her door and hopped into the car.

Anthony frowned. "I'm supposed to get the door for you." His hands went up in mock exasperation.

"That's old-fashioned." She giggled and shut the car door.

Anthony drove them down the short gravel utility road at the back of the parking lot and pulled over in a reasonably secluded spot. It was a private place where all the kids liked to hang out. He turned to her, and a smile spread across his handsome face.

Angelica's heart skipped a beat, and she felt the color rise in her cheeks. "I made you something," she said. She opened her backpack and took out two pieces of cardboard taped together. Lowering her head, she slid out the paper from between them and held it out for him with both hands.

It was a sketch of them sitting on a seawall with a lighthouse in the distance; Angelica's head was resting on his shoulder as they held hands.

"It's unbelievable." His smile widened. "Is this what you were doing during class?"

"You saw me?" She swallowed hard.

"Not *what* you were drawing, just that you were drawing something. I thought Mr. Gillespie was going to catch you."

Angelica cocked her head. "Is that why you kept coughing? To distract him, so I wouldn't get in trouble?"

He ran his hand through his thick brown hair. "Yeah. You should enter the art contest at school."

"I don't think so."

"You know you can probably win."

Angelica twisted a length of her hair and looked down at the picture. "You think I can win?"

"Are you kidding me?" The corner of Anthony's mouth turned up. "You're so talented. There's a reason Mr. Bowman asked you to join the advanced art class."

Angelica looked down at her lap.

"Don't be embarrassed about being talented." Anthony squeezed her hand. "You have a gift."

She turned back to him and gazed into his deep brown eyes. He stroked the back of her hand once with his thumb, and she melted. Slowly, he leaned forward...

And he kissed her.

Tenderly, she kissed him back. As her hand started to relax, her fingers began to slip away from his, but he gently tightened his grip and held on.

His kisses were even better than she'd imagined. The warmth of his lips sent a tingle through her body. He leaned in, and she wrapped both arms around his neck.

Anthony spoke between his kisses. "You—taste—like—cherry—lip—balm."

She giggled.

Their kisses grew in intensity until the car windows fogged up. As they made out, getting lost in each other, Angelica lost track of time.

Finally she looked at the windows. "What time is it?"

"Not sure, but if the late bus has already left, I'll drive you home myself."

She spotted the clock on the dash. She was late. Very late. "Oh no."

The sound of cars churning up gravel down the little road caused the hairs on the back of her neck to stand up. She tried to wipe away the condensation on the windows, but they were so fogged up she couldn't see anything.

Anthony squeezed her shoulder. "It's okay. It's probably just some other kids."

Both front doors were ripped open. Two large men, one in a thick black leather jacket, dragged Anthony out, while a third man grabbed Angelica by the arm.

"Paolo!" Angelica's voice caught in her throat when she looked up to see her uncle's stern face. He was a barrel-shaped man with thick gray hair. His lips were always curled into a snarl, and his eyes were cold.

"You bring shame on this family," he growled.

"Nothing happened," Angelica cried out as he dragged her away from the car.

"Leave her alone!" Anthony yelled, straining to reach her.

"Shut up!" The guy in the leather jacket slammed Anthony against the car.

Angelica didn't recognize the guy in the jacket, but she knew the other man with Anthony. It was Sal, one of her uncle's lackeys. "Who the hell do you think you are?" Sal shouted in Anthony's face. "I'll teach you some respect."

The guy in the leather jacket grabbed Anthony's arms and yanked them behind his back. Then Sal pummeled Anthony in the stomach.

"*Stop!*" Angelica screamed. She tried to run to him, but Paolo held her fast. She turned to her uncle. "He doesn't know who I am," she pleaded.

Somehow, Anthony managed to rip one hand free, and his fist smashed into Sal's face. Groaning, Sal covered his bloody mouth with one hand. The guy in the leather jacket tried to regain control of Anthony's free arm, but Anthony was swinging it wildly. Cursing, the men and Anthony crashed into the driver's side door.

"Stop hurting him!" Angelica screamed.

"Calm that kid down," Paolo ordered.

"Run, Angelica!" Anthony yelled, still wrestling with the men.

"No!"

A loud bang rang out. The driver's side window shattered; glass sprayed in a huge arc.

Angelica blinked and looked at Anthony. His face turned toward her. His big brown eyes grew dark.

"What the hell?" Paolo bellowed.

"He went for my gun." The guy in the leather jacket stared at the weapon in his hand.

The window broke. It wouldn't have broken unless...

Anthony's body slumped and slid slowly down the side of the car.

"*No!*" Angelica's legs gave out, and she sank to her knees. But Paolo's arm wrapped around her waist and yanked her back to her feet. He threw her over his shoulder and carried her to his car.

She couldn't breathe. The ground sped by swiftly, and then she was flung into the back seat of the Cadillac and the door slammed shut behind her. Outside, Paolo swore at the other men. Someone threw her bag in the back seat behind her, and she looked down at it.

Her crumpled picture had landed at her feet. It was spattered with blood. She reached down and let her fingers stroke the paper.

The front door slammed shut and someone threw the car into reverse. Gravel pinged off the car's underbelly as they fled backward, and then gears ground as the car shifted into drive. Angelica slammed herself up against the rear window and looked back. She could feel a burn in her throat as she screamed—but she didn't hear any sound.

The boy she loved lay face down on the gravel.

The boy she loved was dead.

Because of me. Because of who I am.

Because I am Severino Mancini's daughter.

2

I SHOULD HAVE BEEN A MONK

PRESENT DAY

"It's going to be okay. I have a plan." Replacement held her hands behind her back as she stood by Jack's side.

Jack opened the drawer of the little hallway table and grabbed his gloves.

"You look mad." She eyed him sideways. "Is it because of work?"

Jack wanted to respond, *Oh, nooo, I'm demoted to a beat cop but I'm absolutely thrilled about it*, but instead he stuffed down the sarcastic reply and said, "I'm fine."

"I think my plan is going to make you very happy."

"So you've said. What's this big plan you've been cooking up?"

At six foot one, one hundred ninety-five pounds, and with a muscular frame, Jack towered over Replacement, who was only five four and petite. But even when he loomed over her in his most serious manner and raised one eyebrow, she just put her hands behind her back and shook her head, her brunette ponytail bouncing back and forth. She had spunk.

"I'm *almost* ready to lay it all out," she said, "but not yet. Don't worry, though— you'll love it." She crossed her arms while her green eyes looked up at him. She was dressed in a pair of baggy gray sweatpants and one of Jack's faded high school shirts. He loved how she looked, but right now it only added to his rising frustration.

"What's the plan, Replacement?"

"All I'll say is that I'll soon be contributing something."

"You already contribute." Jack grabbed his keys off the table next to the door. "The apartment's never looked nicer."

"I can do more." She handed him his wallet. "You moved just so I could have my own bedroom."

"It was only a floor down."

"Still, you had to move everything. And it's more money." She stepped in front of him.

Jack caught sight of his reflection in the mirror. Brown hair cut short, dark brown eyes, tall, fit, and ruggedly handsome, Jack could have been the police poster boy— but that wasn't what caused his chest to puff up.

Replacement must have noticed where he was looking, because she reached up and gave his badge a quick polish with her sleeve. "You look great, but try to smile a little more." She gave him a big grin.

As Jack looked at those dimples, he couldn't help but grin back. He grabbed his hat and pulled it down on his head. Then he opened the door, and stopped.

Every time he left the apartment, this same awkward moment replayed. She gave him a quick hug. He hugged her back. And each time, a part of him didn't want to let her go.

"See you later," he muttered and hurried into the hallway.

Jack thundered down the stairs and marched out the door. It was a beautiful winter evening. The warmest winter on record meant the air was only slightly brisk. Jack left his gloves in his pockets as he walked toward downtown Darrington. His Impala sat parked at the curb, with Replacement's blue Beetle in front of it.

Jack sighed. There'd be no driving for him tonight. He had been reduced to walking a beat downtown. He wouldn't even get to drive his favorite police cruiser: the Charger.

Jack looked up at the stars. *It's only temporary.*

***

Jack shoved his hands into the pockets of his patrolman's jacket as he paused on the deserted sidewalk. At eleven fifteen on a Wednesday night in Darrington, the place was a ghost town. He looked up and down Main Street, but there wasn't a single car or person to be seen. In the last two hours, Jack had already walked around downtown four times, and had barely heard a peep.

Collins and his creative punishments. Terrific.

During each of his four loops, he had gone past Vitagliano's Tattoo Parlor. On each of his previous circuits, he'd crossed the street before passing it. But this time the lights were off.

She's gone home. Damn. I should have stopped in. But what would I say? I'm out of my mind. I once had Marisa, who's hot as hell and all over me, but I couldn't bring myself to tell her how much I cared for her, so I let her walk away. And then I start thinking maybe Alice, who can drive me crazy in a good way, is sending me signals, and I might have a chance, but...

Jack realized he'd stopped in the middle of the sidewalk and was talking to himself. He quickly looked around and started walking again.

I should have been a monk.

"Are you stalking me or picketing?" Marisa's velvety voice called out from the darkened doorway of the tattoo parlor.

Jack grinned as she stepped into the light. Marisa Vitagliano was tall for a woman at five ten, and her four-inch heels brought her to eye level with Jack. Her black leather pants showed off her curves, and a cropped, black leather jacket did little to hide her generous proportions.

Jack exhaled. She was drop-dead gorgeous.

He locked on to her big brown eyes. He loved to lose himself in them. "Hey, Angel."

She tilted her head back toward the store, and her long black hair flowed around her shoulders. "Do you want a cup of coffee?"

Jack hesitated, but then nodded.

Marisa opened the door. "I already put a pot on. I turned the lights off so you'd come over to this side of the street." She smiled.

Jack tried to hide his embarrassment with a cough. "I fell right into your trap."

She flicked the lights on as they stepped inside. A long counter with stools sat against the back wall, and by the windows were a couple of tall metal tables with high-backed stools.

"Does that make you my prisoner?" Marisa asked. "I like the sound of that." She slid one hand along the counter as she walked halfway down it. "Pull up a stool. Or are you not allowed to take a break?"

Jack caught the edge of concern in her voice. "It's sort of a walking penance, like KP in the army, but they still let me take a break." Jack took a seat at the counter, and Marisa turned around with two cups of coffee already prepared. "You were pretty confident I'd come in, huh?"

She smiled smugly as she handed him his cup. "After your third lap, I was pretty confident."

"You're okay?" Jack asked.

"With you avoiding me?"

"I'm not avoiding you. It's just that I'm trying—"

"Jack, you know how I feel about you." Marisa sipped her coffee but never took her eyes off his. "The ball's in your court."

"You're not making this easy, are you?"

"I'll try to behave and keep my hands off you."

Jack swallowed. "Thanks."

"How's your puppy?"

Replacement would go crazy if she knew that's what Marisa calls her.

Jack exhaled. "Marisa…"

"Sorry. I just want you to be happy."

Jack scratched his jaw and raised an eyebrow.

"I do," she protested.

"It's not that I don't believe you," he said. "It's just—me, happy? I don't know if I'll ever be happy."

"*I* could make you happy." She scanned his toned forearms, and then his muscular chest.

"Marisa…"

"I didn't say I wouldn't try to seduce you; I just said I wouldn't use my hands." She set down her cup and bit her bottom lip coyly.

"You and me, we've been down this road before." Jack blew out a breath. "How about we stick to coffee tonight?"

Her eyebrows lifted.

Jack leaned back. "It's complicated."

Marisa peeled off her jacket. The T-shirt underneath clung to her body, and Jack had to force himself to look at her eyes. "It's not complicated." She shook her head, her long black hair shimmering. "I can give you a refresher."

"Marisa, you're making this hard."

"Hard?" Marisa smiled suggestively, then held up a hand. "Sorry." She leaned back and crossed her tattooed arms over her chest. "You must have your hands full with your new roommate."

"That's an understatement. She's—Why do you say that?"

"She stopped in this morning." Marisa walked over to the cash register. "She said she knew that you and I were close friends. She'd like us all to get along." Marisa picked up a piece of paper and came back. "Then she asked to put this in the window."

Jack took the paper. It was a flyer. On the top half was a picture of a woman holding a magnifying glass. But it was the words underneath the picture that made his eyes go wide.

REPLACEMENT INVESTIGATORS
DO YOU HAVE A PROBLEM THE POLICE CAN'T, OR WON'T, SOLVE? CALL US FOR RESULTS. WE HELP YOU WHEN THE COPS WON'T.

"Oh, crap. Is she out of her mind? She's gonna get me fired."

"At least she used her own phone number."

"Great, just great." Jack folded up the paper and put it in his pocket. "I need Sheriff Collins reading this like I need…" He turned toward the door. "Speaking of the sheriff, I'd better go."

Marisa suddenly stood bolt upright. "Before you do, can I show you something?"

Jack eyed her suspiciously as she walked over to the thick red velvet curtain that covered the entrance to the back rooms and stopped beside the Italian statue of a female gladiator that perpetually stood guard there. "Marisa, I have enough trouble—"

"No." Marisa's cheeks flushed. "I want to show you something I made."

One look at her smoldering eyes drove any thought of the sheriff out of Jack's mind. "Sure. Lead the way."

He followed her down the hallway to her office. His eyes immediately went to the tattoo table, and he grinned when he remembered that hot and heavy night. But his grin straightened when he saw Marisa standing impatiently next to an easel covered with a tarp.

"The Darrington Art Festival is next week," she explained.

Jack pressed his lips tightly together to hide his smile. He noticed her wringing hands, her twisting foot, and her eyes darting from the floor to him and back again. The only times he'd ever seen this confident woman off her game were the times when she showed him one of her pieces.

"I was thinking about entering this." She pulled back the tarp.

It was a painting of a young girl running through a field. Her long hair flowed out behind her, and her arms were outstretched. You could just make out her face and a hint of her smile.

It was beautiful.

"Do you… Do you like it?" Marisa's brows arched up, and her voice was just above a whisper.

"That's the sketch you were drawing on the cocktail napkin the night we first met," Jack said.

With all the heat of a man-melting stride, Marisa sauntered forward. "You remember?"

Jack's gaze traveled around the painting. The only color in the piece was a hint of blue in the girl's eyes. It was truly stunning.

Marisa was right beside him now, and he could feel her breath on his neck. He nodded, but said nothing. He was speechless. Something about Marisa's work had always moved him, but there was something about this painting that truly touched his heart.

Is it the little girl's smile? I want to just jump in and run away with her, too.

Jack inhaled deeply and enjoyed the feeling of warmth that spread in his chest.

Don't say it. Don't. She's going to enter it in the festival. Don't...

"I want it."

Idiot.

He turned to look at Marisa, and she searched his eyes. He felt her hand on his shirt, and her grip tightened as she pulled him closer.

"It's unbelievable," he whispered.

She leaned forward. And the dam broke. They spilled into each other, hands frantically seeking out straps and buttons. All of Jack's tightly restrained, pent-up desires poured into a fiery passion. He wanted her.

A deep, primal moan of pleasure sounded in his chest as he let himself go, giving in to his need. Her full lips found his, and her tongue slid between them. He reacted, claiming her mouth.

He could feel the heat from her body where it was pressed against his, which was just about everywhere. Her hand rose up the back of his neck until her fingers entwined in his thick hair and pulled him forward. He ground his teeth in pleasure. Seizing her waist with his strong hands, he drew her hips closer. A deep, lush purr escaped her lips. Their tongues circled and curled together as his hands traveled over her toned muscles and her hands found their way to his waist, grabbing his lean hips.

Jack's powerful arms wrapped around her, and he pulled her close. "Marisa," he whispered, as their hands desperately searched each other's bodies and their passion intensified.

Suddenly, Marisa froze. Her eyes were inflamed with desire, but the look on her face was filled with fear.

"What's wrong, Angel?"

She swallowed, and her lip trembled. Then she inhaled and stepped back. "My hand touched your gun."

Jack looked down. "The safety's on. There's no way it could go off."

"I know." She let out her breath. "It just brought back memories. That's all. I hate guns."

He held his arms out. "I'm sorry you're upset."

She hung her head and stepped forward. He pulled her into his arms. He could feel her body trembling.

"It's okay." Gently, he stroked her hair as she rested her body against his. Her hands gripped his shirt.

"I'm sorry I ruined the moment," she murmured into his chest.

Jack placed his hand under her chin and lifted her face up. He knew a little of her past, but not all of it. He wanted to know more. He looked deeply into her eyes. "Marisa, you didn't ruin anything. Do you want to talk about it?"

"No." She lowered her gaze and swallowed. "I need a couple of minutes."

He let out a long breath. "I think I'd better get going anyway." He started to straighten up. "I'm supposed to be on duty, and I've already taken too long of a break." He let go of her and grabbed his jacket and hat from the floor. She looked hurt. He tried to soften it. "Besides, I don't think we'd only be a few minutes." He grinned.

She blushed.

"I'll let myself out the back."

"Are you working tomorrow?"

Jack walked out to the hallway and over to the rear exit, with Marisa following. "I have to start at seven," he grumbled.

"Seven? You're working the night shift again?"

"Collins wants to experiment with a twelve-hour schedule of walking a beat, and I'm the lab rat." He jerked his thumb toward himself.

"Why? Is he out for your head?"

"I broke protocol, and I didn't go to him first. Simple as that." Jack pulled on his jacket, then ran his fingers through his hair before putting his hat on. "Well, back to protecting, serving—and walking." He smirked as he pulled the hat down.

Marisa held the door open for him. "Will you stop by tomorrow?"

"Right after you close."

She kissed his cheek.

Jack walked out the door and into the alley. He reached back to catch the door before it closed. "If you enter that picture in the festival, you'll win."

Marisa clasped her hands together and brought them against her chin. "Do you think so?"

"Anyone who doesn't love that painting is crazy. It belongs in a museum."

She didn't say anything, but he knew his words had touched her. They stood there, and although no words were spoken, they communicated.

Jack had to force himself to walk away. "See you around." He let go of the door, and it clicked shut.

The alley was well lit, and Marisa always made sure it stayed clean. Even the garbage bin and recycling container were neatly arranged. The space between the buildings was just wide enough to back a truck down, but tonight it was empty.

As Jack started down the alley, he noticed a pair of legs sticking out from a doorway. He moved over so he could walk along the far wall as he approached, and his hand moved closer to his pistol. He had been trained to be prepared for anything. *Just like a traffic stop*, he reminded himself. It could be a little old lady, or it could be a little old lady with a shotgun…

"How you doing?" Jack called out as he got closer.

The legs pulled up, and whoever it was stayed partly concealed by the wall. Darrington was a small town, but it still had its share of homeless.

"Warm night, huh?" Jack said.

Thaddeus Ferguson stuck his head around the corner and blinked rapidly. "It's a warm winter. A very warm winter. Good evening, Jack." He adjusted his glasses with one hand and scratched his bushy, unkempt beard with the other.

Jack walked over so he could see all of Thaddeus, including his hands. The small, thin man stepped out and thrust one of those dirty hands forward.

Don't make a face. Shake his hand.

Jack shook Thaddeus's hand and cleared his throat. "Not warm enough for camping. Are you sure you don't want to head to Father Bill's tonight?"

Thaddeus moved closer. Jack tried not to wrinkle his nose at the smell.

"Nope. I got layers." Thaddeus pulled at his thick, worn jacket, revealing a rainbow of cloths and materials underneath. "And Ms. Vitagliano gave me a Danish and a coffee." He held up a battered thermos and something wrapped in a napkin.

Jack looked back at the closed door. "She's a nice lady."

"Ms. Vitagliano is a *very* nice lady. Makes a fine cup of coffee, too. Not too much cream, and lots of sugar. Sometimes she even makes me cocoa"

"Well, if you get too cold, be sure to head over to Father Bill's, okay? You have a good night, Thaddeus."

Jack continued down the alley, toward the street.

"I will, Jack. You take care of yourself, too."

3

JACK'S JUNK

As Jack walked into his apartment, the clock on the oven read 7:28 a.m. He tossed the contents of his pockets onto the counter.

"Hey!" Replacement swiveled around in her chair at the desk, which was set against the far window. "I just cleaned the counter in case you wanted breakfast." She hopped up, walked over, and slid his keys and change into a little wire bin labeled "JACK'S JUNK." She had purchased the bin in an effort to domesticate him. It wasn't working. "How was your night?"

"Filled with danger and excitement." Jack tossed his jacket on the chair. "I'm gonna take a quick shower and try to get a couple of hours' sleep."

"No breakfast?"

"Thanks anyway. Will that offer still be open when I get up?"

"Sure. What time? I'll set my alarm."

"Two o'clock? That way I can get a workout in before I go to work."

"You don't need any cardio," Replacement quipped.

"Funny. Have you been up this whole time? You don't have to do that. Collins is trying to put the screws on me by putting me on the night shift; you don't have to be punished, too."

"I don't mind," she said. "This way I get to spend more time with you. Your shower is ready, sir." She bent at the waist and held her arm out toward the bathroom.

"Thanks," Jack mumbled as he walked by.

This part of her is awesome. It's like I have a cute girl butler or something. What guy wouldn't dig that?

Jack closed the bedroom door, pulled off his clothes, tossed them on the bed, and smiled.

I mean, my dirty clothes won't be here when I get out. She'll wash them. She treats me like a king. And I have no idea why.

He walked into the bathroom and closed the door behind him. He turned on the shower and leaned against the sink as he waited for it to heat up.

Marisa offers herself up on a platter, but Marisa and me... Part of me knows it will never work out.

He stared at his reflection in the mirror.

She's special. Be careful not to hurt her.

His reflection glared back.

The steam started to rise, and he inhaled deeply. His shoulders were sore. On patrol, his head was constantly in motion, and even though he tried to relax, his muscles were always tense and alert. Even in a quiet town like Darrington, being a cop was a dangerous profession. He stepped into the shower and let the warm water rush over him, hanging his head forward so he could loosen up as the heat penetrated his muscles.

The door flew open, and Replacement hurried in. "Can I ask you a big favor?" she said.

Startled, Jack twisted around. His left leg slipped, and his toes smashed into the tub. He caught himself with his right hand and managed to remain on his feet.

"Damn it," he snapped as he grabbed his foot.

"Sorry."

"Get out!"

"The shower curtain isn't see-through. I need to ask you something."

"Is this about that flyer?" Jack called out.

"You saw it?"

"Are you trying to get me in more trouble?" He poked his head out from behind the curtain.

"No. No, I just… I need to get a job, so I thought I could start my own business. I thought it would make you less stressed about your job." She grinned sheepishly. "Surprise."

"Why would you want to be a private investigator? Why don't you do something with computers?" He pulled the curtain back and stuck his head under the water.

"This *is* doing something with computers. And look at what I've done so far. I'm good at it. I can make good money, too."

"Money? As a PI? You've been watching too many TV shows."

"I researched it. You don't think I can do it?"

Jack sighed. He could hear the disappointment in her voice. He hated when she was sad. "I didn't say that."

He couldn't see her, but he could just imagine her jumping up and down in delight. "Awesome! I know it will work."

I didn't say that, either.

"I'm bidding on something online, and… I need your credit card. I'll pay you back."

"Fine. Wait." He peeked out again. "Bidding?"

"It's an auction. I think I can scarf it up cheap."

"Well… don't go too high."

"What's my limit?"

"Listen," Jack said, "if we're gonna have an entire conversation here, can you at least go outside and talk through the door like a normal person?"

Replacement laughed. "Normal people don't talk through doors."

Jack sighed. "Normal people don't walk in on people in the bathroom. What're you buying?"

"Just something I need. I can get it for a hundred, I hope. Tops, it'll run me two."

"Three hundred is the limit."

"Thanks." Replacement left and shut the door behind her.

Jack stayed in the shower until the water started to run cold. When he came out of the bathroom, he saw the bedroom door was closed. He debated going out and talking to Replacement about the PI thing, but quickly changed his mind and got under the covers. Right now, he just needed to sleep.

Please, Replacement, don't be doing anything stupid.

4

GRANDBABIES

Jack and Replacement walked through the doors of the nursing home and approached the short woman behind the counter. Jack had seen her before, but struggled to remember her name.

Replacement gave her a big wave. "Hi, Cristalita."

The woman lit up. "Hello, Alice. Aunt Haddie is expecting you both. She's having a very good day."

Aunt Haddie had Alzheimer's, so a good day was wonderful, but temporary. She was still in the early stages, but somehow Jack's foster sister, Michelle, had gotten her placed in Well's Meadow Nursing Home.

They headed down the red-carpeted hallway, past men and women who sat in wheelchairs or pushed walkers. The Alzheimer's unit was locked down for the patients' safety, though Jack had occasionally responded to calls about patients who had managed to wander off even with the security.

A nurse greeted Jack and Replacement at the door to the Alzheimer's unit, and then took Replacement on ahead. The routine was the same every visit: Replacement and the nurse would go to Aunt Haddie first, and then Jack would come in after a couple of minutes.

I guess it helps if there isn't too much going on too fast.

Jack stood just inside the doors to the unit. There was a little common room off to the side, and two women sat at a table covered in puzzle pieces while a man watched TV. The man turned, smiled at Jack, and gave a little wave.

Jack pushed his back against the wall. He hated being locked in anywhere.

It's not claustrophobia. What do they call hate of locked places? I-wanna-get-the-hell-outta-here-phobia?

An older nurse, with a tray in her hands, hurried over to the exit doors and frowned. She closed one eye, looked up at the ceiling, and made a face. After a moment, she closed both eyes and tapped her forehead. She rolled her head at Jack. "I'm filling in. Do you work here? I forgot the code."

Jack read her nametag: MARTHA. He looked her up and down with mock suspicion. "And how do I know you're the *real* Martha, and not someone who's tied the real Martha up in a closet someplace while you're trying to escape?"

Jack's joke was about as successful as a North Korean missile test. The woman's expression went from confusion to amusement and then to anger.

"Funny," she snipped.

"It was just a joke. I didn't—"

"Jack?" the nurse who had taken Replacement ahead called for him from down the hall.

He gratefully hurried toward her and away from the older nurse, who glowered at him. As he passed an orderly, he pointed back at the door. "She needs out." Then he leaned closer and whispered loudly, "Make sure it's really Martha," and winked.

As he walked into Aunt Haddie's room, his face lit up. She was sitting in a big, comfy chair, and as soon as she saw him, her arms reached out to him. He practically ran to give her frail body a careful hug.

"You can squeeze me tighter than that," she said. "I won't break." She rocked him back and forth, then pushed him back and held him at arm's length. Her big brown eyes searched his face.

"How are you, Aunt Haddie?"

"Blessed and happy, now that my babies are here." She reached a hand back and squeezed Replacement's.

Jack caught the nurse's puzzled look—she was probably wondering how Jack and Replacement could be Haddie's babies, since she was black and they were white. Replacement apparently felt the need to offer an explanation: "We're foster kids. Aunt Haddie has lots of babies."

Aunt Haddie reached out and ran her hand through Jack's hair. "This one carries on my husband's name: Jack Alton Steven Stratton."

Jack kept himself from making a face, but Replacement turned away and coughed. Jack had recently added the "Steven," in remembrance of his father, but he had placed it *before* Alton to prevent his initials from spelling Jack A.S.S.

Replacement is going to be cracking up all the way home.

Aunt Haddie settled back in her chair. "Speaking of babies, when are you two going to get married?"

Jack's mouth fell open, and Replacement's face flushed.

"Oh, don't start going all wishy-washy. Two people in love like you two should get married, and I do love weddings." Aunt Haddie turned to the nurse. "I didn't raise them at the same time. Jackie was out of the house when Alice came. She's been head over heels for him since then. She used to keep his picture in her drawer and—"

"Aunt Haddie!" Replacement swallowed, and she frantically shook her head.

"Oh, don't worry; he knows it." She patted Replacement's hand. "And Jackie's been just as smitten with her since they got together. He takes such good care of her, but just watch how he looks at her when he thinks no one else is looking." She winked at the nurse. "That's the key. He just melts like butter and goes all soft."

Now it was Jack's turn to wave his hands for her to stop.

Aunt Haddie ignored his protests. "I'm not getting any younger, and my mind keeps wandering." She put both hands on her legs, but a grin crossed her lips. "I want some grandbabies."

Jack looked at Replacement and burst out laughing.

Aunt Haddie laughed too and squeezed Replacement's hand. "All right." She stroked Replacement's arm. "I won't talk about it anymore… today."

They visited with her for over an hour. She talked about the present, but Jack gently guided her to reminisce; he loved it when she talked about the past. Aunt Haddie told the most wonderful stories, but Jack liked the ones about Chandler and Michelle best.

She went on and on, and they both listened and laughed as she talked about a time he was so glad was not forgotten.

5

IN NEED OF YOUR SERVICES

Jack set down his fork and put his dishes in the sink, then walked over to the hall table to look again for his gloves. It was supposed to be a little brisk tonight, so he thought he might need them.

"What're you looking for?" Replacement called to him. She was doing something on the computer.

"My gloves. I can't find them," he muttered, and went to look in the bedroom again.

Jack cracked his neck. Finding his gloves was a small detail, but his years in the Army had taught him that little details could save your life.

Like I'm gonna die if I… Damn it. Just find the gloves, Jack.

Someone knocked at the front door. Jack went to answer it, but stopped at the bedroom door when he saw Replacement was already ahead of him. Before she opened the door, she straightened her shirt and stood up straight. Then she saw Jack watching, and she froze.

"This may be for me." She cleared her throat.

Jack saw her pause to take a deep breath. Then she opened the door. From this angle he couldn't see who was on the other side, and he didn't hear what they said.

"Oh, *really*?" Replacement's voice was loud, and Jack could tell something was wrong. Then she turned around, her eyebrows knitted together and her shoulders square. She marched stiffly over to Jack and held out her hand. Clasped between the fingers of her trembling fist were his missing gloves.

And then Marisa walked through the front door with an amused grin on her face.

"Here are your gloves." Replacement tapped them against Jack's chest. She jerked her thumb in Marisa's direction. "She said you forgot them when you stopped in to *visit* last night."

Jack swallowed. "I'm on… neighborhood liaison patrol. It's my job to check in with the local businesses, including Marisa's."

Jack looked over Replacement's head to Marisa, who nodded in mock approval.

"Yeah, right," Replacement snapped. She spun around to face Marisa. "Thanks. I'm really sorry you have to go *now*, but I have to see Jack gets off to work—"

"Actually, I came to see you," Marisa said.

Both Jack's and Replacement's mouths fell open.

"Me?" Replacement asked.

"Her?" Jack added.

Marisa took out a folded piece of paper. "I have need of your services." She handed the flyer to Replacement, who beamed. Jack glowered.

Replacement stepped aside and motioned Marisa into the living room. "How can I be of assistance, Ms. Vitagliano?" She rushed over to grab a pen and notebook off the desk. Marisa took a seat on the old couch, and Replacement pulled the wheeled computer chair forward.

"I have a problem," Marisa replied.

"You do?" Replacement said excitedly, then quickly calmed. "I mean… certainly. What's the issue you need assistance with?"

"Graffiti. Someone's been spraying horrible graffiti outside, behind my store. I want to know who it is."

"What? Wait a second." Jack walked over to tower over both of them. "You never told me—"

Marisa held up a hand as she looked at Replacement. "I did go to the police, but it's obvious there's little they can do."

Jack opened and closed his mouth silently a few times, then stormed into the kitchen.

"You want *me* to find them?" Replacement pointed at herself.

Marisa leaned forward and tapped the flyer. "That's what the ad says. The police said it was some local teenager, and they would have to catch him in the act."

"Who said that?" Jack snapped.

"His name was Officer Murphy."

"Murphy? He's a moron, that's why he said that. Moron cops say stuff like that, and Murphy's a moron. Why the hell would you go—"

"Jack, please." Replacement shot a quick glare at Jack, then turned back to Marisa and sat up straighter. "I'm sorry about the interruption. And the vandalism. My rate is…" She frantically flipped through her notebook. "I charge…"

"The first time I had to have the paint removed, it cost me two hundred dollars," Marisa said. "Now they're saying it'll be five hundred because there's a much bigger area that was painted. I'll pay you five hundred to find the person responsible."

"Done." Replacement's hand shot out and she shook Marisa's. "You said you hired someone to remove the graffiti. Have they yet?"

"Not yet. They're coming tomorrow."

"Good. I need to get pictures. I can go back over with you now?"

Marisa's lips pursed, and she clicked her tongue. "Actually, I did need to talk with Jack, and—"

"You can talk with him on the way. He has to go downtown for work anyway." Replacement got up and hurried into her bedroom.

Jack stood at the sink and smirked. Marisa sauntered over.

"I don't know what you have planned," Jack whispered, "but this is about as safe as a cruise ship speeding past icebergs on its maiden voyage."

"Shut up, Jack." She wrinkled her nose. "I do want to catch the little bastard who keeps putting that garbage on the outside of my shop."

"Is it worth half a grand?"

"And I want to talk to you."

"Now *that's* worth a grand." He winked, and she pushed him.

***

Replacement rattled off questions as they made the fifteen-minute walk downtown. As Jack strolled behind the two women, the contrast was obvious. Marisa was tall and sexy—she strutted down the sidewalk as if it were a catwalk. Next to her, Replacement looked like a perky fitness instructor, her ponytail bobbing and her hands gesturing in every direction.

I love being around both of them.

They burst out laughing and turned back to look at him. He raised an eyebrow, and they laughed even harder.

And they can make me a bit crazy, too.

They stopped behind the tattoo parlor, where someone had spray-painted a large section of the brick. Replacement snapped pictures.

Jack tilted his head. "I can't read it. You said it was horrible. What's it say?"

Marisa looked at him in disbelief. "I don't know what it says, but it's definitely horrible. Just look at it." She thrust her hands forward. "You can't read it because of the overspray, and they used flat pastel orange and shiny fluorescent green. It's hideous work." She shuddered. "The color combination alone makes me want to throw up."

Jack coughed and looked down. *She's an artist.*

"I'm going to let you two ladies work on this. I'm going to go try to *not* catch the bad guys—so Replacement here can get more customers."

"That would be great," Replacement called over her shoulder, snapping another shot.

Marisa leaned close to Jack and whispered, "Can you stop by later? I *really* need to see you."

The intensity in her voice bothered him. "Are you okay?" he asked.

Marisa frowned and looked down. When she looked up again, Jack's whole body tensed. Even though the corner of her mouth had curled up, he could see fear in her eyes.

"I keep having this bad feeling," she said, her shoulders hunched. "Like somebody's watching me."

"Have you noticed anything? Seen anything?"

"Maybe I'm just being paranoid. Who'd be watching me?" She put her hand on his shoulder, and a forced smile twitched across her lips.

Replacement walked back to them with a serious expression on her face. "Okay, we need to talk. Do you have an office?"

"I'm fine, Jack." Marisa leaned in to hug him, and whispered in his ear, "It's probably just me missing you."

"I'll stop by and check in on you later," Jack reassured her.

"Bye, Jack." Replacement waved.

Jack watched the two women walk inside. He was worried.

Paranoid? No, with her past, it's not being paranoid. It's staying alive.

***

One of many problems with walking the endless downtown beat was that the monotony made Jack think about things he'd rather leave alone. Like Replacement. And Marisa. And the both of them working together.

And he was honestly concerned about Marisa. She was the type of woman who'd remain calm in an earthquake; nothing got her flustered. And yet something had. Some unknown blackness made Jack's chest tighten and his palms sweat.

He clenched his fists. He hated that feeling. But at the same time, part of him also loved it. He didn't know whether it was the adrenaline or something else buried inside, but there was a part of him that embraced the rush. It had almost cost him his life on more than one occasion, but when the alarm bells rang and every sane person ran the other way screaming in fear, Jack ran straight at the threat with a smile on his face.

He approached Marisa's tattoo parlor. The lights were off. He checked his watch: 11:10. He expected her to walk out of the doorway again, like she had last night, but no, this time the place was deserted. He tried the door. It was locked. He knocked. No answer.

Damn. She was nervous, but it was just a feeling, right?

He peered in the window but couldn't see anyone. A lone car turned onto the road, and Jack eyed the driver. It was just the guy who ran the laundromat on the corner. He waved at Jack as he drove past.

Jack glanced once more at the deserted store. *I'll come by tomorrow. After all, she spent the evening with Replacement. Maybe she's just had enough for the day.*

6

TWO'S ENOUGH

Jack came home to find Replacement asleep on the couch. He quietly dropped everything from his pockets onto the counter and looked at the clock: 7:29 a.m. He slipped his shoes off and walked over to the sofa. Replacement lay curled up in a ball, a blanket wrapped tightly around her body. As always, she had a soft sheet clutched against her face and chest like a security blanket. Jack smiled. He wanted to wake her up to talk to her. *I'm like a little kid. I want to wake her up so she'll play with me...*

It was crazy how his brain kept going back to Replacement and Marisa. *How is that? There are, like, seven billion people on the planet, and I've met the only two I can't get out of my head? Two? What's the percentage on that?*

Jack sighed. He considered trying to get Replacement to her own bed, but he knew she liked the comfortable couch. *She probably stayed up half the night for me anyway.*

So he adjusted the blanket around her, tiptoed into his bedroom, and quickly fell asleep.

***

Jack heard giggling, but he couldn't tell where it was coming from. He looked up to see a field stretched out before him, the tall grass blowing in the breeze.

I'm dreaming.

The sky was a crystal blue and completely clear. He could almost feel the warm breeze on his face.

I like this dream.

A little girl, previously hidden by the grass, jumped up and ran away from him.

"Hey," he called out to her.

She turned her head, and Jack saw the side of her face.

She's laughing.

Her arms went out wide, and her brown hair streamed behind her. Jack ran after her. Her giggling was infectious, and between that and the sun, he felt warmth beginning to grow in his chest. He stretched his own arms out wide so he could feel the tops of the tall grass tickle his hands as he ran.

"Wait for me," he yelled.

The girl looked back. The smile had vanished, and now Jack could see fear in her eyes. Her giggles had changed to shrieks. She wasn't happy; she was terrified.

Jack held out his hand to her and quickened his pace. "No, kid, I'm not going to hurt you."

But the girl's little legs moved even faster. And when she glanced over her shoulder again, Jack could see that she wasn't looking at him, but at something behind him. He turned.

A black cloud was rushing toward them. It looked like a giant wave that had already broken but was still hurtling forward, crushing the grass and shaking the ground as it thundered on.

"Run!" Jack shouted.

He tried to sprint after her, but pain shot through his legs, and he couldn't move. His feet were frozen to the ground.

He looked up, only to see that the little girl had stopped too. She faced him now. Their eyes locked.

"Run!" Jack ordered as he braced himself for the impact of the wave. *"RUN!"*

And then the cloud slammed into him, sucked him under. Darkness enveloped him, and the wave rolled him end over end, dragging him along the ground. Rocks and debris bashed and cut him. He tried to grab on to something, or to swim through the cloud, but his limbs just flailed at the void.

Can't breathe. I can't breathe!

His chest tightened and his eyes burned; he struggled to hold on to what little breath he had left in his lungs. Then, suddenly, his head broke the surface. Below him, the wave continued to grow, lifting Jack higher and higher.

And he saw the little girl below, standing frozen as the wave towered above, poised to crash down upon her.

***

"RUN! RUN!" Jack sat up, screaming.

Replacement rushed into the room. Jack scrambled out of bed and leapt to his feet, panting. His hands were up and ready to fight.

Replacement held out her hands. "It was a dream, Jack. You're okay. Everything's okay."

Jack looked wildly around the room, eyes wide and lips twitching. He slowly lowered his arms.

Replacement started forward, but Jack shook his head. "No. I'm good. I just need a second." He held up his hand and breathed deeply three times. Then he lurched into the bathroom and shut the door. As he grabbed the edge of the sink, he lowered his head and arched his back.

Damn it. Me and my dreams. And to think, some people never dream. Not me. It's like I never stop.

He splashed water on his face and neck, then rested his elbows on the sink and let his fingers dangle in the running water. After a few minutes, he returned to the bedroom. Replacement was waiting for him, a glass of water in her hand.

"Thanks." Jack grinned sheepishly. "I think I should go for a run."

"A run? You only got a couple of hours' sleep." Replacement frowned. "And you've been doing nothing but walking at work."

Jack pulled some sweats out of the bureau. "I won't be able to sleep."

"Can I come?" She tilted her head.

"I doubt I'll be good company."

***

They jogged through a sprawling subdivision. Jack set a hard pace, and Replacement's much shorter legs had to move twice as fast as his, but she still breathed easily. Jack watched her out of the corner of his eye. Her head was in constant motion, and he noticed her lips moving from time to time. She looked up during one of those times and blushed.

"I talk to myself," she huffed.

"Me too. Don't sweat it."

Her head moved from side to side. "No, I mean I really *talk* talk to myself. Like both sides of the conversation. Sometimes aloud. It makes people think I'm nuts."

"I heard it can help you figure stuff out. That's why I do it."

She beamed. "Me too."

Jack smiled too, then focused on the road. He really wanted to push it, hoping the run would wear him down enough so he could sleep without dreaming.

But it didn't work. They ran hard for almost an hour before heading back to the apartment, but even so, Jack just lay in bed wide awake, staring at the ceiling, thinking. Finally he just got out of bed to pace around the apartment instead.

Replacement was crafting a list of the things she needed to start her private investigation business. Every time Jack passed through the living room, she asked whether she could get him something. And every time he would refuse and continue to pace—or he did push-ups, or he opened and closed cabinets, or he headed back to the bedroom to try again.

Eventually when he came out the bedroom, he found Replacement waiting with a big glass of warm milk and a grin.

"Drink this," she said, handing him the glass. She crossed her arms and tapped her foot while he downed the milk in two big gulps. Then she took the glass back and turned him around. "Now, get on the bed. On your stomach."

She pushed him teasingly forward. He lay down on his stomach, letting his head flop onto the mattress. She yanked the pillow out from under him, then climbed onto the bed so she could straddle his lower back.

"You don't have to give me a massage," he insisted.

She pushed his head into the mattress. Her hands ran up his neck and over both sides of his head. He moaned.

"Yes, I do. I want to get some work done, and I'm not going to get anything done with you going around banging cabinets and hovering around me like a puppy."

I'm not hovering.

He had to admit, she was good at this. Very good. He moaned again as she continued to work on his head. When she reached his back, he was almost drooling. By the time she finally reached his feet, he was mush.

Finally she pulled the blanket over him, and before he could mutter "thank you," he was asleep.

7

DEATHTRAP

"Jack." Someone shook him. "Wake up."

Replacement started to pull the blanket off him, but he grabbed it tightly and sat up, scowling.

"Knock it off," he snapped.

"Boy, did you wake up on the wrong—"

"Sorry. I haven't woken up yet." Jack rubbed his eyes. "What?"

"Do you have Marisa's number?"

"In my phone."

"I looked. I have the same number as you."

"Then call it."

"I did; she isn't answering. I was hoping you had a different number. I left a message, but I really need to know if she took pictures the first time someone tagged the store. Can you ask her?"

"Sure. You woke me for this?"

"You need to get up anyway."

Jack did a double take when he saw the clock: 6:45 p.m. "Why didn't you wake me sooner? I have fifteen minutes to get there or Collins will write me up."

"Sorry, I was online and—" Replacement stepped back as Jack rushed past her into the bathroom.

Jack brushed his teeth, splashed water on his face, and hurriedly got dressed. As he yanked open the bedroom door, Replacement called out, "Did you shave?"

"Crud."

He spun around and shaved in less than two minutes. When he raced back into the living room, Replacement was standing next to the door with a bagel sandwich and a thermos of coffee.

Jack grabbed both and then kissed her cheek before rushing out. He was halfway down the hallway before he realized what he'd done—and realized that Replacement had gasped when he'd done it. As he thundered down the stairs, a grin spread across his face.

As he swung open the door to the Impala, he stuck his hand into his pocket for the keys and groaned. "Damn it!" He rifled through his pockets, looking for the keys, and realized they were still upstairs. And he only had maybe four minutes to get to the station.

Luckily, time and use had worn down the ignition on his 1978 Chevy so that if you jiggled it just right, you could start the car without a key. Sure enough, after only two twists, the ignition turned and the engine roared to life.

"Yes!"

Jack gunned the Impala all the way to the police station. He flew into the parking lot, past rows of police cars, and slid to a stop in front of the sprawling two-story building. He turned off the car, hopped out, and hurried up to the double doors of the station, smiling. He'd made it with half a minute to spare.

But just as he reached the top of the steps, he saw something that made him pause. Officer Billy Murphy was pulling out of the parking lot—in the Dodge Charger that Jack loved. And Murphy saw Jack, too. He gave Jack a smug sneer before peeling out of the parking lot and speeding down the street.

Jack stood there, burning. It was like watching your girl walk away with a guy you know is a scumbag.

Sorry, baby.

He sighed and pushed through the double doors. As he entered, Officer Kendra Darcey glanced up at the clock and laughed.

"You like living on the edge, Jack."

"I had plenty of time." He grinned as he walked over to give her a hug. "How've you been?"

Kendra was twenty-four. She wore her blond hair pulled back in a ponytail, and her blue eyes seemed to reflect her constant energy. A four-inch scar ran from the corner of her chin to her eyebrow. A huge smile spread across her face, then vanished just as fast. "Actually, I got your old shift." She shrugged. "Sorry, but it's pretty sweet."

Jack raised an eyebrow. "Yeah, it was."

"Can I make it up to you?" She grinned sheepishly. Jack noticed that when her cheeks flushed, her scar stood out a little more.

"Don't worry about it. What could you do?" He patted her shoulder and headed to the assignment desk.

Kendra followed him. "I still feel bad."

He grabbed his disappointingly thin folder and knew before he opened it what his assignment would be. *Neighborhood relations. Walking a beat around downtown for yet another shift. Fantastic.*

"Maybe you could talk to Collins?" Kendra suggested.

"It won't do any good. I might as well run straight into a wall."

"Do you want me to try?"

"To talk to Collins? Go ahead, but my money's on the wall. Seriously, thanks, but no thanks. If you do, we'll both be screwed. Right now it's just me. At least it's still warm out."

"Can I buy you a drink when you're done?"

"I'm working the late shift. I won't be done till seven in the morning. I'll take a rain check?"

"Anytime."

***

The first thing Jack did on the night's patrol was head straight to the tattoo parlor. A tall, lanky guy stood behind the counter. His head was shaved on one side, but his black hair was long on the other side. He went a little pale when Jack walked in.

"Hi. I'm looking for Marisa."

"Not in."

"What time do you expect her?"

The guy spread his hands out on the counter. "She's the boss, and… she's Marisa. Who knows?" He shrugged.

He's right. Marisa goes where and when she wants. "Can you tell her I stopped by?"

"Sure." The guy grabbed a pen and scribbled a note.

"Has she been in today?" Jack asked.

"Nope."

"Thanks."

The bell over the door chimed, and three kids—who Jack was certain were too young for tattoos—entered, talking excitedly. But when they saw Jack in his police uniform, they nearly fell over each other in their scramble to back out the door. The guy behind the counter laughed, and Jack smiled.

But he thought again of Marisa, and his mood darkened again. *I should go by her apartment. She could at least call…*

He stepped outside, shot a glance up at the stars, and resumed his beat.

***

By eight p.m., Jack was walking along the outskirts of downtown, where larger, older, and very expensive houses were packed together along tree-lined streets. Their lawns were small, but always perfectly manicured, even in the winter. And if a car was in one of the driveways, it looked as if someone had just driven it off the dealer's lot.

Jack twisted his hands and cracked his wrist. Having grown up poor, he had to watch himself to make sure he didn't slip into an automatic dislike of people of means.

The people in those houses worked hard for their money.

Some of them, anyway.

He looked up and down the street. There was one car in the neighborhood that stood out like a sore thumb—an old brown sedan parked haphazardly in front of a colonial.

Mrs. Sawyer is out and about. The drivers and pedestrians of Darrington had best be careful.

He crossed the street and spotted Mrs. Sawyer descending a new handicap ramp on the side of the house. She waved.

"Jackie, it's so good to see you."

He walked over to her, gratefully accepting a hug. The faux fur on her thick brown coat tickled his nose as he gingerly hugged her thin frame.

"It's nice to see you, too, Mrs. Sawyer. How's the General?"

"He's doing well. He doesn't like the cold, but there are plenty of mice to catch inside now." She made a big show of frowning.

Jack laughed. "And how are you?"

"I'm well. I was just visiting my good friend Madeline Hopkins." She held out a gloved hand toward the colonial. "She fell and broke her hip. We used to go to Finnegan's every Sunday for brunch, but since the fall she hasn't been able."

"That's too bad."

"Yes, but she's doing much better now. And now that she had them put this ramp in, she'll be up and about lickety-split."

Jack looked at the new ramp, then noticed the sign beside it on the lawn: A-PLUS CONSTRUCTION. His hands balled into fists.

A-Plus is Murphy's moonlighting business. If he made this thing, it'll probably fall apart and kill someone.

He looked up and down the ramp with a scowl. He took a few steps to one side, glaring at the untreated lumber and joists that even he could tell were spaced too far apart.

"What's wrong, Jackie?"

"A guy I know made this ramp, and he did a pi—" Jack cleared his throat. "A poor job of it. He should have used pressure-treated lumber, and the joists are off. Look at the supports." He pointed. "The cement is already cracking."

"Is he a friend of yours?" Mrs. Sawyer's words were clipped.

"A friend?" Jack snapped. "No. He's a jerk."

"Well, that's a good thing." She turned around and grabbed the railing. "I'm going to go tell Madeline everything you just said and insist she get a full explanation."

Jack suppressed a smile. "I don't mean to alarm you, Mrs. Sawyer, but you should also be aware that the brackets on the railing you're holding are interior brackets—definitely not what's needed here. They could pull right out."

Mrs. Sawyer gasped and let go of the railing. "I'm going to insist that man rip this whole deathtrap down and do it again properly."

"That's what I'd do," Jack said. "But he can be pretty stubborn. If he says he won't do anything, you may have to call the town business board."

"I'm going to do more than that. I'm going to call the inspector's office."

"Good thinking."

Her eyes went wide and she clicked her tongue. "And they have that special TV news segment they're doing now. You know the one? The one with the girl reporter, the little brunette who wears too much eyeliner. She asked for stories about people taking advantage of the elderly. Well, now she's going to get one. Thank you, Jackie."

"Just watching out for the people of the community," Jack said. He waved as she headed back up the ramp.

Sticking it to Murphy had nothing to do with it. Nothing at all.

Jack walked away, whistling.

8

WAS?

It was almost eleven when Jack looked in the door of the tattoo parlor for the fifth time. The tall, lanky guy was still there. Jack pushed the door open and poked his head in.

The tall guy shook his head when he spotted Jack. "She's still not here." He made a face at a short girl dressed all in black, with black eye shadow, who sat at the end of the counter.

"Did she call?"

"Nope. Sorry."

Jack's phone buzzed, so he let the door swing shut and stepped back onto the sidewalk. He had a text from Replacement.

U TALK TO MARISA YET? I NEED PICS!!

Jack sighed. That dumb graffiti job was the least of his concerns. Marisa should not have worried him and then just disappeared like this. But he knew he was probably worrying over nothing.

I'm letting that stupid nightmare freak me out. She probably just started a new painting and got sucked into it. After my shift, I'll go by her apartment.

Jack's heels clicked as he marched down the sidewalk. At the corner, he turned and saw Thaddeus standing near the entrance of the alley, rocking from one foot to the other. The man turned in Jack's direction. Jack waved.

Thaddeus ran, disappearing into the alley.

Jack was so surprised he just stood there for a moment.

Why would...?

Thaddeus's words rang in Jack's head: "Ms. Vitagliano is a very nice lady."

Jack's feet pushed against the concrete as he flew forward like a sprinter off the block. He covered the short distance to the entrance of the alley in ten long strides, just missing the wall as he rounded the corner. He saw Thaddeus ahead, running as fast as his long coat would allow.

Jack surged forward and bellowed, *"Freeze!"* His voice was so loud in the narrow alleyway it echoed off the bricks.

Thaddeus froze.

Jack slowed to a walk and put his hand on his gun. "Turn around slowly and let me see your hands."

Thaddeus turned around and raised two shaking hands. Jack took one look at his face and knew those hands weren't shaking out of fear.

He's angry.

"Thaddeus, what's wrong?"

Thaddeus's eyes narrowed. "You want to know what's wrong? *You.* You're what's wrong. You and the corrupt institution that's been designed to 'protect and serve.' Serve? Ha. Protect?" He spat on the ground.

Jack angled his body slightly and held up a hand. *It could just be another one of his rants.* "Can you give me a little more to go on here, Thaddeus?"

"I told you that girl was the sweetest thing."

Jack went cold.

Was?

"Marisa?"

Thaddeus nodded.

"What about Marisa?"

Thaddeus let his hands drop to his sides, and the anger fell from his face. "I tried." His voice was now soft, and his shoulders slumped.

"Where's Marisa?"

As Jack said the words, bands tightened around his chest. *This is not happening. She's fine.*

"I don't know. I told them what happened."

"Who? Who did you tell?" Jack took two steps forward.

"The police. I told them, but…" His whole body went rigid, and he screamed in Jack's face. *"YOU LAUGHED AT ME!"*

Calm. Soften your body language. Non-threatening.

Jack tried to invoke his training, but instead he threw it out the window. He leaned in and growled, "Thaddeus, you're not going to yell anymore. Got it? Now, when did you last see Marisa?"

Thaddeus shrank back. "Last night. I was coming to get a ham sandwich. Ms. Vitagliano told me she'd have one for me, but there was a car near the back door."

"What kind of car?"

Thaddeus scratched his beard. "Silver. Four doors."

"Did you notice the make of the car? Ford? Chevy? Honda?"

"No. I saw two guys, and then I hid."

"Did you see these guys? What they looked like?"

"Only one. I think he was Asian."

"Asian? Anything else about him? What he was wearing?"

"He had on a black shirt, but it was hard to tell because his whole body was tattooed." He moved his hand all around his upper body. "And he had black, spiky hair, all pointed up."

"What about the other guy?"

"I couldn't see him."

"Marisa was with them?" Jack tried to picture the three people and the car.

"Yes."

"Did they see you?"

"No. I hid."

"What did Marisa look like?"

"Scared. She was really scared." Thaddeus's lip trembled. "I think they took her."

9

THE TITANS

Sirens and lights filled the alley as cruisers continued to arrive. Jack stood outside the rear door until Sheriff Collins's car pulled in.

"Sheriff Collins, I didn't think—"

"You and that statement seem inseparable, Stratton!" Sheriff Collins snapped in his twang. *"You didn't think."*

"Sir, I have a witness who—"

"You have a witness who filed a police report last night, Jack. *Last night.* You're not the only cop in the station, Stratton. Get yourself and your *witness* in my car. We're going back to the station."

"But, sir—"

"It's not a request." Sheriff Collins spun on his heel and marched for the car.

Jack took Thaddeus by the elbow and followed. "It's okay, Thaddeus. We just—"

"Actually, it's not okay, Jack." Collins's tan face was beet red as he got in the cruiser. As soon as Jack and Thaddeus were inside, he rammed the car into gear.

"Sheriff Collins, Thaddeus saw—"

"I know what he saw. You might not think it, but I do my job."

"I'm not saying otherwise, sir, but this is a possible abduction, and nothing was done."

"Nothing?" Collins strangled the steering wheel. "We checked it out, Jack, and that's what it looks like—nothing. But something *was* done. I reported it to the state, and now I have two Feds sitting in my office. They want to speak to the both of you."

"Me?" Jack asked.

"You called it in, Jack. They heard. Why the hell would you call for backup when he filed the report yesterday?"

Jack's hands went up. "I didn't know he filed a report."

"I *told* him I already went to the police station," Thaddeus corrected.

Collins glared at Jack.

"I didn't think—"

"There it is again, Stratton: *I didn't think.*" Collins pulled in behind the police station. "I just got all the news crews out of my lobby, and now two Feds are taking their place. Go fix this."

"*Fix* this?" Jack snapped. "Marisa may have been abducted."

Collins turned in his seat to look at Thaddeus. "Nice to see you again, Thaddeus. Do you remember when you spoke with *me* last night?" He shot a quick scowl in Jack's direction.

"I told you what happened."

"You told me about Ms. Vitagliano?"

Thaddeus nodded.

"You said she was walking and didn't appear hurt?"

He nodded again.

"You said you were upset because maybe she gave them your ham sandwich?"

He hesitated. "She gave me a sandwich, but—"

"And you wanted a coffee because it kept you warm?"

"I keep the thermos in my coat."

"Then you asked me if I knew why this winter was so warm. I didn't know, but you said you did. Can you tell Officer Stratton what you told me?"

Thaddeus pulled himself forward. Jack saw Collins's nose wrinkle at the smell, but other than that, his expression was blank.

Thaddeus cleared his throat. "Well, the Russians and the Chinese have been drilling in both the North and South Poles in search of methane. This is very significant because only a little change in the amount of methane in the atmosphere will spell disaster for humans."

"Now…" Collins closed his eyes and turned his head to inhale before continuing. "Why would the Russians and Chinese be purposely making the Earth uninhabitable?"

Thaddeus held up a finger. "Uninhabitable for *us*. But not for the Titans."

"The Titans. You're not talking about a football team, are you, Thaddeus?" Collins directed the question to Thaddeus, but he looked at Jack with eyes that would have made any drill sergeant proud.

"No, no, no. They're from Titan, the sixth ellipsoidal moon from Saturn."

"So, they live on one of Saturn's moons. That would make them…" Collins held out his hand, indicating that Thaddeus should finish his sentence.

"They're aliens."

Sheriff Collins gave Jack a pointed glare.

Jack swallowed and shifted in his seat. "Sir, I know it sounds crazy—no offense, Thaddeus—but he saw those men, and Marisa told me—"

Collins looked at the ceiling and loudly exhaled. "So you know this girl?"

Jack paused. "Yes. And if you were aware… I know certain information."

"What information, Jack?"

Jack's lips pressed together. *I'm so going to want earplugs in just a moment.* "I can't say, sir," he said.

Jack watched the veins in Collins's neck slowly expand. In a voice slightly lower than normal, and through clenched teeth, Collins asked, "Do I *really* have to remind you I'm the sheriff?"

"No, sir."

Collins waited.

Jack tried to stop himself, but he could feel his right eyebrow arch.

"Get out," Collins said.

Jack opened the door.

Collins turned to look straight out the windshield before adding, "And take him with you."

He didn't even raise his voice. That's bad.

Jack hurried Thaddeus up the steps into the station, where a man and a woman were waiting. The man was close to six feet tall with a thin build. Judging by the gray hair and lined face, Jack guessed he was in his mid-fifties. He wore a blue suit, white shirt with a tie, and black shoes. The woman was dressed in a dark blue business suit. She was close to Jack's age, if not a little older. She had short red hair and wore light makeup. Under different circumstances, Jack would have found her quite attractive.

"Stratton?" The thin man's voice was gravelly. Jack shook his hand. "I'm Walter Prescott. This is Jennifer Rivers."

The woman smiled and shook his hand.

Jack gestured to Thaddeus. "This is Thaddeus..."

"Ferguson," Thaddeus finished. He shook Jennifer's extended hand, but Jack noticed that Walter kept his hands at his sides.

"Is there a room where we can speak?" Jennifer asked.

"I'd like to talk to Mr. Ferguson alone for a few minutes," Walter added. His tone made it clear that this wasn't a request.

"Of course," Jack said. He led Thaddeus down the hall by the elbow, and Walter and Jennifer followed. "We have a room right down here." Jack stopped in front of an interrogation room and held the door open.

Walter gestured for Thaddeus to enter, then closed the door behind him, leaving the three of them out in the hallway. "Is there a viewing room?"

"Right over there," Jack said, pointing to the door and trying not to frown.

"Rivers," Walter said, "I've got this. You watch. Stratton, you stay right here."

Jack glared at the older man. Walter seemed like an old, grumpy, by-the-book type of Fed. "I'm the reporting officer," Jack protested.

Walter moved closer until he was nose to nose with Jack. "Let me explain a few things to you, son." His low voice sounded like grating rock. "If it's an abduction, I have jurisdiction. If it *isn't* an abduction, I have jurisdiction anyway. That means you have squat. I just spent a half hour with your boss, and reading between the lines, he doesn't like you. Now, do you want to push this?"

Jack's fist tightened.

Jennifer stepped forward. "Listen. We're on the same side. If something happened to that girl, we want to know. If it didn't, we all want to rule that out, too. Let us talk to him and we can go from there."

Walter grabbed the doorknob to the interrogation room. "This isn't my first dance. I'll find out what happened." He entered, then closed the door behind him.

Jennifer walked Jack partway down the hallway to some benches along the wall. "Thank you for bringing him in, Officer. Walter wants me to observe, so—"

Jack shot her a look. "Wait, are you new to fieldwork?"

Jennifer's nostrils flared. "I'm a federal investigator."

"But you've never done fieldwork?"

"There you go again. I'm trying to help you, Jack."

"I just want to know who's working this case and what their background is."

"I've been an analyst for over three years. I've been recently reassigned to fieldwork."

"Desk analyst? You haven't been in the field? Is this the first time Walter's brought you out? A kidnapping is your debutante ball?"

She winced at the jab. "*Possible* kidnapping. So far this is just a routine welfare check on a woman. But trust me, Walter's been at this for twenty years. He's very good."

Jack wanted to say more, but he bit his tongue. Arguing about Walter picking the wrong time to train a newbie was a no-win situation.

"Just wait here," Jennifer said. She marched over to the observation room door, shot Jack a glare, and went inside.

***

Jack paced the hallway for over half an hour. When his phone buzzed, he looked down to see a text from Kendra.

JUST HEARD YOU'RE AT THE STATION. HOPE EVERYTHING IS GOOD. K.

He clicked the phone off and went back to pacing.

Finally, both doors opened. Jennifer's lips were pressed together, Walter looked as if he'd drunk paint thinner, and Thaddeus just looked sad.

"Thank you for your time, Mr. Ferguson. Ms. Rivers will see you out."

Walter turned to Jack and tilted his head toward the interrogation room. "Inside, Stratton."

Jack brushed by him.

"Have a seat."

"I'm good."

"No, you're not. We may have a problem, Jack. Have a seat."

Jack folded his arms and glared at the man.

"Fine. Be a hard-ass. I just spent an hour of my life talking to a fruit loop, and you want to cop an attitude?"

"Listen. I know Thaddeus is 'out there'—"

"*Out* there? Out there is believing reality TV is real. Totally nuts is what that guy is."

Jack rubbed the back of his neck. "There's more to it than what Thaddeus told you. With your access as a federal agent, if you look into Marisa's background…"

Walter cocked his head. "What about her background?"

"If you have access, you need to look. It's all there."

The door opened, and Jennifer walked in. Walter turned toward her, and Jack caught the slight shake of his head.

"Jack," Jennifer said, "I just spoke with Sheriff Collins, and he said you have more information?"

"You have to be kidding me," Walter snapped.

Jennifer held up a hand to Walter and continued to face Jack. "She told you?"

Jack tried to get a read on Jennifer, but her expression was neutral. *They have to know who Marisa really is. Why else would they have come out so fast?*

"Yes," he said. "She told me."

Walter placed his hands on the table. "I'm going to ask you a few questions, Officer Stratton."

"Ask away."

"Right now I have a *witness* who's been in and out of institutions. All he's saying is Marisa Vitagliano left with two guys. That doesn't even register as far as sending out a beat cop. So—how do you know Marisa, Jack?"

"We're friends."

"Friends?" Walter repeated skeptically. "Have you slept with her?"

"Yes."

"Are you and Marisa still a thing?"

"No."

"Jack." It was Jennifer's turn to speak. "Can you try to see how this looks from our perspective?"

Jack stared at the metal table. He thought about what he would do if their positions were reversed. Jennifer was right. They needed more to go on.

He opened then closed his mouth. If Marisa were here she'd be furious with him for breaking her trust.

But she's not here, and she needs help.

"It's not just Thaddeus," Jack said. "Marisa was nervous. We were supposed to talk about why she was scared. Marisa Vitagliano isn't her real name. She has a past. If someone found out who and where she was, it would be dangerous for her."

Jennifer and Walter exchanged a look.

Walter rapped his knuckles on the table. "I know all about her past. I'm the guy who put her here. But I don't think that's what's going on right now."

"Hold on." Jennifer shot Walter a shut-up look and turned back to Jack. "We can go back and forth like this all night. Instead, how about I start, and you finish. Angelica…"

"Mancini." Jack sighed. "Now you know why I'm worried."

Walter leaned down and whispered something in Jennifer's ear. Her lips pursed.

"I'll tell you what I think, Jack." Walter's rock-chewing voice was back. "I think I've got a crazy homeless guy who was furious because someone else got his ham sandwich and cappuccino. He goes to the cops, but they laugh at him, so he gets real mad. Then he comes to you, the jilted ex-boyfriend. You strike me as the hot-headed, jealous type. You get paranoid, and want us to track her down because you think she ran off and is banging her new guy."

"You're an idiot," Jack snarled.

Jennifer stepped between the two men. Unlike her partner, she remained calm. "Jack. I understand your concern. We know that Marisa Vitagliano is Angelica Mancini, daughter of Severino Mancini. We know that she went underground eleven years ago, and that she's had no contact with him since. In fact, nothing about her has been raised on any agency's radar—until last night, when you guys contacted the state and her name tripped a flag. That's why we're here. We even went so far as to make inquiries with Severino himself. Just to do our due diligence, and for Angelica's sake.

"And you know what we found, Jack? No one's been in touch. We found nothing." Jennifer folded her hands. "Jack, I know you're worried, but this looks like nothing. Right now, all we have—"

Walter cut in with a sneer. "All we have is that your ex-girlfriend got in a car with her new Asian boyfriend." Jack took a threatening step forward, but Walter just grinned. "Go ahead, smart guy. You're already walking a beat. Take a swing and then see what kind of duty you'll be pulling."

The two men stared at each other. Jack just barely kept his anger in check.

Finally Walter growled, "I'm gone," and he turned and stormed out the door.

Jennifer put her hand on Jack's arm. "Jack, please sit down."

Jack clenched his jaw. But he pulled out a chair and sat.

"I know you're concerned about your friend," Jennifer said, "but we've got this. It's important that you let us handle this from here."

Jack shook his head. "If you think I'm just going to sit back and do nothing, you don't know me. I can't just leave her out there."

Jennifer frowned. "Jack, let me talk to Walter and Sheriff Collins to see what we can do about it. Did you tell the sheriff who she really is?"

"I haven't told anyone."

"Good. I know you think something happened, but sometimes a lady just needs to get away. If that's what's going on, we want to make sure she has a place to come back to, so we need to keep this low profile. Give me a minute?"

Jack nodded, and Jennifer walked out the door.

Jack got up and paced. *Could it be nothing? Could she have just gone away? All I'm going on is Thaddeus… No. It's not just Thaddeus. She was frightened. Something spooked her.*

He paced the small room and debated with himself until Jennifer returned.

She did not look happy. "You failed to convey to me the current state of your relationship with the sheriff."

Jack shrugged. "It's been better."

Jennifer shook her head and sighed. "Listen, Jack. This is off the record, okay? We have Severino's house under twenty-four-hour surveillance now. All the phones are tapped. If anyone reaches out to him, we'll know. But if you want my opinion? I think she's just taken some time off for herself. You know her. Has she ever just gone off to be alone?"

Jack said nothing, but his silence surely gave Jennifer all the answer she needed. It was definitely not the first time Marisa had gone off to be alone. *Even when we were together.*

"This is also off the record." Jennifer leaned forward. "Stay the hell out of it. Collins was adamant: *stay out of it.* I know Walter can be a real bastard, but he knows his job, and beneath his crusty exterior, he cares. He placed Marisa here; he'll look out for her. But we can't tell Collins who she is. Go home, Jack. We'll look into it, and I'll let you know what we find."

Jack didn't like it, but he had calmed down enough to realize there was nothing to be gained by arguing. "I have to go finish my paperwork," he said.

As he started for the door, Jennifer caught his arm. "Actually, Collins said… well, the censored version is he's ordering you home. Immediately. You're off for the next three days. Just go home, Jack."

10

I LOVE THAT STUPID BED

Jack walked up to the third floor of Marisa's apartment building and took out the key she had given him. The building had once been an old mill, and Marisa had fallen in love with it. Aged wood, brick, and recently added brass and glass made it an artist's dream. And she had the penthouse suite. *She felt safe here.*

Jack tried the door. Locked.

He unlocked the door, poked his head inside, and listened. Nothing.

"Marisa?" he called out.

It's two o'clock in the morning. If she's here, she's going to kill me. Please be here anyway.

Jack walked inside and shut the door behind him. The darkness in the corners of the room seemed to close in on him. He listened for the slightest sound, but could hear only his heart pounding in his chest.

"Marisa?"

Everything was just as it had been when he was last there. The living area was open and cluttered. Magazines lay on the sofa; open sketchbooks and pencils covered the little table in front of it. Clutter was Marisa's normal. She was always messy.

Jack marched into the kitchen. A small pile of coins, receipts, and papers littered the counter.

Looks like she empties her pockets like me.

He picked up a receipt. It was for coffee, from two days ago. There was also a business card for a de Lorme Fine Art Galleria. He flipped it over. Written on the back were the words: DON'T ENTER THAT PIECE. I'LL BUY IT NOW. NAME PRICE.

I told her people would want it.

He put down the card and kept walking. His footsteps rang out in the silence, as if to remind him that he was intruding. Marisa was a private person, and this was her sanctuary.

The bedroom door was closed. Jack knocked, then pushed it open.

The king-sized bed wasn't made, and clothes lay crumpled on the floor. But Marisa wasn't there. He checked the bathroom, too. Also empty.

He stared at the bed and pictured her lying there wrapped in a sheet, gazing longingly at him with those big brown eyes. He could see her biting her lower lip and invitingly pulling back the sheet.

I love that stupid bed.

He'd spent more than a few nights in it, and the smell of the room now brought back memories that swelled his chest and squeezed his heart. She had lain with him here, and he had been with her. They had been lovers in this room; they had forged a bond.

Jack hung his head.

Bonded.

Chandler had told him that. Sex wasn't just sex. Making love with someone was something more. It bonded you with the other person. Young and cocky, Jack had laughed when his friend told him that, but now he knew how right his friend had been.

She needs me. I'm her friend. I have to find her.

He walked over to the largest room in the house, which Marisa had converted into an artist's studio. Easels, paint, clay, and papers were everywhere. Jack surveyed it all, then hit the wall with his fist.

Damn it. On the one hand, I'm glad I didn't find anything, but—where the hell is she?

Taped to the corner of a half-finished painting of a lighthouse was a flyer for the Darrington Art Festival next week. He thought about the little girl in the field from the painting and, now, his dream.

She was afraid. She was running.

Jack bowed his head.

"God, please…"

***

After an hour of searching the apartment, he'd still found nothing to give him the slightest indication where she might have gone. That wasn't surprising; he knew searching his own apartment wouldn't tell anyone where *he'd* gone, either. But he had hoped to find… something.

He stopped and closed his eyes.

I didn't see a purse or her phone.

He pulled out his phone and called Marisa's number. While it rang, he walked around the apartment and listened. He heard nothing. Her phone wasn't here.

That's not surprising either. And it was good news. She would never leave her phone behind on purpose, so if it had been here, something would definitely have been wrong.

Jack walked back to the bedroom, where he spotted Marisa's Bible next to the bed. He flipped it open to the back and took out the old photograph he knew was there. She'd shown it to him one night after too much wine—and then turned melancholy.

Why did she show me this again? Jack closed his eyes and tried to remember. *That's right, I commented that there were no photographs in the apartment. And so she showed me this one.*

He looked at the old photo. It was of Marisa when she was about seven. She and a young boy—both of them chubby kids with huge smiles on their faces—were hugging a short older man. On the back of the photo, she'd written three names: Angelica, Ilario, and Orsacchiotto.

Orsacchiotto? That can't be a name. Maybe it's a title in Italian? Like Uncle?

He put the photo in his pocket and walked back through the apartment, flicking off the lights.

The darkness felt like a punch in the chest.

11

CRAPBLIZZARD

When Jack returned home, the clock read 4:14 a.m. The chair in front of the computer was empty, and Replacement was asleep on the couch. He gently shook her shoulder.

She opened one eye and grinned. "Sorry," she mumbled. "I tried to stay up. Oh, man. It's after four. What happened? Why are you home so early?"

"It's nothing. Go to bed."

Her eyes widened and her mouth fell open. "You got fired?"

"I didn't get fired."

"Are you okay?"

No. "Yes. Go to bed."

Jack walked into his bedroom, closed the door, and took a quick shower. Ten minutes later he was lying awake in bed, staring up at the ceiling. The light from his clock gave off a dim glow, but it was too dark to make out the cracks in the paint, so he just stared at the void.

He heard a faint tap at the door, but didn't answer it. After another tap, the door creaked open.

"Jack?"

"What?" *I sound rude.*

"Can I come in?"

No. "Why? Is something up?" His words were still clipped.

Replacement hopped into bed next to him.

"Stay over on that side," Jack said.

"I will. Why?"

"I'm in my boxers."

Replacement stuck out her tongue and started to lift up the blanket to peek.

"Stop." Jack pulled it back down.

"What happened?"

"Nothing. Get out."

"Is it about Marisa?" Replacement rolled up on one elbow.

Jack closed his eyes. After a moment he asked, "Did you have any friends when you were little?"

Replacement shook her head. "My brothers, but after they died... not until Aunt Haddie's. Not until Michelle."

"What would you do for her?"

Replacement rolled onto her back. The longer she stared, the more Jack's resolve grew. After a few moments, she whispered, "Anything."

Jack inhaled. "Yeah."

They lay in silence after that. Jack listened to her breathing until he finally fell asleep.

***

"Are you out of your mind?" Chandler asked.

"Shut up," Jack said.

Chandler glared at him. "Seriously, Jack. The CO is ripping everyone. You're not going in there."

"I know, but…" Jack bit his cheek. "Did you see him?"

"See him nearly take all of our heads off? Yeah. He was ticked."

Jack looked past the sea of tents at the stucco building that served as their command center. A soldier stood guard outside the front door. Then Jack turned back to his friend and tried to explain.

"He doesn't drink, but he bought a bottle after mail call."

"So? Maybe he's going to have some guys over. I heard they have a TV in there."

"He looked right at me. It was wrong."

"Wrong?"

"Here." Jack patted his chest. "I know something is wrong."

"You're going to start a crapblizzard, and for what? Because you have women's intuition? Maybe it's just cramps." Chandler smirked.

Jack stood up and started to walk.

"I'm not coming," Chandler said.

Jack stopped and looked back at his friend.

"Seriously, Jack. You do this, you're on your own." Chandler squared his shoulders.

"Fine."

Jack walked alone to the building. As he approached, he saluted the guard.

I don't know him. Same rank as me. Williams.

The man saluted back but raised an eyebrow.

"I need to see the CO, Williams."

The guard rolled his eyes. "He left orders not to be disturbed. No exceptions."

"This is an exception."

"Not happening. Get your superior."

Jack reached past him and pounded on the door.

"Are you crazy?" The young soldier thrust his hands down at his sides.

Jack shrugged. "Yeah." He waited a second, then pounded on the door again.

"Stop it," the guard said in a loud whisper. He looked down at his gun, then back at Jack. He was clearly trying to figure out what to do.

"Are you thinking about shooting me for knocking?" Jack asked incredulously. Then he pounded again. "Sir! I need to see you now, sir!" he shouted.

Chandler came jogging up beside him. Jack raised a questioning eyebrow, and Chandler scowled. "Aunt Haddie would kick my ass if I left you alone," he explained.

Jack shook his head and tried the door. It was locked.

"You got a key?" he asked the guard.

The guard looked puzzled. "It's not supposed to be locked."

Jack stepped back. *Well, I've gone this far.*

Chandler groaned. "Oh, man…"

Jack kicked the door open. Bits of wood flew from the latch.

The guard's hands went to the sides of his head. "Are you out of your mind? What the hell is wrong with you?"

"Sir!" Jack yelled as he walked in. "I need to—"

The CO had thrown a rope over a beam in the main room. His feet swung a few inches off the floor, and his face was a hideous blue. The guard screamed. Jack and Chandler ran forward. Chandler grabbed the CO's legs and held him up while Jack cut him down.

"Get the doc, now!" Jack shouted at the guard, who turned and bolted.

Chandler started rescue breathing while Jack pushed on the CO's chest.

Breathe. Just breathe. I waited too long… Breathe.

As they worked, Jack noticed scattered pieces of construction paper on the floor. They were covered with crayon drawings.

Stick figures. He's got a kid.

The picture closest to him was of a little girl holding a soldier's hand, and beside them a woman and a man were holding hands. Names were written in crayon beneath all four figures: Daddy, Kylie, Mommy, and "my new Daddy."

"Keep going," Jack ordered.

Jack pushed down on the CO's chest while Chandler blew into his mouth. After a minute, they stopped, and Chandler tilted the CO's head and leaned in to listen.

The CO's chest rose, and a raspy hiss escaped from his mouth.

The guard, a doctor, and several other soldiers raced into the room. As they went to work on the CO, Chandler and Jack moved aside.

Chandler looked at Jack. His eyes narrowed, and then he hung his head. "If you didn't… If you hadn't…"

***

Jack woke up gasping and grabbing his throat. Replacement was instantly at his side. "It's okay. It's just a dream. It's okay, Jack."

He sat up. Replacement rubbed his back while he stared straight ahead.

"Do you want to talk about it?" she asked.

He looked down at his trembling hands and slid them under the blanket. "Iraq. Chandler and me." He arched his back, closed his eyes, and tilted his head up.

"What happened?"

Jack slipped out of bed and walked over to the bathroom. He stopped at the door and looked down at the wood floor. When he shut his eyes, he could still almost feel the oppressive desert heat.

He ran his hand through his hair. "Chandler saved this guy. I was just remembering it." He headed into the bathroom.

When he came back out, Replacement sat up and stretched. "Are you going out?" She flipped over on her stomach and looked at the clock. "It's only seven. You got no sleep."

"I have to do something."

She tossed the blanket aside, but Jack shook his head.

"No. I have to do this alone." *Don't take her. Too dangerous.* Way *too dangerous.* "It's nothing dangerous. I just have to do it alone. Please?"

Replacement's mouth opened, then snapped shut. "Okay." She exhaled and lay back down. "Thank you." She snuggled back under the covers.

"For what?"

"For being honest. It makes me feel safe."

I'm trying to keep you safe.

Jack closed the door.

I'm still a liar.

12

DON'T BE A SMARTASS

The Impala's engine roared to life. Jack pulled out his phone.

Be in here. Please be in here.

The GPS program appeared. Jack had never used it, but Marisa had.

Last Christmas. That's when she told me her real name. Maybe it was Christmas that made her homesick. She wanted to see her little brother. So we drove all the way out there, and then she just looked at the house. We didn't go inside.

But she used my phone to get us there.

Jack selected PAST DESTINATIONS and searched for December 25—Christmas Day.

The address was still there.

He pulled away from the curb and hit the gas.

***

Jack turned into an upscale neighborhood with large houses set back from the road. Huge trees lined the street, which curved around in a long, lazy loop. Jack followed the instructions on his phone, but when he reached his destination, he rolled right past it.

Two-story Tudor home. Attached garage. Two big SUVs in the driveway.

He went another block, turned right, and then drove for a bit more before pulling over to park. To be safe, he took all the cash out of his wallet.

A hundred and twenty dollars.

Jack pulled the door panel out with a snap, dropped his wallet and phone inside, and replaced the panel. He had started to hide things inside the door when he first moved into a pretty rough neighborhood. Meth addicts would smash your window in, looking for loose change, but if they didn't see anything valuable they would leave you alone.

Jack patted his gun and got out.

Mancini's son's house. He could have security. Unprofessional thug security, but security.

He circled back to the home. Small lights lined both the long driveway and the brick walkway that led to a huge oak door. Marisa's brother had one hell of an expensive house.

Jack rang the bell and waited. He resisted the urge to look in the window. Just when he was about to reach for the buzzer again, the door swung open, and an older, barrel-shaped Italian man stood smiling in the doorway. He had thick, curly gray hair that still had some streaks of black. Jack guessed he was in his sixties.

It was the man from the picture. *Orsacchiotto.*

"Hi," Jack said. "I'm looking for Ilario."

"Ilario?" The old man smiled. *"Buongiorno. Come stai?"*

Jack blinked. *Shoot. I don't know Italian.*

"Ilario," the old man repeated, and then stepped back. *"Ilario si prega di entrare."* He motioned for Jack to follow him.

Jack tipped his head and smiled back. "Thank you." He stepped inside.

As the old man closed the door behind them, the lock clicked. "Nice and slow, kid." The voice was the old man's.

So. He speaks English fine.

As Jack raised his hands and turned around, seven other men came into the entranceway: two from the hallway, two from a door off to one side, and three from an open living room, where the sound of a TV could be heard in the background.

Six pistols. One pump shotgun. Old guy has a damn hand cannon. Smith and Wesson .500 Magnum. That would blow me through the door.

Jack kept his hands up.

"Pat him down." The old man looked Jack up and down.

"I have a gun in a shoulder holster," Jack said.

A very fat man stepped forward, took Jack's gun, and handed it to a medium-built guy with a big nose. He then proceeded to pat Jack down, but as he was unable to bend past his huge belly, he stopped at Jack's knees.

I have to get a boot gun, Jack thought.

"Bring Ilario out," the old man ordered.

Two of the men stepped into the living room and came right back escorting a young man. He was short, with thick, curly black hair, but Jack could immediately see the resemblance to Marisa.

Ilario. Marisa's little brother.

Ilario shook his head. "I don't know him."

The fat guy with the shotgun raised it, and the guy next to Jack screamed out, "Stop, you freakin' idiot! I'm right next to him."

Jack kept his hands up, but he shifted his weight to the balls of his feet. "Wait. I'm a friend of Angelica's."

The two guys next to him kept moving away.

"What do you know about Angelica?" The old man walked forward and stuck the barrel of his huge gun in Jack's face.

"She's missing. I think someone took her."

Ilario darted forward, but the old man held out a hand. The old man's bushy brows knitted together. "If she is… missing, how do we know that you didn't have anything to do with it?"

"First—and no offense intended—why would I come here, trying to help, if I was a bad guy?"

The old man cocked the revolver.

"And second—in my shirt pocket, Orsacchiotto." Jack tried his best with the difficult Italian word. "I don't know what it means, but that's what Angelica called you."

The old man nodded to the guy with the big nose, who reached into Jack's pocket. He took out the photograph and handed it to the old man. Ilario's eyes went wide. He grabbed the photo out of the old man's hand and held it up to Jack.

"Where did you get this?" he asked.

"It was the only photograph she had. Like I said, Angelica's my friend, and I'm trying to help find her."

Ilario turned to the old man. "Paolo, we need—"

Paolo backhanded him in the mouth. Ilario stumbled backward but didn't fall. Paolo lowered the gun to point at the floor, and Jack exhaled.

"What's your name?"

Don't say anything that could tell them where she is.

"Friend."

Paolo's eyes narrowed, and the other men shifted restlessly. "Why do you think something is wrong with Angelica?"

"Someone saw her being taken into a car."

"Who?"

Jack hesitated. "A friend of mine."

Paolo's lips pressed together, but Jack watched the old man's eyes. *He knows I'm watching out for her. Part of him respects that. The other part's bad.*

Paolo looked Jack up and down once more before holstering his gun. "Follow me."

He led Jack down a short hallway to a door. Paolo held up a hand, went inside, and then closed the door behind him, leaving Jack to wait in the hallway with two of the men—Big Nose and Fat Man. After a few minutes, Paolo opened the door and waved for Jack to enter.

The room was a large study, and from its thick red carpet to its paneled walls, it felt expensive. At the far side of the room was a thick oak desk, and standing beside it was a man who could be none other than Severino Mancini. He was almost six feet tall and looked as though he belonged in a boardroom. Black Armani suit, red tie, and perfect hair created the picture of a powerful businessman—far from the butcher Jack had read about.

Severino was in his late fifties. He was a handsome man, but his eyes were hollow. As he looked up, Jack could almost feel the man's pain.

"You're a cop. I already got a call from the bastard who took my little girl away from me. Why are you here?"

His voice was so smooth it took Jack an extra second to take in what he'd just said. "Who called you?" Jack asked.

"You don't get it. I ask—you answer." He looked at Paolo, and Jack saw the way the old man shifted his gun so he was now palming the cannon.

He's holding it to pistol-whip. Don't be a smartass. That thing would cave my face in.

"I'm a friend of Angelica's." Jack regretted his choice of words when he saw Severino's scowl, but he continued. "She's missing."

"So Prescott told me when he called. He said two guys *might* have driven off with her. Asked me if I was having any issues with anyone." Severino scoffed. "The list of people who have 'issues' with me is long. Prescott had no details. He thought she could be... away on a vacation. What do you think?"

"She was scared about something. She thought someone was watching her."

Severino growled, and his arm swept everything on the desk onto the floor. Glass broke, and papers went flying. The door behind Jack flew open and Fat Man and Big Nose came running in.

"Clean it up!" Severino bellowed at them. "That prick takes my daughter and can't keep my little girl safe? Now *I'll* fix it." He took two steps forward. "Do you know what they look like?"

"No."

"Race?"

Jack hesitated. Prescott must not have told Severino that one of the guys was Asian. Jack decided to hold back that fact too. "No."

Severino stared at Jack for almost a full minute. Jack could feel sweat forming on his back. He had been called on the carpet by just about every authority figure he'd ever met, ever since he could remember. In school, it was a weekly visit to the principal's office. In the Army, he had true experts try to stare him down. But none of them came close to Severino's cold examination.

"You got anything else?" Severino finally snapped.

"No."

"You did your bit. Now get out."

Jack met his gaze. "If you get a call, I need you to let me know."

Severino looked at the floor, then raised his eyes again. "You think I'd go to the cops? You? For help?" He pounded his chest. "I'll get my daughter myself. *Me.* Since you had the balls to come here, I'm going to repeat myself. Get the hell out while I let you keep them." He turned and smashed everything the two men had been putting on the desk back off. Then he turned back and stood there, panting and glaring at Jack.

Jack felt Paolo's hand on his arm, and he looked at the old man. Paolo's eyebrows raised, and he tilted his head toward the door.

He isn't threatening me. He's helping.

Jack looked once more at Severino, then walked out. Paolo escorted him to the front door. The guys in the hallway eyed him with awe and puzzlement.

I guess they're not used to seeing people walk out of that office still breathing.

Jack stopped at the door and held out his hand. Paolo tilted his head to the side, and one of the men handed Jack his gun.

Jack turned to the old man. "Paolo, if you hear—"

"Look, kid. You just asked Severino. Are you going to insult me and ask me now?"

The two men stood toe to toe for a moment—and then Jack holstered his gun and walked out the door.

Damn it. He wanted to scream. *Mancini hasn't heard from anyone. If someone abducted her... it has to be related to her father.*

Jack marched down the driveway and started down the street, heading away from his car—he planned to double back around. But as he walked, he saw a man at the corner, standing in the shadow of a tree. He couldn't make out the man's face.

Jack unzipped his jacket, letting it hang open, giving him faster access to his gun. And as he walked toward the man, he did his best to make out details.

Short. Five five or five six. Curly hair.

Ilario.

Marisa's brother nervously shifted back and forth as he waved Jack closer. "Is my sister okay? Have you talked to her?"

The family resemblance to Marisa caused a pain in Jack's chest. "No. I told you all I know. Did anyone—?"

"Bull."

"What?"

"That's BS. Either the guy who called knows more than you, or you're lying."

"Why would I lie?"

Ilario took a step back. "How do I know you even know my sister?"

Jack's hands went out. *Besides the photo, what can I tell him?*

"How am I going to prove to you...?" As Jack's head tipped to the side, he looked down the block. "There." He pointed toward a side street. "Last Christmas I parked with Angelica right there."

Ilario's eyebrows arched. "She didn't come in?"

"We sat there for an hour and she didn't even say anything. Your sister, she's good to me. I would have sat there all night with her. At midnight, she laughed. I asked why, and she told me the two of you would exchange one present early. You forgot to get her something one year when you were little, so you took one of your father's presents from under the tree and wrote her name on it. She gave you a Power Ranger and you gave her a corkscrew."

Ilario kept looking down the street, but Jack knew that wasn't what he was seeing. He held his hands up to his head and pressed them into his temples. "The Fed who called kept asking about knock-offs. My father went crazy afterward."

"Knock-offs?"

"Counterfeits." Ilario looked at Jack as if he were slow. "You know, handbags, jackets, crap like that. It's one of the rackets. Big money, low risk, low cost. My father has a piece of it but doesn't control it."

"Who does?"

"The Yakuza."

"Are the Yakuza against your father?"

"Everyone is against my father, but I don't have anything to do with his business. I'm actually going to medical school. But my sister..."

"If someone did take Angelica, they're going to contact your father."

"Yeah. My father's already getting cash together. But what if they don't call? What if it isn't about money?" Ilario wiped his eyes with the back of his hand.

"Ilario, they'll reach out to your family. You need to let me know right away when they do."

"How can I contact you?"

"You won't. I'll reach out to you. What's your phone number?"

"You don't trust me?" Ilario glared at Jack.

"The trust isn't mine to give. It's Angelica's. I can't betray that."

Ilario's eyes smoldered. Now Jack could see the resemblance to Severino. Ilario reached into his pocket and took out a cell phone. "Here." He handed it to Jack. "It's a burner phone. I have a drawerful. I'll call you on it."

13

I ACTUALLY SAID *DROP* THE KNIFE

As Ilario hurried back to the house, Jack continued down the block and started working his way back to the Impala. Before he took the last turn, he waited and scanned the area thoroughly. Besides a woman walking a dog, the streets were empty.

He quickly strode over to the Impala and slid behind the wheel. Exhaling, he stretched and flexed his hands. He focused on his breathing, trying to calm the tremor in his leg.

So—Severino already knew about Marisa, from Prescott. Prescott must have been fishing about the connection between the Asian guy Thaddeus saw and the Yakuza and Severino. Why else would Prescott call Severino if he didn't think there was anything to it? Unless he just wanted to rub salt in the man's wounds. Severino was a bastard, after all.

Jack popped the panel again and dropped Ilario's cell phone inside. Then he spun the car around and headed for the highway. But when he reached an intersection, he stopped abruptly. Four SUVs flew by in front of him, with Big Nose driving the lead car.

They're on the move.

Jack waited for a few moments before pulling out after them.

Four cars. Easy to spot. And easy for me to get spotted if we bunch up.

Jack didn't have to worry too much about the caravan getting bunched up. To them, stop signs and traffic lights seemed to be merely suggestions. They quickly made their way to the highway and headed for the city.

Jack slipped through traffic as the row of cars moved into the left lane. The lead car, a giant black SUV, repeatedly ran right up on the bumper of the car in front of it until the driver pulled out of the way. It was tough for Jack to keep up without drawing attention to himself, but he thought he managed okay. As the outskirts of the city approached, the caravan suddenly shifted toward an off-ramp. Jack felt like a fighter pilot as he eased back and followed them. He no longer had to wonder where they were going. At the end of the off-ramp, a huge red archway with giant yellow letters said it all.

Chinatown.

It's not a caravan. It's a war party.

Jack followed from a distance until he saw the cars double-park in front of a restaurant. There were plenty of people on the streets, but the traffic here was light.

Damn. I can't drive right by them.

Jack cut in front of a taxi and swung onto a side street. The cab driver laid on the horn while Jack turned his body to hide his face as he flipped off the cabbie. He thought he was far enough away that the Italians couldn't see him anyway, but he wasn't taking any chances.

Up ahead, a van was pulling out of a parking space, so Jack slipped right in to the vacated spot. He hopped out of the car, popped the trunk, then yanked his jacket off, grabbed his gray sweatshirt, and slipped it on. He shoved a gym bag aside and found a white baseball hat. The baseball hat's strap was too tight, so he loosened it and then pulled the brim down low. Finally he slammed the trunk shut and walked back toward the caravan.

As he turned the corner leading to the restaurant, he slowed and fell into step behind two couples who were just ambling along. When the people in front of him stopped to look in a jewelry store window, Jack did too.

He glanced across the street to see Fat Man and Big Nose by the cars. Fat Man was talking to someone inside one of the cars.

At least three guys stayed with the cars. Did the others go into the restaurant? Or the department store next door?

Big Nose kept looking up to the second floor of the restaurant.

They have to be in there.

Jack looked at his reflection in the window and realized why the baseball hat was too tight. It was Replacement's. He scowled at the pink logo.

The people Jack was using for cover moved on, and he followed. The next store was a coffee shop—perfect—so he slipped inside. He ordered the closest thing on the menu to a regular cup of coffee, while keeping his eyes on the cars across the street. Then he took a seat by the window and waited.

He didn't have to wait long. Soon Paolo walked out of the restaurant accompanied by a giant. The man had to be six foot six and over three hundred pounds.

That guy was definitely not back at the house. Either he's new, or he stayed out of view.

Big Nose held the SUV door open, and Paolo and Goliath climbed in. Then all the cars pulled away.

Jack sipped his coffee. *They went to see who they thought was responsible. Prescott clued them in that the guy was Asian, and Ilario said they're arguing with the Yakuza. So Paolo came here either to give an ultimatum or to arrange a deal.*

Either way, someone in there knows something.

Jack tossed his coffee cup in the trash and headed to the restaurant.

The building's entryway was dominated by a wide staircase covered in red carpet. Two gold lions stood on either side of the stairs, and next to one of the lions was a sign with an arrow pointing up and the words GOLDEN BLOSSOM. Off to one side, a short hallway led to a door with a keypad entry.

Jack headed up the stairs.

At the top was a large, dated restaurant. The room was filled with huge round tables, each of them easily large enough to seat eight, covered in white tablecloths. All the places were already set with silverware, water glasses, plates, and napkins. There were perhaps three dozen customers and half a dozen employees moving around with carts and trays of food.

A young girl hurried up to Jack and greeted him with a customary Chinese bow. "How many, please?"

"One." Jack took his cap off.

"This way." She bowed again and led Jack over to a square table with four place settings. Another waitress rushed over and quickly removed three of them.

"Would you like a drink?"

I'd love you to leave a bottle.

"Tea, water, and I'll get the buffet." Jack returned the smile that seemed to be constantly on the young girl's face.

"Very good. Thank you." She bowed again and hurried off.

Jack put his hat down on the chair next to him, got up, and headed back to find the restrooms. Along the way, he noted the large uncarpeted area in the middle of the restaurant.

Dance floor? Maybe they do weddings.

The restrooms were in the back, down a small hallway. The men's and women's rooms were the only two doors in the narrow corridor.

Jack frowned. *Where are the offices?*

He entered the men's room and walked over to the sinks. He had just finished washing his hands when the door opened behind him and four men walked in. All four were Asian, and all were slender and around five foot six, except for one guy who was much bigger, maybe five ten and two hundred pounds. They were all dressed in business suits, but Jack knew from the way they lined up in front of the door that they weren't businessmen. Three wore blue, and one wore black.

Three are Japanese and one's Korean. Looks like I've come to the right place to find the Yakuza.

"Why are you here?" Black Suit asked.

Jack looked over at the urinal, then back to the guy, and smirked. The big guy laughed and then quickly stopped himself.

Black Suit bared his teeth. "Talk."

Jack turned his hands out. "Why don't we sit down over a cup of tea?"

Black Suit shrugged. "Kick his ass."

The three others started forward.

Jack didn't wait for someone to throw a punch. He lunged forward, grabbed the big guy's shoulder with his left hand, and hit him in the throat.

Fight them one at a time. Drive them toward the urinals.

Then he grabbed the large guy with both hands. His muscles fired from his feet, traveling up his thighs, and his strong back muscles kicked in. The big guy's legs were already wobbling, so Jack used him like a battering ram and drove him into the other three. All but Black Suit tumbled into the back wall. The laughing guy fell, and Jack heard his head crack on a urinal before he hit the floor.

But Black Suit was too fast. He sidestepped the big guy and kicked at Jack's ribs. Jack twisted out of the way so the kick just missed. Jack punched hard, but Black Suit tilted his head out of the way and Jack's fist passed his face. Jack just grabbed the back of Black Suit's head and slammed him face first into the stall door.

The laughing guy wasn't moving, but the other small guy got to his feet. He didn't stay there long. Jack's first punch broke his nose, which made him fall back onto the big guy. Like playing a drum set, Jack unleashed a flurry of blows on both men, and then, panting, he straightened up.

Black Suit was back on his feet. A thin blade was in his hand, and he wiped his bloody nose with the sleeve of his suit. Jack's lip curled into a wiseass grin.

"That blood's going to be hard to get out of that suit. If you don't drop that knife, there'll be more of it."

"You want the knife?" Black Suit swung the blade in a big arc.

"I actually said *drop* the knife."

Black Suit lunged with a straight thrust, but Jack blocked it with his right forearm and grabbed Black Suit's arm. His legs settled into a deep horse stance, and he pulled the man's arm straight, yanked up with his right hand, and smashed his left forearm into the man's elbow.

The bone snapped, and the man gasped—but he didn't have a chance to scream, because Jack's left fist crashed into the side of his head, and he crumpled onto the tile floor.

Jack looked down at the four men on the ground.

"Excuse me?" a girl's voice called out from the doorway. A young girl, her eyes wide, had poked just her head in. "Excuse me. Please come now. The owner needs to speak to you." Her forced smile trembled slightly.

The owner?

With one last glance at the men, Jack followed the girl down the hallway and back to the dining area. All of the customers were gone. One man sat at a large table in the middle of the room, and Jack counted at least seven guys standing around him, all armed.

You really thought this through, didn't you, Jack?

Three of the men walked forward. Two had pistols pointed at him while the third patted him down and took his gun. Then the man at the table held out his hand and gestured to the chair across from him. Jack walked forward and sat down.

The man was in his late thirties with short gray hair, gleaming white teeth, and black eyes. He didn't glare or scowl, but simply sat and studied Jack. Finally, he spoke.

"I am the owner. Why are you here beating up my employees?" His voice was even and calm.

"They started it. I didn't come here to fight. I came looking for my friend."

The owner angled his head, and the waitress came over to pour Jack a cup of tea.

"I have already given my answer to the Mancinis, but you are not with them." He looked at Jack's gun. "You are a police officer."

There are no markings on my gun. He's guessing. Jack said nothing.

"You are a friend of Angelica's? Do you have a name?"

"Friend," Jack replied.

The owner nodded slowly. "Now I understand. Angelica Mancini went into witness protection. Even though you fear she has been kidnapped, you still try to hide where she was relocated. That is why you will not tell me your name. It also explains why you have no wallet or phone."

This guy is good. Dangerous.

The owner took a sip of his tea. "Since you are alone, I wonder if your colleagues even know you are here?"

"I don't have an issue with you, and neither did Angelica."

"True. Since you are a policeman, and I do not want to deal with any repercussions from you not walking out of here, I will explain something to you. Look around. Look at me. We operate a business. Not like the old ways. You followed the Mancinis to the same blind conclusion. Severino's daughter goes missing, and your knee-jerk reaction is that it must be my organization? You need to ask the right question, friend. Even if we are not allied with the Mancinis, why would I kidnap Severino's daughter?"

"I don't care about why. I just want her back."

"You have to look elsewhere, then. I know nothing about her."

Jack studied the man's face. The owner met his gaze calmly. Jack put his hands on the table. "You should know this: if something happens to Angelica, I'll hold you responsible."

The owner grinned crookedly, and his head gave the slightest shake. "That is the second time today I have heard those words. Are you a friend of Paolo's?" He set his teacup down. "My answer to you is the same I gave him. I had nothing to do with the girl's disappearance. Do not come back to Chinatown."

Four men walked around the table and stood by Jack, two on each side. Jack stood and looked down at the owner, who took a sip of his tea without looking up.

The men escorted Jack to the door. At the bottom of the stairs, another man handed him back his gun. As Jack walked out into the sunshine, his mood turned black.

I have no idea where she is, and now I'm in way over my head.

14

ANOTHER CASE

Once again, Jack had no intention of leading anyone back to his car. So when he came out of the restaurant, he walked a couple of blocks, crossed the street, and then glanced back. Just down the road, two Japanese men in suits were walking side by side. One crossed the street.

Thank you for being so obvious.

Jack turned a corner and saw a men's clothing store two doors down. He entered. The store had mostly urban clothing for young men. Jack grabbed a baggy T-shirt, a thin jacket, blue jeans, sunglasses, and a bottle of hair gel, then tossed them on the counter. A pimply faced teenager, who looked bored out of his mind, rang him up, using one finger to press the cash register keys. Jack used all his cash except a twenty-dollar bill.

"Hey. I'm trying to surprise my girl," Jack began. "You know what that's like, right?" The kid puffed up. "I'm going to change real quick into this stuff. Does this place have a back door?"

The teenager's mouth opened and then closed.

Jack held up the twenty. The kid snatched it and nodded.

Jack hurried into the dressing room, where he threw all his clothes in the bag. He dressed quickly in the new getup and ran the gel through his hair, spiking it straight up.

Leave the bag. Go. I've been in here too long.

When he stepped out, the teenager looked surprised by his new appearance.

"Thanks. She's really gonna flip out." Jack grinned.

"Go this way," the kid said. "It says fire exit, but it's turned off so we can sneak a smoke."

Jack went out the door to the alley. It ran both ways, so Jack doubled back in the direction of his car. He stuck one hand in his pocket and let the other one swing wide.

This should work... from a distance.

He adopted a pace that was slightly hurried but would fit his look, and he stayed close to the buildings as walked. When at last he reached the street with his car, he walked right past it to make sure no one had followed. He looked around. Nothing raised any flags.

Best I can do.

He headed to the car. One last look, then he slipped into the driver's seat and headed out. But instead of going back to the highway the way he'd come, he decided to drive into the city and get out a different way. Just in case.

After a half hour of winding around, Jack made his way to an on-ramp. And once he hit the open highway, he gunned it all the way back to Darrington.

He pulled up in front of his apartment building and started to get out of the car. A muffed hum made him freeze. He looked down, puzzled. His car door was buzzing. *What the hell?*

He looked down at the door and tilted his head. *Of course.* He popped the door panel and pulled out the burner phone from Ilario. According to the screen, it wasn't the one that had rung, so he pulled out his wallet and his own cell phone. He had a voicemail from his parents.

Nothing from Replacement? I'm going to hear it from her.

He stuffed both phones and his wallet in his pockets and headed inside. It was after four p.m., and he was starving.

Inside the apartment, he found Replacement working on the computer. "Hey," she called, without turning around.

"What're you working on?"

"I got another case." She didn't stop typing. "A real scumbag. This lady hired me. The disgusting pig of a man she's married to is stepping out on her."

"Replacement..."

"She's sick, and he starts fooling around with someone else? She had her head all wrapped up in a scarf, you know. You do that when you have cancer and your hair falls out. Seriously, how low can you go?"

"You can't start a case automatically thinking the guy is guilty."

"Yes, I can." She still didn't stop typing. "I'm not a cop."

"It's not about being a cop; it's about being right. What if he didn't do it?"

Now she turned away from the keyboard. She had a look of total disgust on her face, but when she looked up at him, it instantly vanished.

Jack shrugged. "I'm just saying. Maybe he's not seeing someone else. Did you find anything out?"

She sat there with her mouth open.

"Hello?" Jack said.

That's when Replacement burst out laughing. She stamped her feet and grabbed her sides. She laughed so hard, Jack thought she'd fall out of the chair.

"What?"

Replacement *did* fall out of the chair.

And then Jack caught his reflection in the microwave. *Damn it. My hair.* He saw how goofy he looked with gel in his hair. *I forgot.*

He marched through his bedroom and into the bathroom. He stripped off the new clothes and tossed them on the floor.

"Wait, wait," Replacement called as she knocked on the door.

"Stay out," Jack snapped. He turned the water on. "What?"

He slipped behind the shower curtain just before she barged in.

"Can I get a picture before you wash it out?"

"No."

"Please? *Please?*"

Jack stuck his head under the water.

"Darn it, Jack."

"I'm not in the mood."

"What happened? Where did you go?" She hopped up on the sink.

Don't get her involved in this. Just don't.

"I had to do some stuff. That's all."

"I can't believe how the day flew by. I'm working a new case, and you get so sucked in you forget about everything else. Have you talked to Marisa? I can't get her on the phone, and she hasn't gone to the shop."

"No." Jack's voice was low. He scrubbed his hair hard.

"Well, I've got nothing on the scumbag. The lady is nice. Susan Taylor. It's sad."

"She thinks he's cheating on her?"

"Yeah. Her husband, Darren—he's some office manager. He doesn't come home from work until almost midnight, and he goes out all weekend, too."

"What's his side of the story?"

"He tells her he's working. Some special project."

"Is he?"

"I don't know. I just got the case this morning. I started with online stuff. I got zip. No social media. She said their finances are pretty thin. She had to stop working."

"Maybe that's why he's working more."

"Nope. He's salaried."

Jack rinsed out his hair.

"What's with the weird clothes and your hair?" Replacement asked.

"Huh?"

"The clothes. They're totally not you, and—" He heard her hop down from the sink. "Did you go undercover?"

"No, it was—"

"You did!" She tried to pull the curtain open, but Jack yanked it back.

"I didn't. I'm not going to get into it now."

"I can't believe you went—" Replacement stopped. "My phone's ringing! I think this is about my case. I have to go." She dashed out of the bathroom.

Jack stood in the shower for another few minutes before turning it off. He watched the drops fall from his body and splash below. When the last of the water swirled down the drain, he climbed out of the tub. He heard the front door close; apparently Replacement had a lead to follow, or whatever it was she was doing.

He walked into the bedroom and checked the phone Ilario had given him. There were no messages. He picked up his own cell phone and tried Marisa again, but got only voice mail.

He laid both phones on the table next to his bed and set the alarm on his clock. He needed some sleep. Two hours—then he would go back and check Marisa's apartment again.

15

BRASS KNUCKLES

Jack sat bolt upright and looked out the window. It was already dark. He looked at his alarm clock: 6:30 p.m. Someone must have turned it off. *Damn.*

He kicked his blankets back and stormed into the kitchen. A note was propped on the counter.

> HI. LEFT A SANDWICH IN THE FRIDGE FOR YOU. SINCE YOU HAVE THE NEXT FEW DAYS OFF, I FIGURED YOU WANTED TO SLEEP. BE HOME LATE. A.

"If I set my alarm clock, I do it for a reason," he growled in the general direction of the empty computer chair.

He crumpled up the note, but when he opened the refrigerator, his scowl softened. Replacement had made him a roast beef sandwich and an iced tea. It was hard to stay mad at someone who was trying to watch out for you.

He tried calling Marisa again. Still nothing.

God. Please let her be okay.

He ate the sandwich and drank the tea, then got dressed and ready to go. He took his gun and both phones with him. Out front, he looked for Replacement's blue Bug, but it was gone.

He drove to the tattoo parlor, parked out front, and marched up to the door. Three girls and seven guys hung out at the tables. All of them looked up as he flung the door open.

The lanky guy held up his hands. "She hasn't showed," he said quickly.

"She call?" Jack asked.

"Nothing. Not a word."

Jack turned to address the groups at the tables. "Have any of you seen or spoken with Marisa?"

Silence and blank faces were the only responses.

Jack stepped up to a table with three guys in their early twenties. "I asked a question. Have any of you—"

A guy with wide-set eyes and an angular nose scoffed, "Like we'd tell you if we did."

Jack grabbed him by the hoop in his ear. The man shrieked.

"Sorry, but my hand accidentally caught your earring. What did you say?" Jack growled.

"I haven't seen her. I haven't." The man's voice was now two octaves higher.

"What about the rest of you?"

More silence.

Jack flexed his finger, and the man whined, "Answer him, answer him."

They all shook their heads, and he heard at least one mumble, "No, sir."

Jack let go of the earring and turned to the guy behind the counter. "What's your name?"

"Shawn. Shawn Miller. I'm the assistant manager."

"Are you sure she hasn't been here? Maybe she came in and went right to her office?"

Shawn shrugged. "Only she's allowed in there. If she did, I wouldn't know."

"I need to get in there." Jack walked over to the curtain that led to the back rooms.

A short girl with black eye shadow—Jack recognized her from an earlier visit—scurried over to Shawn. "Don't be spineless," she whispered to him.

Jack walked past the statues and pulled the curtain aside. "Come on," he growled, and then stormed down the hallway, with Shawn nervously following.

Jack tried the door to Marisa's office. It wasn't locked. He looked at Shawn.

Shawn shrugged. "I don't know if she keeps it locked. No one would go in there anyway."

Jack stepped inside. The room looked just how he remembered it. Her computer was on one desk in the corner, and there was a separate desk covered in papers.

He walked over to the computer. *I need to get Replacement to come and take a look at this.* "Does she use this for work?"

"I don't know. The building doesn't have Internet access."

Jack walked to the other desk and started going through some of the papers.

"You can't—"

Jack looked up, and Shawn stopped mid-sentence.

"I'm going to need a couple of minutes," Jack said.

"Listen. I know you can kick my ass." Shawn nervously shifted. "But Marisa wouldn't want anyone going through her stuff."

"Shawn. Has Marisa ever said anything about me?"

"Once she offered any takers a million dollars to put a bullet in your head, but I think she was just mad."

Wow. I know I got her upset, but...

"Women get like that. Marisa and I are more than friends, and right now I'm worried about her. That's all I'm going to say. So ask yourself this: When Marisa comes back, would she be more bent out of shape if you let me look around in here, or for the mess that happened because you tried to stop me?"

Shawn swallowed, looked around nervously, then turned quietly and walked back down the hallway.

***

It was a good hour later when Jack at last got up from the desk chair and rubbed the back of his head.

Bills. Receipts. Payroll. Nothing.

He tossed the curtain back as he walked out. Everyone looked up.

"If she calls, or you see her, tell her I have to talk to her. It's an emergency. Got it?" Everyone nodded.

Jack stormed back out to his car. He saw the guys in the tattoo parlor talking animatedly inside, and he could only imagine what they were saying about him yanking the guy's earring earlier.

Jerk should have just answered the question when I asked nicely. If he has an earache, it's his own fault.

***

Jack walked up to the third floor of Marisa's apartment building. The old wood stairs creaked, and the higher he went, the lower his spirits sank.

She could be anywhere. She could be safe, or...

He knocked on her door, unlocked it, then walked in. "Marisa?" he called out. He went through all the rooms, but everything was just the same as when he was there last. "Marisa?"

He grabbed a sheet of paper and a pen.

MARISA, PLEASE CALL ME AS SOON AS YOU GET THIS. IF YOU DON'T REACH ME, COME TO MY APARTMENT. JACK

Was there anyone she talked to? The people at her store? Artists?

That festival.

Jack went into her studio, grabbed the flyer for the art festival that was taped to the easel, and dialed the number. An answering machine picked up. "Thank you for calling the de Lorme Fine Art Galleria—"

Jack hung up.

He taped his handwritten note to an empty easel, then placed the easel where she'd be sure to see it the minute she walked into the apartment. Then he turned off the light and left. The click of the lock echoed in the hallway.

He knew Marisa wouldn't be happy about him talking to her neighbors, but at this point he couldn't care less. Hers was the only apartment on the third floor, so he went down to the second floor and knocked on both of the doors. Unfortunately, no one was home in either unit. Jack considered going back up for paper and leaving a note, but decided against it. He knew she didn't like her neighbors; if she *had* gone somewhere, she wouldn't have told them anything anyway.

He walked downstairs and got in his car. For a minute, he just sat there, gripping the steering wheel tightly. *Dammit, Marisa.* But then he forced down the panic that was trying to rise in his chest, pulled away from the curb, and headed home.

He only made it two blocks before he stopped again.

No. I should leave a damn note for the neighbors. If there's even a chance they know something...

He spun the Impala around.

But as he got out of the car back at Marisa's building, he happened to glance up— and for a brief moment, he could have sworn he saw a sliver of light illuminate Marisa's window. It wasn't the light in the apartment, but there was something.

It must have been the light from the hallway. Someone opened the door to the apartment. Marisa's home!

Relief washed over him as he ran for the entrance and raced up to the third floor, taking the stairs two at a time. It wasn't until he hit the third-floor landing that it hit him.

Marisa would turn on a light if she walked into her apartment. It's not her.

Jack drew his gun. He flattened himself against the wall, and with his left hand, he reached for the doorknob. It wasn't locked.

Instinctively, his hand started to move for his radio. Of course, it wasn't there. He frowned.

You're on your own, Jack.

His breathing slowed as he waited and listened. Should he let them come to him? No one was in danger, and there was no other way out. He could just stay here and let the snake come out of the hole.

And he was prepared to do just that when he heard a window in the apartment being flung open.

Fire escape.

Jack's foot hit the door and he went in.

He was too slow. He was fast enough to get his head out of the way, but something long, fast, and hard—a broomstick?—slammed into his arms just above the elbow. Even with a double-handed grip, he felt the gun fall from his hands, and before he could recover, the stick came back up again to thump him solidly in his face. As he staggered backward and fell into the hallway, his assailant shot from the apartment, dashed past him, and tore down the stairs.

Jack screamed in rage and pushed himself to his feet. As he shook his head to clear his vision, he could feel the blood splatter from his cut lip. He took two steps into the apartment and looked for his gun. It was nowhere in sight.

Forget it. Move.

He turned and raced for the stairs. He could hear the guy already reaching the first floor. Jack flew down the stairs, caught the front door before it closed, and tore outside. He spotted the guy just down the street. He was small, about five six, dressed in black pants and a sweatshirt with the hood up, and he was sprinting toward downtown.

Jack's muscles exploded. His long legs stretched out and his feet dug into the pavement. His arms pushed him forward while he focused his breathing.

You can't lose him. He knows where she is.

As he thought of Marisa, his speed increased. The figure darted between two buildings, but Jack gained on him. And as they raced forward, Jack knew exactly where they were. The route they were on would lead them behind the supermarket. Jack had walked this route a hundred times now.

Everything's locked down. I can go to the right and cut him off.

Jack split off to the right and pushed even harder. At the next corner, he tapped into the furnace of rage that burned inside him, and his legs became a blur. He was running at top speed when he saw the guy reappear just ahead of him. The man saw Jack coming, but it was too late for him to do anything about it. Jack lunged.

If there could be replay reels in life for hits, this one would easily land on Jack's top ten. His shoulder slammed into the guy's midsection and he wrapped his arms around the man's waist and literally launched the guy backward onto the tar. Jack flew with him and landed right on top of him, then raised himself up and slammed his left hand into the guy's chest, pinning him to the ground. With a growl he pulled back his right hand, ready to slam it into the man's face.

But then he realized something. His left hand, which held the man down, didn't rest on a man's chest—but on a woman's breast.

The woman turned her head, and Jack could clearly see her. She was a beautiful Japanese woman, and she glared up at him with a mixture of pain and rage. Taking advantage of Jack's surprise, she managed to pull her legs up almost to her face, and then they shot up toward his head. In one quick movement, her calves scissored around his neck, her strong thigh muscles yanked him forward and sideways, and his head was driven into the pavement.

Jack's vision blurred. As the woman scrambled to her feet, he raised his hands to protect his head, but she delivered a heel kick straight to his solar plexus. Jack doubled over.

The woman reeled back and grabbed the wall. Then she turned and walked calmly down the alley.

Jack spotted a discarded glass bottle lying against the wall. He grabbed it, pulled himself up to his knees, and threw it as hard as he could. He aimed for the woman's head, but hit her in the lower back. She cried out in pain and fell to her knees.

Growling, Jack forced himself to his feet and staggered forward, his steps labored. He kicked at her head. With another quick movement, she blocked it and threw him off-balance, which opened up his back. That's where she hit next. Pain blasted through his exposed kidney and he dropped to his left knee. Then her fist slammed into Jack's cheek, and his whole upper body twisted around with the impact.

Brass knuckles...

Everything went black.

16

DO I HAVE TO CUFF HIM?

Jack opened his eyes, then immediately closed them again as pain raced through his head. He rolled up to his knees and willed his eyes to open again. The alley was deserted.

He looked at his watch: 7:22 p.m. He'd only been out for a couple of minutes. He ran his tongue along his teeth. They were all there.

Small miracles.

He quickly patted down his jacket to do a quick inventory. *Two phones. Keys. Wallet. All I'm missing is my gun.*

Ignoring the pain in his head, he started back toward Marisa's apartment. As he walked, he flexed his muscles, checking for injuries. Nothing felt broken, but he could tell he was going to have one heck of a bruise on his cheek, and he was sure his lip must look like hell. He could still taste the blood in his mouth, and his ears were ringing.

A woman. And seeing as how she kicked my ass, she definitely knows how to fight. I'm lucky she left me alive. But what was she doing in Marisa's apartment?

Back at the apartment building, he hurried up the stairs. On the second floor, he encountered a young couple carrying groceries into their apartment, but before he could question them, they took one look at his face and hurried inside.

"Wait!" he called after them, but the door had already slammed shut with a loud thud. He heard the tumblers as the door was locked and bolted.

Great. Get your gun back first, and then try to talk to them.

Marisa's door was still open, and Jack was relieved to find that his gun had merely slid underneath a chair. He retrieved it, then scanned the room. One window was open.

Girl was smart. She knew I was waiting outside the door, so she threw open the window to draw me in. I fell for it.

Jack closed the window, then headed for the kitchen. He opened the little cabinet next to the refrigerator, grabbed the aspirin bottle, and took four. Then he opened the freezer and dumped two handfuls of ice cubes into a plastic bag. He didn't know which hurt worse, his lip or his eye, so he held the ice bag midway between them.

As he leaned against the counter, trying not to think about the throbbing in his cheek, he glanced down at the coins and the receipt for coffee. *Coffee.* The sight of the receipt—such a simple, ordinary thing—brought on an unexpected wave of emotion.

What he wouldn't do to have a simple cup of coffee with Marisa right now. To have her back. To know she was safe.

He looked once more at the receipt and the coins, and the hairs on the back of his neck went up. Something was missing.

The business card from the art gallery.

He looked all around the counter, but it was gone.

"FREEZE!" someone yelled from the hallway.

Jack drew his gun and ducked down.

"Police officer!" Jack bellowed back. "Officer Jack Stratton. Police."

"Jack? Is that you?"

Jack recognized Officer Donald Pugh's voice. Donald wasn't the brightest bulb on the force, but he was a good guy. "Donald, it's me. I'm alone, and I'm going to walk out of the front door. *Don't shoot me.*"

Jack holstered his gun and stood. He took a deep breath and held his hands up before leaving the kitchen. "I'm walking out."

Donald strolled through the front door but pulled up short when he saw Jack. "What the hell? Who beat the crap out of you?"

"Donald, for future reference," Jack growled, "make sure it's safe before you just walk in."

"But you said it was you." Donald shrugged. He was Jack's age and height, but Jack had twenty pounds of muscle on him. Donald was the type who never could seem to gain weight even if he wanted to. He pushed his hat farther up his sandy brown hair and then put his hands on his hips. "Are you okay? The neighbors called in a break-in. When Collins heard the address—"

Before Donald finished, Jack was headed for the door. "Donald, I have to go. Why don't you run downstairs and explain this to the neighbors."

"Explain it? I don't even understand it. What's going on? You look like someone rolled you for your wallet. Is this your apartment?"

"No. It belongs to a friend of mine. See?" Jack held up the key. "She gave me a key and permission to come and go."

"Then what happened to your face?"

"That's a little more complicated. Someone did break into the apartment, but before Collins gets here, I need to think—"

"Too late for that, Jack." Sheriff Collins's twang shook the walls as he strode through the door. But he stopped as soon as he saw Jack's face. His mouth opened and closed twice before words actually came out. "Do you need medical attention?"

Jack shook his head. His eye throbbed from the movement. "Sir—"

"Don't." Collins's index finger snapped up. "Is this *her* apartment?"

"It is."

"Did you break in?"

"No." Jack held up the key. "I have permission to come and—"

"No, you don't. Not from me," Collins growled.

"With all due respect, I don't need your permission to go to my friend's apartment, sir."

"Actually, you do." Collins stomped forward. "You work for me, so you *do* need my permission. I made it clear. Stay away. There was no wiggle room in what I instructed."

"Actually—"

"*Save it.* You think something happened to this girl. If that's so, you have now contaminated a crime scene."

"What? Are you kidding me? You tell me nothing happened, and now you want to jam me up for—"

"*I'm* not doing the jamming, Stratton. *You* are." Collins turned purple. "Take him in," he snarled to Donald.

"What?" Donald and Jack exchanged incredulous looks.

"I'm not going through this now. You're not on duty, and you've been found in the apartment of a girl who was reported missing."

"You disregarded that report, and I have a key."

"You can tell me all about it down at the station, Jack."

"Sir, there was someone in here—"

"What part of 'shut up and tell me back at the station' do you not understand, Officer?" Collins's right eye twitched.

"Fine." Jack headed for the door.

Donald just stood there like a deer in the headlights. Collins snapped at him, "What the hell are you waiting for?"

Jack didn't look back, but he heard Donald whisper, "Do I have to cuff him?"

17

CAN I GET THIS ONE IN AN EIGHT-BY-TEN?

Cindy Grant opened the door of the interrogation room and frowned. Cindy was in her sixties, but whether it was due to her round, chubby face or her constant smile, she looked twenty years younger. She had short, light-brown hair, and today she wore a modest dark-blue skirt and a blouse with a bright butterfly brooch. Cindy was the police dispatcher and also Jack's friend.

Her little heels clicked on the floor as she walked over to the table. "I don't know what you're smiling about, Jack." She set down an ice pack, a bottle of water, and three aspirin, then sat down next to him.

"Thanks." Jack took the pills and put the ice pack on his eye.

"What were you thinking? If you're trying to make the sheriff explode, you're on target."

"I'm not trying to tick him off."

"Well, you have. And those two Feds are back. Now everyone is screaming."

Jack put his elbows on the table and leaned into the ice pack. "What am I supposed to do?"

"Are you going to throw away your career on a gut feeling?" She rubbed his shoulder.

He looked at her and then at the ceiling. "Yes. Yes, I am. I'd rather throw it away than do nothing."

Cindy frowned. "Can you just try to back off for a little while?"

Before Jack could answer, Walter Prescott surged through the door. "Oh, your boy is going to back off for a while, all right. He's been suspended."

"What?" Jack and Cindy both got to their feet.

Jennifer came in behind Walter, a disapproving look on her face.

Cindy wagged a finger in Walter's face. "You don't have the right to suspend him."

Walter sneered. "*I* don't. But Collins does. I'm sure he'll want to officially notify Jack once he's done signing the paperwork."

"Jack"—Cindy put her hand on Jack's shoulder—"don't say anything without your delegate."

"Jack's a big boy—he can talk to me," Walter snapped.

"Just stop it, Walter," Jennifer said. Then she turned to Cindy. "Cindy, we need to talk to Jack alone."

Cindy looked at Jack, and he nodded. She patted his arm, leaned in closer, and whispered, "If you need Peter, I'll get him. You have a right to a delegate." She glared at Walter as she left the room.

Jack dropped the ice pack onto the table. "There's no way I'm getting suspended because I went into a friend's apartment—*with a key*."

Walter sneered. "You're right, Stratton. You're not suspended because you went to a *friend's* apartment. You're not suspended because you went to meet with the head of the Mancini crime family. You're not even suspended for going to Chinatown and meeting with the Yakuza."

I guess they really did have all those places under surveillance.

Walter pulled out a chair and sat down. "No, Stratton, you're suspended because you used an authorized police account to send an unauthorized email."

"What? That? They've been dragging out that investigation for weeks. You're trying to tell me they made a decision now, and it has nothing to do with any of this?"

Jack didn't even send that stupid email; Replacement did. But he couldn't tell anyone that or he'd jam her up.

"Stratton, you're one stupid son of a bitch."

Jack walked around the table and stared down at Walter. "You know what? I'm sick of hearing words come out of your mouth," he snarled.

Jennifer stepped between them and raised her hand. "Walter, can I please have a moment alone with Officer Stratton?"

Walter grunted, then stood. "You'd better listen to her if you want to see the sun in the next couple of weeks." His voice was grating. "Since 9/11, we have a little bit more leeway, if you understand me. And since you just crossed the line when you met with two groups I can lump with terrorists, you'd better sit down or we'll handle you how *I* want to handle you."

As Walter walked out, Jennifer scowled and took his seat. Jack remained standing.

"I tried to warn you," Jennifer said. She crossed her arms and leaned back. "You met with Severino? Seriously?"

"You said I did," Jack said. "I haven't confirmed that."

She set a manila folder on the table and flipped it open. Inside were pictures of Jack walking up to Ilario's house. Jack casually flipped through them. They only showed him arriving at the house—not leaving, and not meeting with Ilario. *These photos were taken from someone standing on the opposite side of the street. From this angle, they may not have seen us.*

Jack held up a close-up and grinned. "Can I get this one in an eight-by-ten?"

Jennifer laughed. "Maybe you can get yourself a job in stand-up since you seem so intent on throwing away your police career."

Jack's smile vanished.

Jennifer continued. "So. What did they say?"

Jack shrugged and sat down. "Nothing. Severino told me Walter had called him, and he thought Walter was a bastard, and that's about it. They haven't heard anything."

"How many men were inside?"

"You're asking me?" Jack leaned back. "Why don't you check the drone surveillance?"

Jennifer frowned. "So Severino didn't say anything. Did he give you any idea who could be involved?"

"He's not a real great conversationalist." Jack looked directly at the two-way mirror and raised his voice. "But it went something like this: 'Walter sucks. You're a cop. Get out. Walter is a piece of garbage. I haven't heard anything. Tell Walter he sucks.'" Jack held up his hands innocently and leaned back in his chair.

"Shut up, Jack. Severino hated Walter long before Marisa." Jennifer rolled her eyes. "What about the Yakuza? Who did you meet with?"

"Well, four guys rushed me—"

"Four?"

Jack grinned, but winced when his lip curled. "Four guys came at me in the bathroom, and then I talked with a guy."

"Who did you meet with?"

"I think he was Japanese. He called himself the owner."

Jennifer frowned and took out her smartphone. She pressed a few buttons, then slid it across the table to him. "This the guy you met with?"

It wasn't the type of picture Jack expected. He'd assumed she'd have some grainy, slightly blurred photo from a surveillance van at dusk. This was a professional headshot.

"Did he pose for the FBI Christmas calendar?" Jack asked.

Jennifer smirked. "Funny. Really. That was funny. He's Takeo Ishikawa. He's part of the new Yakuza. Business suits and board meetings. Don't get me wrong: they're still very happy to kill you."

"He didn't."

"*Yet,*" Jennifer said, taking back her phone. "Why did you go see him?"

"I followed Severino's men."

"Smart." Jennifer scowled. "Why did Severino's men go there?"

"Ask Walter. He called Severino. Did Walter tell him the only description we have is of an Asian man with tattoos?"

Jennifer's hand clenched. "What did Takeo have to say?"

Jack rubbed the back of his neck. "He said they had nothing to do with it."

"Did you believe him?"

"Do you care if I did?"

Jennifer pressed her lips together. "The problem with you, Jack? You don't think before you act. That said, you also tend to figure out things that other people don't."

Jack put his elbow on the table and ran his thumb against his lip. "Have you been reading my file?"

Jennifer laughed and brushed back her red hair. "No. I've been reading the newspaper. I'm surprised Collins doesn't have your picture up on a dartboard in his office."

"I thought he did. So, do you guys have anything?"

"We're in the same place we were before you went all rogue, ex-boyfriend crazy. What happened to your face?"

"That's what I've been trying to tell you. I went to Marisa's apartment, and there was a Japanese woman there. She broke in."

Several different expressions played across Jennifer's face: disbelief, anger, confusion, amusement. "A woman? Are you trying to tell me a woman did that to you?"

"I take it you're not a big believer in the whole women's equality thing?"

"I did read your file, and I find it hard to believe you got your ass kicked by a woman. Are you also telling me she got away?"

"Yeah. She's good."

"Description?"

"Japanese."

Jennifer turned to the window. Jack heard the viewing room door open, and then Walter stormed into the room.

"Now you've done it, Jack! You've gone and kicked the bear." He thrust a finger in Jack's face. "You had to go and see Takeo, and now you've stirred everything up. You let them know where Severino's daughter is. You put a huge target on her head!"

"No one followed me from Takeo's."

"Get real, kid," Walter said. "I've done this for twenty years. Anyone can be followed." He walked back to the door and smacked the frame with the palm of his hand. "I hope you at least got a good look at this Japanese woman. You'll need to look at some mug shots before you go." He shook his head. "You know Sheriff Collins is ready to hang you out to dry? But if you're a good boy and look at the pictures, then you get to go home. And if you can manage to keep your nose out of our investigation, well... I'll see what I can do for you with Collins."

Walter shot a look at Jennifer, then left.

Jennifer turned back to Jack. "I don't have to tell you, if someone was in Marisa's apartment, that's not good. Give us a little time. Let's see what we can do with what you found out."

"Do you believe me?"

Jennifer paused. "I believe your face. And... it doesn't feel right. I'll talk to Walter."

"Like he cares."

She put her arms on the table. "You don't know him, Jack. Give him a chance. I know he comes off as an old curmudgeon who's about to retire, but if he hadn't given me a chance, I'd be stuck behind a desk. I had no way to move up at the Bureau, and I was going to transfer. He knows what he's doing. He's an expert on the Mancinis."

"An expert?"

"No one in the agency knows the Mancinis like Walter. He knows not only them, but their enemies. Just let me work on him, okay?"

Jack's hand tightened into a fist.

I'd like a chance to work on Walter.

18

THE LITTLE FAT MAN

Jack returned to his apartment shortly after midnight. He emptied his pockets on the counter, and then, almost out of habit, called Marisa. Once again, the call went straight to her voice mail. He hadn't expected anything different, but… he had hoped.

Stepping into the kitchen, he went straight for the aspirin. He was just about to wash down a couple with some stale Diet Coke when the front door was flung open. Replacement rushed in looking close to tears.

Jack hurried over. "What's wrong? What happened?"

Replacement held her hands up. "Nothing. Nothing." She ran past him into her bedroom and closed the door behind her.

Jack rubbed his head. *Should I give her a minute, or—*

Before he could finish that thought, a little fat man rushed into the open doorway of the apartment. Jack reacted. He grabbed the man's shoulder with his right hand and yanked him forward. Twisting at the waist, he pulled him down with his right hand, and with his left grabbed the man by the belt. The move launched the man through the air. He crashed to the floor and slid into the living room wall.

Instantly, Jack drew his gun. *"Don't move."*

The flushed-cheeked man lifted trembling hands in the air as he looked up at Jack.

Jack eyed the startled intruder. He was short, fat, and balding—probably in his late forties. His eyeglasses now rested at a crooked angle.

"I didn't mean to—" the man started.

"Why were you chasing her?" Jack snapped.

His lower lip quivered in fear. "I wasn't—"

Replacement whipped open the bedroom door. "Jack!"

"Get back in the bedroom. *Now,*" Jack ordered.

"Jack, no!" She rushed over to the fallen man.

"Alice, get away from him. He was chasing after you."

"Jack." She crouched over the man and shielded him with her body. "Put the gun away."

Totally confused, but still on guard, Jack lowered his aim toward the floor.

Replacement helped the man to his feet. "Are you okay?"

He took off his glasses, rubbed the bridge of his nose, and nodded.

"Who the hell are you?" Jack snarled. "And why did you just barge into my apartment?"

"I'm sorry. I'm sorry," he blathered.

Jack could feel his frustration building. "Who are you?" He walked toward the little man, who seemed to get even smaller as he approached. "You answer me. Who are you, and why are you here?"

The man shifted his weight from foot to foot. "Darren Taylor. I'm looking for her." He pointed at Replacement.

"Jack, I can handle this." Replacement raised her hand.

Jack raised his hand back to her as he continued to glare at Darren, making it clear he wanted some answers from him. "Continue."

Darren rubbed his arm, looked at the gun, and swallowed. "I thought I saw this lady following me, then earlier today she showed up at my work and started talking to my boss. I figured my wife had hired her." He looked at Replacement. "That's what you're doing, right? You're an investigator, and my wife asked you to follow me."

Replacement hesitated to answer.

Darren began to beg. "You can't tell my wife what you saw."

"I have to."

"You can't."

Jack wondered what vile thing Replacement had caught Darren doing.

"Does she think I'm having an affair?" the man asked.

"Yes," Replacement answered.

"I'm not. I swear it."

She nodded. "I know."

Jack raised his eyebrow and looked to Replacement for some answers. "What did you catch him doing?"

"Cleaning dishes over at the O'Donell Pub."

Jack shook his head. *You've got to be kidding me.* He took a long breath and holstered his gun. He knew the place. It was a dive. But the man's appearance and demeanor didn't match that of a dishwasher at a cheap restaurant. "Why were you..."

"My wife has had some medical problems. She had to stop working, and with the hospital bills... well, she's been feeling like she needs to go back to work. It's just too soon though—she has therapy, and recovery... I don't want her to feel that financial pressure. So I took a second job and told her we had plenty of money to pay the bills."

Replacement sighed.

"I'm sorry I barged in. I panicked. My wife can't know."

"You have to tell her the truth," Jack said. He retrieved the aspirin bottle and offered a couple to Darren. "Listen, Mr. Taylor. Your wife has no idea you're working a second job, is that right?"

"Yes. If she knew, she'd feel guilty and—"

Jack held up his hand. "Don't talk—just nod, okay?"

Darren obediently nodded.

"Good. You've obviously had to make up reasons why you're not home. Right?"

Darren nodded again.

"Well, that made your wife suspicious—" Darren started to speak but Jack held up his hand. "Sorry, she became *concerned*, so she hired a private investigator."

Darren's face fell. "She doesn't trust me."

"Darren, don't feel bad or take it personally. Your wife's sick and probably thinks you're unhappy. Her illness is hard enough on both of you, and now you're working two jobs so you're tired and stressed, on top of that. Your sex life has to have tanked. You come home late, and you don't tell her what you've really been doing."

Darren nodded.

"Women can sense when you're lying."

"But it was for a good reason."

"He was trying to help. He needed the job," Replacement added.

Darren looked at Replacement. "Please don't tell my wife. If she finds out, she'll insist on going back to work herself."

Replacement hesitated. "I could just tell her that you're not having an affair."

"No, you've got to tell his wife," Jack interjected.

"But—"

"If you don't, his wife will just hire another private investigator, or this whole thing could blow up worse than it has. Listen, Darren. Trust me. Tell your wife the truth. She'll understand you're being a stand-up guy, and I'm sure you can convince her to hold off on going back to work. It's a hell of a lot better than her thinking you're getting some action on the side. Just go tell her you love her so much that you took a dishwashing job for a little while."

"I—I don't want her to think less of me."

"Believe me, she's going to go crazy in a different way than how you think, and you can thank me later. For now, get the hell out."

"You think?"

Jack arched a brow.

Darren practically sprinted for the door. "Thank you. Thank you very much," he mumbled as he left.

The second the door closed, Replacement put her elbows on the kitchen counter and let her head flop into her hands.

Jack eyed her with sympathy. "There's more to being a good detective than just following somebody around."

"I'm so sorry. I was... I was..."

"Wrong," Jack finished as he headed into the kitchen.

"Yes. Wrong," she admitted. "I don't know what I'm doing. I just wanted to help, and since I didn't need a license in Darrington to be a private investigator..." She trailed off.

"We're one of the last states where you don't need a license. Next year that all changes. They're going to require mandatory firearms training, certification, and a minimum age of twenty-five."

"I'll be grandfathered in. I registered with the state. And how do you know all that?"

"I, ah, looked into it. But don't be too hard on yourself. You probably helped save their marriage. You did good... except for being seen."

"Thanks for getting me out of that mess."

He smiled at her.

Just then his phone buzzed. The screen lit up, displaying a text message from Kendra.

ARE YOU @*&^%#!= KIDDING ME?!?!?! YOU GOT SUSPENDED?!?!? I'M @ BOAR'S BUTT. COME SEE ME IF YOU NEED A SHOULDER.

Replacement lifted her head off her hands. From the expression on her face, she had obviously read the text as well. Her eyes were rounded in concern, and her little hands were tightly balled into fists.

I should let her go give Collins a piece of her mind.

"I didn't want you to see that." Jack sighed. "Before you say anything, just… wait a couple of minutes. We can talk after I take a shower."

He went into the bedroom and shut the door behind him. In the darkness, he paused.

All my life I wanted to be a cop. Have I just thrown that away?

19

NO, NO, NO...

As Jack peeled his shirt off in the bathroom, he winced.

"What the hell happened to you?" Replacement asked from the doorway.

Jack turned around and leaned back against the sink. "Can't I get any privacy?"

"You're not doing anything I shouldn't see, and you're hurt." Replacement opened the medicine cabinet and began to take things out. "You need to wash that scrape off now. It looks like you cut yourself and rolled in a mud puddle."

Good guess.

Replacement turned on the shower and pulled the curtain back. "Pants." She reached for his belt buckle.

He slapped her hand away. "I've got it. Turn around."

"No. I can't take care of you with my eyes closed. Here." She handed him a towel. "Just think of me like a nurse, okay?"

Replacement looked up at the ceiling and grinned while he took off his pants and wrapped the towel around himself.

"Let's start at the top," Replacement said. "Let me see your face." She turned the water on in the sink and got a washcloth wet.

Jack shut his eyes and leaned over the sink. "I feel like I'm four," he muttered.

"Open your mouth." Replacement tilted his head toward the light. "You've got a big cut in your mouth, too. You'll need to rinse with salt water."

"Yes, Mom."

She dabbed at the cut on his lip; he winced. "What hit you?"

"A broom handle to the lip and brass knuckles in the jaw."

Replacement made an awful face. "What's the other guy look like?"

Surprisingly, she looks pretty good, Jack thought, but he kept his mouth shut.

Replacement turned him around so she could work on the dirt in his shoulder. She felt around with the tips of her fingers, then gingerly pulled out a thin shard of glass. "Darn it, Jack. You might have to go to the hospital."

He rolled his eyes.

"Seriously, you might need a shot or something."

"I need a shot *of* something. I'm going to go get one when we're done here."

"You getting drunk won't help anything. I can't get this clean this way. Get in. I'll be right back." Replacement headed out of the bathroom.

Jack grudgingly dropped his towel on the floor, got in the shower, and pulled the curtain closed behind him. He shook when the water hit his wounds, but he stood still and let it run down over his body. After a minute, the sting started to fade, but the warmth just made him drowsy. He closed his eyes.

Replacement ripped the curtain back.

"Hey!" Jack yelled.

Jack tried to quickly cover up, but Replacement had her eyes closed and was holding a towel out to him. "Wrap this around you. You won't do a proper job of cleaning your wounds, so I'm coming in."

"You are *not* coming in—"

But Replacement had already grabbed the sides of her pants and yanked them to the floor. Jack's eyes went wide. At least she was wearing one of his T-shirts, and it hung halfway down her thighs.

Without waiting for an invitation, she stepped into the shower with him. "I have a shirt and panties on," she said, "so don't worry about it." She grinned as she held up the washcloth. "Turn around."

Jack complied.

She didn't say a word after that, just gently cleaned his wounds. But despite the obvious care she took not to hurt him, after a few moments Jack was clenching his teeth and balling his hands into fists.

"Congratulations on solving your first case," he said with some effort.

"Shut up." Replacement rubbed a little harder.

"Look, trust me, his wife will be a lot better off knowing."

"Well, still. I did all that for free," Replacement pouted.

"What? You're not taking any money?"

"No way! She's sick and he's washing dishes. How can I?"

Of course she wouldn't take it.

"Maybe they'll refer you?" Jack grinned, but it quickly faded. "You need to be careful following people."

"It was easy. I just waited and drove over to where he was."

Jack stuck his face under the water. "How did you know where he was?"

"GPS."

"GPS? That's not going to do you any good, unless—" *She wouldn't.* "Did you put a GPS device on his car?"

Jack could almost sense Replacement's shrug behind him. "Where else would I put it?"

"Are you out of your mind? That's illegal. You can't do that. Where the hell did you get it?"

"Online. I won it in an auction."

Jack spun around so fast he almost fell. "You used my credit card. Is that thing in *my* name? Damn it. Great. Just great."

"Relax. I always use a throwaway account and get a different card when I'm doing anything online. The FBI couldn't trace it back to you."

Interesting choice of words.

"Replacement. You can't put a GPS device on someone's car without a court order."

"People do it all the time." She grinned, and the water running down her face detoured into her dimple.

"On TV. That's not real. In reality, you go to prison for that."

She tilted her head to one side. "Well then, I'll try to be more careful."

If you didn't look so stinking cute, I'd... Damn.

"All right," Replacement said. "I think you're good up top. Now I just need to look at your leg."

"My leg?"

"It's cut too. Face the wall."

Jack turned to the side, and Replacement knelt down.

"Put your leg back," she commanded.

As she slid the towel up his leg and pulled the cut apart, Jack fought back a string of profanities. "I think that's enough," he said through gritted teeth. "This is weird. You're always walking in and seeing me half naked in the shower."

"It's not weird." Replacement scrunched up her face, leaned her head back under the water, and grinned. "You're smoking hot. It would be weird if I *didn't* want to see you naked."

She stood back up, and Jack looked down at her. His soaking wet T-shirt clung to her body and showed every curve. He watched the water run down her neck and travel down her chest—and he felt his hand tremble as he realized just how badly he wanted to be with her right now.

Replacement gazed up at him. He thought he could see desire in her eyes, too.

She stiffened.

Jack quickly reached over and turned the water off. He straightened up and brushed his hair back. "I think... I think I'm clean."

Replacement jumped out of the shower, grabbed a towel, and clutched it to her. She bit her lower lip as she looked him up and down. Then with a muttered, "I'm sorry," she ran out of the bathroom.

20

IF SHE DIDN'T HAVE THAT LASSO...

Jack's bedroom door opened, and Replacement's head appeared.

"Not tonight," Jack grumbled, staring at the ceiling.

"Can we talk?" She walked to the edge of the bed.

"No."

She hopped onto the bed next to him.

"You don't get 'no,' do you?"

She scooted over and looked down at him. "Is that why you got suspended? You didn't listen to a 'no'?"

Actually, you didn't listen.

"Something like that," Jack muttered.

"What's going on? What happened?" She arranged herself into a crossed-legged position beside him.

"I don't know where to start."

"Well, how about telling me what happened to your face?" Replacement's hand went out to touch his cheek.

"I told you. I got in a fight. I got my ass kicked."

"You?" She leaned back. "Really? Was it a few guys?"

"One."

Replacement pressed her lips together. "He must have been huge. Like, real big. It's okay. You said anyone could get in a lucky shot."

"It wasn't luck. She got the drop on me from the start and—"

"*She?*" Replacement shook her head as if she had water in her ears.

"She," Jack repeated.

"A girl?" Her voice rose in amazement.

Jack sat up. "Yeah. Is that so out of the realm of possibility to you?"

"I didn't mean to hurt your feelings."

Jack glared.

She dipped her chin down. "Was she like an Amazon or something?"

Jack rolled his eyes. "Yeah. I got in a fight with Wonder Woman, and if she didn't have that lasso I'd have kicked her ass."

"I'm just..." She closed her mouth and waved her hands. "Why did you get into a fight with her to begin with?"

"I went to Marisa's." Replacement frowned, but he ignored it. "This woman had broken into Marisa's apartment, and—"

"She broke in? Is Marisa okay? Is that why we haven't heard from her?"

"Hold up. A couple of nights ago, Thaddeus reported—"

"Who?"

"Thaddeus. He's this homeless guy who hangs out behind the tattoo parlor. He reported two guys had grabbed Marisa and had taken her in a car."

"Taken her? Kidnapped her?" Replacement scooted off the bed. "What the hell, Jack? You could have told me."

"I'm sorry. It's complicated. Anyway, like I said, the homeless guy reported it, but Collins didn't believe him."

"Collins is an ass."

"He's by the book, but he looked into—"

"He looked into Michelle, too." Replacement's eyes blazed, and her words hung in the air. "Don't defend him."

Jack swung his legs over the side of the bed. She was right.

Replacement's fists clenched and opened repeatedly. "They won't even look? *You're* searching for her, though, right?"

"Yes. Of course I am." Jack stood up.

"The clothes. That's why you had the weird hair. You did go undercover..." Replacement's voice trailed off, and she looked at the floor.

"Yeah. But I couldn't tell you."

She looked up. Jack wished she looked mad, but she didn't. She was hurt.

Way to go, Jack.

"I... I had my reasons, and most of them sound stupid now. I'm sorry. Marisa has a past, and I can't..."

Replacement's eyes narrowed.

"If *you* told me *your* darkest secret, would you want me to tell someone?" Jack asked.

Replacement stood there, fidgeting. "Fine. Let's get started." She marched into the living room.

Jack followed her. "What?"

"You haven't found her. Let's start at the beginning." She sat down and picked up a notebook.

Jack studied her. Sometimes she amazed him. She barely knew Marisa, but here she was, in the middle of the night, ready to go rescue her.

It would *be nice to talk through it with someone*, Jack thought. *But Replacement is* not *going out in the field on this one. It's way too dangerous.*

Jack paced while he talked. "Okay. The night that Marisa came over to talk to you about the whole graffiti thing, she told me she was scared. She felt like someone was watching her. I went back later that night, but she wasn't there." He walked over to the window. "I didn't think anything about it. I thought she just went home."

"That was Tuesday night."

"Yeah. And Wednesday, while I was walking my beat, I saw Thaddeus. He'd already gone to the police, but nothing happened."

"*See?*"

"Collins had his reasons. Thaddeus isn't the most reliable witness. Anyway, when Thaddeus saw the guys, he hid, so he only *thinks* they took her."

"But you believe him. And you believe Marisa."

"It might not be as black and white as that. What if... What if she just went away and—"

"I'm only going to say this once, Jack." She glared at him. "You were right about Michelle even when everyone doubted you. Don't doubt yourself now."

Jack looked out the window.

"Did Thaddeus get a good look at the guys?" Replacement asked.

"Only one. He said he was Asian and had his arms covered with tattoos."

Replacement scribbled that down. "Okay. Then what?"

"I took Thaddeus to the station, and we met these two Feds, Walter Prescott and Jennifer Rivers."

"Feds?"

"FBI."

"FBI? Oh, because it's a kidnapping? They sure came fast." Replacement put down her pen. "But I thought Collins didn't believe Thaddeus? So why were the Feds already there? And why would someone kidnap Marisa anyway? She isn't rich. Is she?"

Jack exhaled. *She can't help me if she doesn't know.*

He looked at his reflection in the window. "It's because Marisa has a past. Her father is a man named Severino Mancini. Her real name is Angelica."

Replacement turned to her computer and started typing. After two minutes, she looked up at Jack, wide-eyed. "Are you kidding me? This guy is a serious badass. He's ruthless. Even his name means *severe*. Do you know how many times he's been put on trial?" She leaned closer to the monitor.

"He's never been convicted," Jack said dryly.

"You dated *his* daughter? Are you insane?"

"She left her family when she was seventeen. That was almost eleven years ago."

"Why did she leave?"

Jack shrugged.

"She didn't tell you?"

"I didn't ask."

"Is that why she was kidnapped?"

"I don't know." Jack resumed pacing. "For all I know, it may not be related. But... why *else* would someone grab her? Like you said, she's not rich. And if it *is* a kidnapping, why hasn't anybody reached out to Severino?"

Replacement started to write something in her notebook, then froze. "How do you know no one has reached out to Severino?"

Jack stopped pacing. "I asked him."

Replacement spun around. "You went to see *him?*"

Jack could see fear and anger on her face, but also a little pride. "I did. He didn't know anything. But his son, Ilario, gave me a phone." He walked into the bedroom and brought out the phone. "He's going to call me if he finds anything. Don't worry, it's a burner—he can't trace Marisa back here."

"And has he called?"

"No."

"Okay, keep going."

"After I left Severino's, I followed his men to Chinatown. They met with the Yakuza. And then I met with the Yakuza. They didn't know anything either."

"*What?* Jack, even *I* know the Yakuza are Japanese Mafia. You met with them alone? No backup? Jack, that's… It's…"

Now she's ticked.

Jack stuck his hands in his pockets. "What else was I going to do?"

Replacement scribbled hard on the pad. "How about something not so… stupid?" She shook her head. "Fine. What reckless and dangerous thing did you do next?"

Jack ignored the attitude. "I went to Marisa's apartment. I'd already gone there yesterday morning before I went to see Severino, and found nothing. I went back again last night to check it out again, and it was still untouched. I left, but I forgot to leave a note with the neighbors, so I turned around to go back, and when I did, I saw the light from the hallway in the apartment. I went up there, and this woman was inside. She got the jump on me and took off. I chased her down and caught her, but… she knows how to fight."

"What did she look like?"

"Thick black hair, blue shorts with white stars, and this gold headband and lasso."

"Shut up." Replacement threw the pen at Jack. "I said I'm sorry about the Amazonian thing."

"Sorry. It's just hard, knowing I let her get away."

Replacement set the notebook down and looked at the clock.

"You need sleep." She stood. "Let me see what I can get online. You go back to bed. You're no good to me if you turn into a raging beast."

21

NOW IT'S MY TURN

The bullet ricocheted next to Jack's head. Someone screamed. A shell exploded just beyond the wall in front of him. A wave of sand lifted high into the air, and then darkness descended as the cloud enveloped him.

Jack rolled onto his stomach and started to crawl. His hands felt a body, and he pulled himself closer. Another shell blew up nearby, making Jack's ears feel as if they would burst.

The swirling sand burned his eyes. Jack's arm lay across the man's chest, and he felt no movement. He pulled himself up to look at the soldier's face, but only lifeless eyes stared back at him.

***

Jack opened his eyes and stifled a scream; Replacement's sleeping face was right there next to his own. He quietly slipped out of the bed. His whole body shook as he stood there, gasping.

Get it together. Nightmare.

Jack remembered the firefight. He remembered the dead soldier. But he couldn't recall the man's name. He turned and looked out the window.

You're alive. Be grateful.

Why me?

Shut up. Be grateful.

The first rays of the rising sun peeked through the window. Outside, bare tree branches clawed at the lightening sky.

Dead trees. No. They're not dead; they're dormant. Come spring, they'll be beautiful. Alive. Breathe. Just breathe.

Jack remembered the soldier's name.

Private Henry Waller. Twenty-two. North Carolina. Loved fishing.

As he stared out the window, a gray two-door coupe pulled away from the curb. Just before it took the left and disappeared, the driver turned her head.

Dark hair, porcelain skin...

Jack couldn't be certain, but she was a close match for the woman he'd fought in Marisa's apartment.

He leaned against the window frame and closed his eyes. When he opened them again, Replacement was watching him from the bed.

"You okay?" she asked sleepily.

He exhaled. "It was just a dream."

"You want to talk about it?"

"No. You find out anything?"

"Marisa has no social media footprint. I researched her father, and that totally freaked me out. You're right, he has no convictions, but that's only because no one will testify; they're all dead, missing, or terrified. What did you say was the name of the FBI guy? Prescott?"

"Yeah, Walter. Why?"

"It's another trial Severino walked on. It was almost twenty years ago. Prescott testified." She stretched. "Shootout. Prescott's partner was wounded. Karl Weaver. He ended up in a wheelchair."

"That explains why Prescott hates him. Did the article say why Severino got off?"

"Not enough evidence. Two witnesses. One changed her story, said she never saw anything, and the other one disappeared—permanently." Replacement yawned. "Ilario Mancini is in med school, by the way. I found a photo. He totally looks like her." She hopped out of bed.

"Stay sleeping."

"I want to see if my program's finished."

"What program?"

"Well, you said you went into the city to see Severino, right? I figure if someone was after Marisa to get to Severino, they would have come from the city, right?" She shrugged.

"Okay…"

"And if they came from the city, they'd take the highway and get off at the toll. It has cameras, and—"

"You didn't hack any government websites again, did you?"

"No."

He eyed her suspiciously.

"You know how there are public websites where you can watch traffic cameras from around the world?"

"The Internet and I aren't on speaking terms, but I'll take your word for it."

"Well, there are. Sites like Trafficland and the DOT. New York City even has its own cable television station: NYC Drive. They stream the video to help drivers. Some guy wrote a computer program that scans the video and records all the license plates. It compiles them into a database. I just pulled up the cached video from the state tollbooths on Tuesday and ran it through the program. Then I logged in to the police database as you and started cross-referencing."

Jack looked at her with awe.

"I narrowed the search to look only for cars registered in the city, but I could also try limiting it to whether it's stolen, rented, or arrests, or something else."

"Wow." Jack rushed over, grabbed her, and kissed her forehead. "That's brilliant. Illegal, but brilliant. I didn't hear any of this, by the way."

Even Replacement's ears blushed. "I don't know if it will work. It may take too long trying to access the different systems and trying to pull those records."

"It's something, and at least we're moving. Thank you."

They walked into the living room together. Replacement headed straight to the desk. "I'll start looking at the results."

"Can I help?" Jack asked. "You want coffee?"

"Yes to both." She smiled.

They spent all morning and afternoon poring over the records of the cars that had driven through the tollbooth. Jack frequently checked his phones, still hoping for a message from Marisa. By the time the sun started to set, he was pacing.

"It was a stupid idea," Replacement said. "I'm sorry I—"

"It was a good idea. Don't be upset." Jack patted her head, but she swatted his hand away.

"That doesn't help."

"I know." He grinned and headed for the bedroom. "Maybe they didn't come over on Tuesday. They could have already been here."

Replacement followed him. "What now?"

Jack leaned against the wall and glanced out the window. He hadn't seen the gray coupe again, but he was sure that woman was still following him.

"We try to find the Asian woman."

"How? We have no idea where she could be."

"No, we don't. But I have a plan to lure her out. Now it's my time to turn the tables."

Replacement smiled.

Jack put on the new baggy pants he'd bought, right over the top of his jeans. He turned around. "Can you tell I'm wearing two pairs of pants?"

"Why?"

"I have an idea. Can you tell?"

Replacement put her weight on her left leg and bit her lip. "No." She shrugged. "They're so baggy you can't tell. But isn't it uncomfortable?"

Jack grabbed the shirt, pulled it over his head, then paused.

What do I do about Replacement? I shouldn't take her with me. It's too dangerous...

"Are you thinking about leaving me behind?"

Am I that transparent?

"What? No!" He pulled the shirt on the rest of the way. "Of course not."

22

_____

A GOOD PLACE TO TALK

Jack hurried down the sidewalk toward the apartment building at the end of the street. He was two blocks from Marisa's apartment, four from the tattoo parlor. There was a light rain falling, and because of the cloud cover, it was very dark. The weather was perfect for what he had planned.

With his head down and the collar of his jacket up, he rushed up the steps, nervously looked around, and rang the bell. He was buzzed right in. He walked into the entryway, and Donald Pugh leaned out of his apartment and waved him over.

"Thanks, Donald."

Donald's apartment was a small one-bedroom. The kitchen was tiny, and the living room was only slightly bigger, dominated by a giant TV. Jack heard the sound of claws on linoleum, and a little collie ran up to him. He gave the dog's head a quick pat and then turned to Donald.

"Let's go over the plan—" Jack began.

Donald waved his hands to cut him off. "Jack, you've got to promise me this won't get back to Collins."

Donald may have been a cop and Kendra's partner, but he didn't have the typical temperament for the job. His face was pale, and Jack could see he was sweating.

"It won't. I promise." He yanked off his shirt and handed it to Donald.

"Do you even know how mad you make him?" Donald said. "Now everyone asks 'How Jacked-up is Collins?' when we have to go near him. It's like measuring an earthquake, but instead of a Richter scale, we use a Stratton scale. You got suspended, and it was a ten. If the sheriff finds out I'm helping you, he'll go off the chart."

"He won't find out." Jack kicked off his shoes and pulled off the baggy pants. "Here. It'll only take fifteen minutes. Just head out of the apartment and walk the route we talked about."

Donald pulled his shirt off, revealing a bulletproof vest. Jack tried not to frown, but his lips curled down regardless.

Donald must have noticed. "Do you not want me to wear it?" He stopped with the new shirt halfway over his head.

"No. It was good thinking. I have a couple pounds on you."

Donald pulled the shirt down. "Can you repeat the route for me?" He took the hat off Jack's head and swapped it with his own.

"You're going to just do a big *S*, okay? You'll end up at the Old Mill Apartments, if you make it that far. If you do, go around to the parking area and just wait."

"Should we switch shoes?"

Jack looked down at Donald's feet and shook his head. "We may be the same height, but what size shoe do you wear, a four?"

"Shut up. I have small feet. Here I am helping you, and—"

Jack held his hand up. "Sorry. Keep your shoes." Jack pulled Donald's cap down lower and flipped the collar of his jacket up. "Ready?"

"Did she follow you from your apartment?" Donald rolled his shoulders and took deep breaths.

Jack shrugged. "I hope. I want her guessing what I'm up to, so get out of here fast. I'll give you a minute, then I'll go out the back and circle around."

Donald straightened up and took a step back. "How do I look?" He turned around.

"You look like good bait." Jack grinned.

Donald's eyes widened.

Not the right time to joke, Jack. "You've got this, Donald." Jack put his fist up; Donald swallowed, then bumped it.

Donald took one more deep breath, patted his gun under his jacket, and headed out.

"Keep your head down," Jack whispered before the door closed.

Jack hurried to the back door of the apartment, the little dog following happily behind him. He slipped out the door, holding the dog back, then jogged to the corner of the building, making sure he kept close to it and in the shadows.

Wait. She followed me without my knowing before. She knows what she's doing. She'll let Donald get a good distance away from her before she starts to tail him. There aren't many people on the street, so she'll have to keep farther back.

Jack's eyes stopped scanning when he saw a woman walk down the far side of the street. He strained to see her clearly through the rain and darkness. The weather would definitely help sell his deception, but now it worked against him, hiding her as well. The woman held an opened black umbrella, and she wore a black, waist-length coat, high heels, and a medium-length black skirt.

Not really the outfit for shadowing someone.

The hairs on the back of Jack's neck rose. He let her get almost to the end of the block before he started forward. He tried to relax as he followed.

The umbrella is going to screw her up. Limits her view. Maybe she's too focused on him.

Jack stuck his hands in his pockets and tipped his head slightly forward against the rain. He hoped he just looked like a guy heading downtown who was too stupid to bring an umbrella.

The woman's stride was steady and purposeful. He couldn't see her head, but the whole umbrella shifted like a giant arrow whenever she looked somewhere. She looked like someone trying to get out of the rain. Maybe it wasn't her?

The woman stopped at the corner of Elderberry, the street Jack knew Donald had gone up. He could feel his chest tighten as he waited to see whether she'd turn or continue on her way. Elderberry was more of a side street. If she picked it, odds were she was following Donald.

The black umbrella shifted on her shoulder when she looked up Elderberry. Jack forced himself to keep walking. Then the umbrella straightened back up and she stepped off the curb and crossed the road.

Damn. It's not her.

But just before she reached the other side of the street, she leapt effortlessly over a large puddle. She landed on the balls of her high heels and turned left so she could continue up the road after Donald.

It is her. She jumped that puddle like Baryshnikov. She's either a dancer or a martial artist. She's following him. Great… Now I just have to try to catch her.

Jack started to run, his feet splashing in the puddles. The plan was to circle around; with the route he'd sent Donald on, he'd be able to cut them off. He flew down the street and ducked into an alley that led to a spot where Donald would pass. But as Jack swung into the back of the alley, he grimaced. Donald was already walking by, and he was walking too fast.

He's too nervous. She's going to know something is up and back off if he doesn't slow down.

The woman walked into view on the other side of the road. When she reached the alley directly across from the one Jack was in, she turned to head straight down it.

Damn. She knows he's onto her. She's rabbiting.

Jack bolted from the shadows and sprinted across the street. He could see Donald in the distance, still walking too fast with his head down, unaware the woman was no longer following him. Then Jack raced into the alley after the woman.

The front portions of the alleys crisscrossed downtown and were kept clean. However, the back ends of the alleys, through which Jack now raced headlong, were lined with boxes, dumpsters, shipping pallets, and trash.

Jack turned a corner. The alley ahead of him was deserted. Jack sprinted forward.

As he approached a big green dumpster on the right, he saw a discarded high-heel shoe sticking out from underneath it. He was just able to get his arms up in time to block the attack as the woman leaped out and swung the closed umbrella in a wide arc at his head. Jack's forearm deflected the blow, but he growled in pain as the umbrella bent around his arm.

He slid to a stop and turned to glare at the woman.

She was Japanese and stood around five six. She casually slipped her jacket off, revealing clearly defined muscles in her arms. Her skin was a pearly white, and her eyes and teeth gleamed in the rain. She was uniquely attractive; her jaw and cheekbones were so angular it gave her an almost wolfish appearance.

She tossed the broken umbrella behind her, but Jack noticed her left hand stayed low and drawn back. He moved half a step toward the wall.

Take her down fast and hard. Wonder Woman kicked your ass before. It doesn't matter that she's a girl.

She moved the opposite way, her eyes never leaving his chest. Jack saw the tip of a knife in her left hand.

She's faster than me. Much faster.

Jack's foot touched the edge of a metal trashcan. He grabbed the trashcan and heaved it at her.

I have to be meaner.

The contents of the trashcan flew out in a spray. Jack lunged at the woman, thinking she had only one way to go—through him—but he was wrong. She grabbed the top of the dumpster, flipped herself onto the cover, and then flipped again over the side.

Jack grabbed a wooden pallet and launched it at her.

She tried to block it, but it hit her solidly and sent her sprawling backward. She groaned as she landed hard on the pavement. The knife skittered out of her hand.

Jack started toward her again, amazed at how quickly she regained her feet. But just at that moment Donald came running around the corner, his gun held low, and almost crashed right into her.

Donald hesitated. The woman didn't. She grabbed his gun hand and elbowed him in the face. Jack drew his gun, but he was too late; she was already shielded behind Donald. She pressed Donald's gun into his back. Donald's hands went out, and he looked desperately at Jack.

"Easy…" Jack kept his gun pointed at the woman.

"Put down your weapon, Officer Stratton." The woman's voice was remarkably calm.

"Not a chance. Drop the gun."

"We want the same things, Officer."

"Good. Start with me wanting you to put the gun down." Jack moved forward, and she moved back with Donald.

"I would prefer to have this conversation some other time."

Jack's jaw tightened, and he raised his gun a little higher. He eyed her shoulder. *It's not a good shot. No one else would take it…* "Last chance, lady."

Donald lifted his hands up further and waved them. "Don't. Please, Jack."

"You will not shoot, Officer."

"*I* will," Replacement yelled from behind the woman.

The woman stopped moving. Jack stepped sideways to see Replacement with her feet shoulder-width apart, holding a gun aimed at the woman's back.

Where the hell did she get a stupid gun?

"You won't shoot. Neither of you will." The woman's eyes narrowed, and she looked first at Replacement and then back to Jack.

She's not sure of that.

Jack watched Replacement.

Neither am I.

"Easy, Alice," Jack said. He tried to catch her eye, but Replacement's cold glare was fixed on the woman.

The three of them stared one another down.

Jack kept his gun level. "What's it gonna be, lady?"

"I guess here is a good place to talk after all." The woman spun the gun around and held it out to Donald, grip first.

Donald grabbed the gun and took two quick steps back.

The woman straightened her shirt, then turned to face Jack. "I am looking for Angelica Mancini, too."

"And you are?"

"My name is Kiku."

Her words were clipped and crisp, with an edge of refinement to them. She stood with one foot forward, the other slightly angled. There was a sense of action about her even though she didn't move.

Poised. She's not breaking a sweat. Three on one, and she doesn't bat an eyelash. Girl is a pro.

Her medium-length, feathered hair was a rich charcoal that matched her outfit. She could have easily been waiting in a beauty salon instead of standing in an alley with two guns pointed at her. She met Jack's gaze and raised a dark eyebrow.

"Where is she?" Jack kept his gun pointed at her chest.

"That is what both of us are trying to figure out." She inhaled, and her entire body seemed to relax. She cocked her head. "I think our little tête-à-tête may have attracted unwanted attention."

Jack could hear a siren in the distance. Replacement kept her gun up but looked at Jack. He could see the question in her eyes.

Jack addressed Donald. "Head toward Cushing Street. Go home that way." Then he turned to Replacement. "You've got my back. Stick with me. Put your gun away. I'll keep her covered." Finally, he turned to Kiku. "Start walking."

"Jack, I can help. What do you want me to do?" Donald asked.

"You've done enough. Thanks. I don't want you mixed up in this."

Donald's eyes bulged. "I think you meant 'mixed up any more than you already are' in this."

Jack grinned crookedly. "Exactly."

"Before you go," Kiku said, "would you please retrieve my shoes and jacket?" She pointed under the trash container.

Donald looked at Jack to make sure it was okay. Jack nodded his approval, and Donald picked up her things.

Replacement took the things from Donald with a frown. "I'll hold on to them. She can get her feet dirty." Replacement dangled the shoes in one hand and tucked the jacket under her arm.

She'll be slower in heels. "Give her the shoes," Jack said. He shot Replacement a look, and she tossed them at Kiku's feet.

The sirens drew closer. "I'd better get going." Donald turned and jogged away.

"Move," Jack ordered Kiku.

"Gladly. I have no desire to meet with the police."

The three of them walked quickly down the alley. Jack kept his gun concealed by his jacket and cringed when Replacement put hers in her waistband.

"What are you doing, Jack?" Replacement whispered fiercely.

"She's looking for her, too."

"Aren't you believing her a little too easily, even for your truth meter?"

"I have my reasons."

"Where are we taking her?"

Replacement was trying to walk beside him, but he kept his arm out to keep her slightly behind him.

"My apartment."

"Home? *Our* home?"

Again Replacement tried to push forward. Jack had to hold his arm firmly so she didn't get between him and Kiku, who marched five feet in front of them.

"Will you stop pushing me for a second?" Replacement began.

Kiku looked back, annoyed. "Can you get her under control, Officer? The police are getting closer."

She definitely doesn't want to talk to the cops.

The rain came down more heavily, making the night even darker. As they neared the end of the alley, the woman looked back again. "If your intention is to march me down the street with your gun in your pocket, may I please save us the trouble and flag down a police car?"

Jack knew she was right; they couldn't leave the alley like this without drawing unwanted attention. He looked at Replacement. "Pat down her jacket, then give it to her."

"You're not taking her back to my home," Replacement protested.

Jack ran a hand through his hair. "She's already been there."

Replacement's jaw dropped slightly, and her head turned slowly toward Kiku.

"Very impressive, Officer," Kiku said.

Thanks for confirming a guess.

"You broke into my house?" Replacement's fists quivered at her sides.

"Just give her the jacket," Jack said.

Replacement rifled through the pockets. A little grin formed on her face as she balled it up. "Nothing." She tossed it at Kiku.

"You stay on my left and a foot and a half out, the same distance behind," Jack instructed.

Replacement's eyebrows arched, but she did as she was told.

Jack switched hands with his gun and turned to Kiku. "Don't try anything."

"I'll be good." She grinned, and Jack saw her large canine teeth, which only added to her wolfish appearance.

Jack grabbed her by the elbow, and the three of them walked at a faster pace, the rain pouring down.

At the first intersection, Jack stopped suddenly. Kiku pulled forward, and Jack was surprised at the strength in her arm. Replacement bumped into him from behind.

Jack frowned and started to walk again. "I said keep a foot—"

"Yeah, yeah, stay two meters out and at a forty-five degree obtuse angle." Replacement shook her head. "You're the one who just seized up."

"He's keeping you away from me," explained Kiku. "He also stopped to check my strength."

"Stop talking until we're back," Jack grumbled.

***

When they got back to the apartment, Replacement clomped up the stairs, making her displeasure known. Inside, Kiku went straight toward Jack's bedroom. "Do you mind if I dry my hair?"

She said the words so casually that Jack almost nodded, but he caught himself and shook his head instead. "Sit. Big comfy chair." He pointed to the recliner in the corner. He knew it was awkward to get out of.

Kiku stopped in the middle of the living room, then turned and looked at Jack and Replacement. Replacement drew her gun.

Jack put his hand out to Replacement. "Put it away. She could have killed me three different times now. She didn't."

"Who says she won't try for four?"

Kiku took off her jacket and held it out. It was soaked, and water dripped to the floor. "Can you hang up my coat?"

Replacement frowned but stepped forward.

Jack reached out to stop her walking between them, but he wasn't fast enough. Kiku flipped the jacket up and over Replacement's head, hit Replacement's forearm with her left hand, and grabbed the gun with her right.

Kiku pointed the gun at Jack's chest. "*Now* it's four."

23

STRANGE BEDFELLOWS

Kiku had Replacement's gun pointed at Jack's chest. Replacement held her left arm with her right hand and glared at the woman, who grinned triumphantly. "Sit down, Officer." Kiku angled her head slightly. "May I call you Jack?"

Jack ignored the command and took off his jacket instead. "Like I said, you could have killed me before, but you didn't. You won't now."

"Don't," she said. The gun didn't waver.

A wiseass grin spread across Jack's face. "Shoot me then." He took off his jacket and walked over to hang it up on the back of the door.

Kiku's eyes narrowed.

She's dangerous.

"You are correct. I won't shoot you... now," she said in an even tone. "I want to speak with you. But in a civilized manner."

"Sure, we can talk." Jack held out his hand. "After you give me her fake gun."

Kiku's eyes widened. She looked down at the gun in her hand.

Replacement pouted. "How did you know?"

"Fake guns are a cop's nightmare," Jack said. "Besides, it's an M9. I had to clean a thousand of those in the service. It's not the best replica. The barrel is too short, the dust cover is too fat, and the sight is huge."

Kiku let the gun swing around her finger. She handed it to Jack, then gracefully bowed her head. "May we talk?"

"Right after I stab you in the face." Replacement took a step forward, but Jack grabbed her arm.

"Why are you here?" Jack asked.

Kiku smiled. "When I said civilized, I didn't just mean without guns. May I please have a towel and something to drink?"

Replacement looked back and forth between Jack and Kiku twice, then, with a dramatic sigh, she walked into the bedroom and returned with three towels. "What kind of name is Kick-u anyway?"

"It is pronounced KEE-koo," she replied coolly.

Replacement stood toe to toe with Kiku. "Tea, coffee, orange juice, or drain cleaner?"

Kiku ignored the gibe and began toweling off her hair. "Tea, hot."

Jack dried off his own hair, then leaned against the kitchen counter. "How did you find me?"

"The spiked hair and baggy pants were a good look on you." She smiled, turned to the window, and drew the blinds. "You lost one group of men sent to follow you, but you still have a lot to learn."

"If Takeo didn't have anything to do with her disappearance, why are you here?"

Kiku shrugged. "Someone has taken Angelica Mancini, and I've been sent to find out who. The Mancinis believe it was my employer. Tensions are high between our two… organizations, and if something were to happen to Angelica, the Mancinis will think Takeo is responsible, and tensions could escalate. The Mancinis are preparing for war, Jack. My orders are to prevent it."

Jack shook his head. "I know the Yakuza are trying to move in on Severino's knock-off operations. How do I know they didn't grab Angelica because of that?"

"Regardless of any business, the *ninkyō dantai* were not involved in the abduction of that woman."

"The who?" Replacement asked as she laid out cups.

"*Ninkyō dantai.* Jack prefers to call them 'Yakuza.' That is a label placed on them by the media at the behest of the Japanese police."

"I forgot." Jack crossed his arms. "You prefer to be called a 'chivalrous organization.'"

"You continue to impress. That is correct. It is also true."

"And you thought it was me who kidnapped her," Jack said.

Replacement dropped a teacup into the sink.

"I had to rule you out," Kiku replied.

"Have you?"

"You were looking for her too hard." She wrinkled her nose. "You hunt for Angelica like a drowning man seeking air."

"You went to her apartment," Replacement said to Kiku. "Did you find anything?" Her voice was much lower than normal.

"I found some very interesting sketches of Jack." Kiku smiled. "I wondered if you had posed, or if she had drawn you naked from memory. They were quite stunning. You seem to be Marisa's favorite art subject. That is her preferred name now, isn't it?"

"You weren't in there that long," Jack noted.

"The first time, no," Kiku replied. "I did go back."

"So you have nothing?" Replacement walked over with a cup of tea.

Jack was a little nervous that Replacement might be about to do something stupid.

Kiku took the cup and handed the wet towel to Replacement, who accepted it with a frown. The tea cupped in both hands, Kiku took a seat. "I know of two parties that have no involvement in her disappearance: you and I. Other than that, I know a few nice details about Officer Stratton." Her eyes roamed over Jack's body, lingering pointedly on certain locations.

She's pushing Replacement's buttons on purpose. Testing her.

"Did you take anything from Marisa's apartment?" Jack asked.

Her head tilted just a fraction and her lips pursed. Both motions were very rapid and she stopped them just as quickly. "Nothing."

She's telling the truth.

"Well then," Replacement said, "thanks so much for coming by, since you have zip info. Now, sorry, but you've gotta go." Replacement pointed toward the door. "Bye-bye."

Kiku didn't move.

Jack leaned up against the counter. "She has a point."

Kiku looked into her teacup. "I think it would be beneficial if we shared information. Would it not?"

"'Share' is the key word," Jack said.

Kiku looked at him coolly. "Mancini's men are on the way here."

Jack's chest tightened. *How?* She *followed me, but I couldn't have led* them *back here, too. Could I?*

"What was missing from her apartment?" Kiku asked.

Jack debated what to tell her. "Nothing."

She frowned. "You still do not trust me, Jack. Pity. I would think with our similar backgrounds, you would realize we are kindred spirits."

"You work for the bad guys. We're not on the same side."

"You have some knowledge of my organization. I have some of you. I have been reading up on you. You are the son of a murdered boy and a prostitute. If you had been born in Japan, you would have been one of us. We're the outcasts, but we protect each other."

"By hurting other people?"

She sipped her tea. "We watch out for those of us who are too weak to protect themselves. If someone comes after them, or us, we deal with the issue. Look at you and Alice. You are her protector, no?"

"It's the other way around." Jack smiled wryly at Replacement, who glared at Kiku. "So, you protect each other? Then what happened to your pinky?"

Kiku's teacup froze halfway to her lips. Her little finger had been cut off just after the second knuckle.

He saw the flash in her eyes. It wasn't anger he saw there; it was shame. The memory of his own shame caused a bitter taste to rise in his mouth.

"Every organization has rules," she said. "They keep order. I violated one."

Replacement's lip curled. "And they chopped off part of your pinky? It's a good thing Jack's not in the Yakuza. He wouldn't have any hands left. He's not good with rules."

Kiku's face hardened, and her jaw flexed. "War is coming, Jack. If we do not find Angelica quickly, Darrington will be the battlefield. Severino Mancini is a butcher, and he will tear this town apart to find his daughter." She rose and walked over to pick up her jacket. "Or he will burn this town to the ground to avenge her."

She handed the teacup back to Replacement with a slight bow, slipped into her jacket, and looked up at Jack. "Do you know what else they say about war, Officer? It makes for strange bedfellows." A leer spread across her lips. "I appreciate the tea. And I am sorry about your face."

24

CRAZY SMART

Jack paced. "The Mancinis are coming to Darrington. This is not good. If I led them here..." Jack knew he would never forgive himself. Even if he got Marisa back, she could never come back to the life she'd had here. Not now that Severino had found her. *I'm sorry, Marisa.*

Replacement flipped open the burner phone, pressed a few buttons, then tossed it back on the counter. "No calls in or out. Ever. If they're coming, why didn't her brother call you?"

Jack stopped pacing. "I don't think he's involved in the business."

"The business?"

"His father's organization. His uncle backhanded him in front of me. Wise guys don't show weakness within the ranks." He shot her a look. "Ilario is going to medical school. I venture that Severino keeps him at arm's length."

Replacement put her elbows on the counter and leaned her face into her hands. "I don't get it. Don't kidnappers call right away?"

"That's the movies. They're all different. Sometimes there's no call. And if it's related to her father, they could be giving him time to raise cash."

"It's crazy to kidnap a crime boss's daughter. Why not just rob a bank?"

"It's not *that* crazy. In fact, it's crazy smart. Severino has to have cash. Untraceable cash." Jack resumed pacing. "And with the whole Omerta thing, they're not going to the cops."

"Omerta?"

"It's an honor code. They handle things themselves. It's how the Mafia started. Back in the old days, the police were corrupt, so you couldn't go to them even if you wanted to."

"So..." Replacement stuck her tongue in her cheek. "You kidnap the boss's daughter, get ready, untraceable cash, and you're sure they won't go to the cops. That *is* smart."

"*Crazy* smart though, because it's also dangerous. The Mancinis aren't a family to take lightly. Whoever has Marisa is willing to take them on. They have serious guts."

"What was that deal with Kiku's pinky? How did you know all that?"

Jack shrugged. "The pinky thing I learned in kendo. It's like Japanese fencing—sword fighting. You hold the sword real loose with your fingertips. When my instructor taught me to hold it with just the tips of my fingers, he told me how they punish people in the Yakuza. They start with your pinky to weaken your sword grip. They don't mess around."

"So what now?" Replacement said. "Kiku knew nothing, so we're back to square one."

"Well, we know she didn't take the business card."

"What?"

"I forgot about it until Kiku started talking about Marisa's apartment. There's an art contest or something Marisa's entering next week. There was a business card on her kitchen counter, and someone had written a note for her on the back of it, offering to buy the piece she's entering in the festival. After Kiku attacked me, I noticed the card was gone. I thought Kiku took it, but she obviously didn't even know it was gone—which means someone else took it."

Replacement moved for the computer. "What do you remember about the card?"

"It was for the de Lorme Galleria."

Replacement began to type. After a few minutes, the screen was covered with various websites regarding the gallery and the upcoming art festival. "It's a local thing. It doesn't look that big," Replacement said.

It was to Marisa. "Who runs it?"

"Arber de Lorme. French. Thirty-something years old. Tall. Very handsome. Rich."

Jack frowned. "He's not that tall. Go back to the gallery."

"One second. I want to see his biography." She tiled different windows on the screen.

"This guy's in love with his own face." Jack reached for the mouse, but Replacement blocked him with her shoulder.

"He could be a model." She clicked on another page. "Oh, he was one."

She looked up at Jack, who scowled. "Just go back to the gallery page already."

"What? Are you jealous?" A little smirk spread across her face.

Jack scoffed. "No."

"Good. You shouldn't be." She winked.

She clicked on the link for past festivals. Jack scanned pictures of people dressed in their formal best, sipping wine and looking at paintings on the walls. He cringed at the thought of being there.

Replacement made a face. "I think I'd last about five minutes at that party."

"I'd race you for the door. I—"

Jack's hand tightened on the back of the chair. Marisa was in one of the photographs—in the background, but it was definitely her. And next to her was Arber, his arm around her waist. From the way his hand rested on her hip, it was obvious the two were more than acquaintances.

"What year was that festival?" Jack asked.

Replacement scrolled around. "Not sure. I think three years ago. It may have been two. It wasn't last year's."

"Go back to that guy's website. Where does he live?"

"Jack, just because they're standing like that doesn't mean—"

"They dated. Someone mentioned it in passing once. Don't ask. Get the address. Please."

Replacement smiled. "Does this mean we're taking a ride?"

25

SOMEONE'S COMPENSATING

The Impala drove up a long, winding driveway to Arber's huge stone house. On the edges of the pavement, small lights illuminated the way.

"What's he park here, a plane?" Jack quipped.

"He owns one." Replacement looked up from her phone. "And a yacht. Look at the picture. It's massive."

"Someone's compensating," Jack jeered.

"For what?"

Jack laughed, then saw her puzzled expression. "Uh... nothing."

They parked the car and strode up a wide stone walkway. Replacement looked at Jack as they stepped up to the door. "You ever want a boat?"

Jack grinned roguishly. "I don't need one." He rang the bell.

Replacement still looked perplexed, but kept her mouth shut as they waited at the enormous black door for someone to appear. After another minute, the door opened.

Arber de Lorme looked just like his photos: tall, fit, and handsome. His black hair was swept back. His feet were bare, and his loose shirt was untucked, and he held an almost-empty wine glass in his right hand. His frown at Jack and Replacement turned to a look of annoyed disgust when his gaze turned to the old Impala parked in his driveway.

"There's a gas station about four miles down the way." He rolled his eyes and turned back into the house. "Push the car out of the driveway before you go. I don't want it to leave any spots." He started to close the door.

"Actually, Arber." Jack felt his hand tighten into a fist as he pressed it against the door to hold it open. "I'm here to ask you a few questions."

The disgusted look remained on Arber's face. "Are you with the authorities?"

I'm suspended. I don't even have my badge.

Replacement flashed a badge. "Do you want to answer our questions here or downtown, Mr. de Lorme?"

I'm going to kill her.

"We're here to ask you some questions about Marisa Vitagliano," Jack said. "Or should we speak with your guest first?"

Arber looked back into the house. "This isn't the best time." He angled his head inside. "I have company. Come back later, okay?" He smiled thinly.

He started to close the door again, but again Jack's hand stopped it. "It won't take long,"

Arber glared. "You can't force your way in here."

"Really?" Jack rolled his shoulders.

"Jack." Replacement put her hand on his arm.

He cast a quick glance back at her, and as he did, he spotted someone moving in the shadows at the far edge of the yard.

Arber sighed. "I'm sorry if I sound rude, but I've had a glass or two to drink. And I do have company tonight. So if you don't mind, call the gallery and I'd be happy to speak with you later. Goodnight."

Jack stepped back. "We'll do that. Thanks for your time. Have a good night."

The door closed, and they heard the lock click.

Replacement looked at Jack, perplexed. As Jack headed down the stairs, she hesitated at the door.

"Come on," he called back.

She jogged to catch up with him. "That's it? You're just walking away?"

Jack kept moving. "We'll talk in the car."

They hopped in, and Jack started down the long driveway.

Replacement did a double take when he turned right instead of left. "Where are we going?"

Jack drove around the corner. Up ahead, a car was parked on the edge of the road. He shut off his lights and pulled up behind it.

"Roll your window down."

"What?" Replacement asked, but she still cranked the window down.

"Wait," Jack instructed.

A few seconds later, Kiku appeared silently out of the brush and walked over to the car.

"Officer." She smiled.

Jack leaned over. "A business card was missing from Marisa's apartment. The guy who lives here owns an art gallery downtown that's sponsoring an art festival Marisa entered. His name is Arber de Lorme. He dated Marisa. I have no idea how often or how long. He didn't want to talk to me. There's one other person in the house, he said. I didn't see who it was. I assume it was a female. He'd had a couple of drinks, and the alarm was off. The alarm panel is just to the right of the door."

Replacement's mouth hung completely open.

"Dogs?" Kiku asked.

Jack shrugged. "Didn't see any. I assume cameras."

"Let me have a look. I'll stop back at your apartment." Kiku turned and disappeared back into the darkness.

Jack pulled back onto the road, turning the lights back on.

"You sent her after him?" Replacement peered back into the night.

"She's the best way to get the information I need."

"But she's... she's Yakuza."

"Kiku's looking for Marisa. That guy's a scumbag."

Replacement held up her hands. "I'm fine with that." She laughed. "I knew you were too easy about leaving."

Jack gripped the steering wheel. "What the hell was that back there?"

"What?" Her smile vanished.

"The stupid, fake, plastic badge."

"It worked, didn't it?"

"It's called impersonating a police officer! It's a felony, Alice."

"I never said I'm a cop."

"You flashed the badge. You implied it. That's the law."

"They do it all the time." She crossed her arms.

"In the *movies*. But they don't go to jail in the movies. In real life you do."

"No offense, but didn't you just instruct a ninja to go break into his house?"

"But *I'm* not breaking in."

"So if I let you pull out your badge when you're suspended—"

Jack interrupted her. "You didn't know I was going to pull out my badge."

"I saw your arm twitch, and you looked at your jacket pocket."

Jack exhaled loudly. "Okay, I appreciate you watching out for me, but still. We have to sit down and go over what you can and *can't* do."

Replacement sat up straight. "I can handle myself."

"You had a fake gun and a fake badge. You're going to end up really shot."

Replacement huffed and turned to look out the windshield. "Actually, I didn't think you were going for your badge. You don't have your badge. I thought you were going to try to bluff him."

"How do you know I don't have my badge?"

"I learned it from movies. When you get suspended, they take your badge."

"What about my gun? Do I have it or not?" Jack raised an eyebrow.

"Not. No, wait. You had it in the alley. Collins didn't take it?"

"No. The movies get that wrong. It's my gun. I own it."

They came out to the main road. Ahead, ambulance lights mingled with the lights of police cruisers and a tow truck. Jack stiffened, then pulled over behind the last cruiser.

As he stepped out of the car, Officer Tom Kempy called out, "Hey, Jack."

Jack jogged over. "What's up, Tom?" Replacement came up behind him.

Tom pointed toward the ambulance. "He'll be all right. He said he hit black ice and slid off the road. He clipped a couple of trees, but the paramedics said he looks fine. Not even a scratch."

"Who?"

"Murphy was driving. But he's fine."

Jack's heart skipped a beat.

"The car took the brunt of the impact," Tom added.

Jack darted around Tom and looked off the road, into the ditch. "No!" Jack screamed. His stomach turned.

Replacement rushed up beside him, and they both looked down at the police car that rested on its side in the rocky ditch.

The Dodge Charger.

Damn it. Not the Charger.

The ambulance pulled away, leaving Jack to turn and scream a string of obscenities after it. All of them were directed at the man who was on his way to the hospital— Billy Murphy.

Two tow truck operators were winching the Charger out of the ditch. The whole left side was smashed in, and the rear window was broken. Jack stormed furiously around the car. The right rear quarter panel had a large dent in it, too.

"Did he bend her frame?" he growled.

The two tow truck drivers looked at each other, then back at Jack. They shrugged.

"Idiot!" Jack muttered as he walked onto the road. "Stupid moron can't drive a freakin' lawnmower."

Jack studied the tar as he paced back up the street. After a minute, he waved at Tom. "Tom! Come here. You have to note this in your log."

Tom walked over.

Jack pointed at the road. "There's no black ice. None. The road is bone dry—and look. *Look*." Jack walked along the road and thrust both hands at the pavement. "He was doing *doughnuts*. That moron was screwing around and lost control. Did you write that down?"

Jack got right up next to Tom as the policeman pulled out his notepad and began to hurriedly write.

The sound of broken glass caused Jack to turn back to the tow truck. The Charger listed to the side as it came to rest on the flatbed.

Murphy killed her. I'm going to kill him.

26

THE BOAR'S BUTT

As Jack passed their exit, Replacement raised an eyebrow, but she kept her mouth closed. He glanced at the speedometer: *82*.

At the next exit, he eased his foot up just a bit and tightened his grip on the steering wheel. Replacement shifted in her seat. Then Jack hit the brakes and the Impala flew down the off-ramp. Replacement slid into the door, clinging to the ceiling handle. The rear of the Impala slipped into the curve, and Jack pressed down on the gas a little and adjusted the wheel.

"I'm sorry about your police car," Replacement said.

Jack slowed down as they turned onto the side road. "Thanks." He tapped the steering wheel. "I swear he beat on that car just to get to me."

He rolled into the parking lot of the Boar's Butt. Kendra's car was parked near the stairs, and he pulled up next to it.

"What're we doing here?" Replacement eyed him suspiciously.

"They have great pizza. Want a slice?" Jack smiled, but he could feel his shoulders tighten even more.

"We could've ordered delivery."

"I need to ask someone a favor."

"They don't have a phone?"

"Some favors you want to ask in person." He got out of the car. "Is there some reason for the third degree?"

Replacement tilted her head. "Oh, I don't know. Maybe it's because the last time you went to a bar, you beat a guy senseless and the police had to drive you back to the inn." She shut her door with a frown. "Or maybe it's because of the warm fuzzies I'm getting heading into a place called the Boar's Butt. Come on—what restaurant has 'butt' in its name?"

As they climbed the steps that led to the outside deck, Jack cautioned, "Don't touch the railing."

Replacement yanked her hand away from the metal. "Well, that warning came a tad too late." She rubbed her hands together to wipe off the rusty orange color.

"Anyway, the Boar's Butt isn't a restaurant," Jack said. He opened the door for an older couple who hurried out. The man smiled and the woman mouthed "thank you" as they passed.

"It's not?" Replacement said.

"No. It's a strip club."

Replacement froze. She looked at the open door, then to Jack, then back again. "I'm not going in there," she blurted out. "And neither are you." She pushed the door closed.

Jack burst out laughing.

"What?" She stamped her foot. "Are you—" She spun around and looked at the gray-haired couple getting into their car. "Oh, very funny. Ha ha." She shook her head.

"Sorry," Jack said. "It's just a bar, but it was too good a joke to pass up."

"Yeah, thanks. I love being the *butt* of your jokes."

Jack debated about making another butt joke, but thought better of it.

As they walked through the door, Jack scanned the room. The entire restaurant was just one large, open room with a kitchen at the back. There were five booths against the wall, and five big tables, each covered with a checkered red-and-white vinyl tablecloth. On the opposite wall from the door was a long serving bar with a dozen stools. Jammed into the corners were two pinball machines and a jukebox. Sawyer Brown blared over the speakers, and the smell of pizza and beer filled the air.

"It's still a stupid name for a restaurant," Replacement muttered.

The staff at the Boar's Butt did call the place a restaurant, but that was a bit of a stretch. The only food they served was pizza and chicken wings. Mostly they sold beer, hard liquor, and cheap wine—all the essentials for a local bar.

Jack scanned the faces for Kendra, and spotted her in the corner talking with a young woman dressed in hospital scrubs. Kendra's friend was around five eight and a little on the chubby side, but despite an exhausted appearance, she wore a bright smile. Jack and Replacement walked over to them across the painted wood floor.

Jack leaned in. "Hey."

Kendra spun around, saw who it was, and hugged him hard. "I'm so sorry." She kissed his cheek, and then he felt her tense up.

Oh, great. Replacement must have her happy face on.

He let go of Kendra. Sure enough, Replacement stood next to him with her arms crossed and her brows knit together.

"Kendra," Jack said, "this is Alice. Alice, this is Kendra and her friend Tina."

"Nice to meet you." Replacement shook their hands.

Tina's mouth opened, and she exchanged a look with Kendra.

"Name tag." Jack smiled, and the woman chuckled.

"It's been one of those days." Tina unclipped the badge from her pocket and slipped it into her purse. "I work at the ER, and it can get a little crazy."

Kendra and Tina scooted in to allow Jack and Replacement to sit, and the waitress hurried over. "How you all doin'? Can I get you some drinks?"

"Whiskey, neat, and an iced tea," Jack said.

Replacement frowned at Jack, and so did the waitress.

"She's getting the iced tea, right?" The waitress stuck her thumb toward Replacement.

"My designated driver." Jack flashed a big, toothy grin.

"Great," Replacement said.

"Were you on today?" Jack asked Kendra, as the waitress went to get their drinks.

"Nope. I'm on tomorrow, though."

Jack eyed the two empty glasses in front of her. "What time?"

"Not till six. Donald and I are doing the late night. Downtown."

"Just watching your back," Jack explained.

Kendra leaned into Jack. "You're usually watching my—ow!"

"Oops, sorry," Replacement said. "Was that your shin? I thought I was kicking the table leg."

Jack reached over to squeeze Replacement's knee, and gave her a quick dirty look.

Tina stirred her drink. "Do you know that officer who was in the car accident?"

"Jack, did you hear that Murphy...?" Kendra trailed off as she saw Jack's grimace. "Guess you did."

"He's gonna be fine. But that moron killed the Charger. And do you think anything will happen to him?" Jack's hands went out. "No. Of course not."

Kendra snapped, "And you get suspended for sending an email! Where's the fairness in that?"

The waitress showed up with their drinks. Jack picked up his glass and pounded the shot.

"What email?" Replacement asked.

Kendra looked up at the waitress. "I'll take another shot." Then she grabbed Jack by the elbow. "Can I talk to you?"

"What email?" Replacement repeated.

"It's nothing. Why don't you order a pizza?" Jack called back as Kendra dragged him away.

"Does she not know?" Kendra whispered as they walked over to the small square of tiles in front of the jukebox that served as the dance floor.

"She doesn't need to know."

"What's the deal with you two?" Kendra started to dance, which made Jack uncomfortable.

"I don't dance." He nervously chuckled.

The song changed to a slow country ballad, and Kendra looked up at him through her long lashes. "One dance?" She took his hand in hers and put her other hand on his shoulder. "It can't hurt."

"It actually could," he muttered. Jack looked back at Replacement, but she was talking with Tina.

"Seriously, Jack. She's living with you, right?"

"Yeah."

"Are you two... you know?"

Jack laughed.

"What?"

"I never volunteer an answer when someone doesn't ask the question. Come on, we use that trick all the time." Jack lowered his voice. "Do you know why I pulled you over?" He clicked his tongue. "When I ask that, I'm just fishing to see what someone did wrong. I want the guy to say, 'I was speeding, I ran the red light, and I have a body in the trunk.'"

Kendra laughed. "Fine." She took a deep breath. "Are you two doing the wild thing?"

"No."

"Because I didn't know if it's a roommate type thing or you're, like, hot and heavy, going at it."

"We're friends."

Kendra squeezed his hand. "Do you think Collins is going to press about the email?"

"Sure as the sun's coming up."

"What're you going to do?"

"I'll think about it tomorrow." Jack shrugged. "Right now, I need to ask you a favor."

Kendra's hands moved a little lower on his hips. "Really?"

"Seriously. I need you to keep an eye out for a group of guys. Either Italian or Asian."

Kendra smirked. "I guess you didn't get that memo about racial profiling."

Jack cracked his neck. "Look. You know I'm looking for Marisa, but some other people are, too. Could be only two guys, but I'm thinking maybe three or four."

"And what do you want me to do if I notice a group like that?"

"Call me. I have some free time on my hands."

Kendra moved her hands up his sides. Jack was used to her flirting, but he could tell this was something different. "Well, I was thinking," she said, "if we're not working together… and if you're not hot with her…" Kendra raised an eyebrow and pulled him a little closer. She was apparently a little bolder after a couple of drinks.

"Kendra, right now—"

"Don't tell me tonight. I'm still holding out hope you'll stay on the force."

"Me too." He glanced back at the table, where Replacement was still talking with Tina. The conversation looked animated. *That's not good.*

Kendra pulled Jack's chin around to face her.

He shrugged. "I gotta go check on her."

"Tina's with her."

"She could be upset about the email." *And I'm amazed she didn't go ballistic over me dancing with you.*

"Why would Alice get upset about the email?" Kendra asked.

Because she sent it, Jack thought, but aloud he said, "Just don't say anything, okay?"

Kendra gave a heavy sigh. "Fine. But next time, I'm really going to make you dance."

They headed back to the table. And when they got there, and Replacement looked up at Jack, her face said it all. There was no need for Kendra to keep her mouth shut: Replacement already knew.

"That stupid email I sent? *That's* why you're suspended?"

"*You* sent it?" Kendra put her hand on her hip.

"I was pretending to be Jack. I sent the email. Can I tell someone? Collins? They shouldn't… I'm so sorry." Replacement's lip trembled.

"Don't you start worrying." Jack put his hand on her shoulder. "I'll figure it out." He flagged down the waitress. "Two cheese pizzas. One for the table, one to go, please."

"Are we leaving?" Replacement asked.

Jack nodded. "We need to get back to the apartment."

Tina sniffed. "Alice was just telling me about all you've done for her, and I just want to say… you're the nicest man."

"I'm not, really."

"Why don't you just tell Collins?" Kendra whispered.

Jack glanced at Replacement. "What? I can't say *she* wrote the email."

The three women started to speak at once, all of them offering their opinion on what he should do.

Jack held up his hands. "Hold up. Let me explain something. I can't say anything. If I do, I jack up Alice and—"

They all started talking again.

Jack waved his hands to quiet them again. He turned to Kendra. "Just do me a favor, and don't say anything about that stupid email. And keep a lookout for those guys." He saw the waitress approaching with the pizzas. "I've got to go."

The waitress set one pizza on the table and handed the pizza box to Jack. He passed her a handful of cash, then turned to Tina. "It was nice meeting you."

"You too."

"See ya," Kendra said. She gave him a sideways sulky look as he and Replacement headed for the exit.

"What was all that with Kendra?" Replacement asked as they got to the car.

"I don't get you." Jack put the pizza box in the trunk. "And don't forget—you're driving." He tossed her the keys.

"What did I do now?"

"I'm going in there to ask Kendra a favor, and you keep giving her looks like she should back off."

"No, I didn't." Replacement started the car, but when she put it in reverse, she gave it too much gas, which made it hop back. "But she should back off," she added.

"Why?"

"Why?" Replacement started to flush. "Because… you said you shouldn't date someone at work." She nodded for emphasis. "You said that. She's not your type anyway." She jammed the gas down.

Jack was pushed back into the seat. "Let's just get back to the apartment and wait for Kiku."

27

MISS MANNERS

Jack paced the apartment. It was already 2:15 a.m.

What's keeping her?

He stopped, dropped to the floor, and started doing push-ups. Replacement was typing away at the computer.

"Can you look up a translation for Orsacchiotto?" Jack asked from the floor.

"Orsa-what?"

"Orsacchiotto. It's Italian. Marisa called Paolo that." He spelled it for her.

Replacement typed, clicked, and started to read. A moment later, her shoulders slumped. "It means teddy bear."

Jack got up, walked over to his jacket, and took out the photo again. He handed it to Replacement. "The guy in the middle. His name's Paolo."

"He looks like a teddy bear," she remarked.

Jack remembered the old man's eyes. "More like a grizzly. That guy's scary." He walked back, dropped to the floor, and started doing sit-ups.

"This Arber de Lorme is a scumbag," Replacement said.

"I thought you said he was a supermodel."

"He's a rich supermodel scumbag. The translation on these pages isn't the best, but look." Replacement clicked through a few different windows. "He went to three different universities in France, and I think he was booted out of all of them. His father is loaded. That's where he gets his money. He has a huge shipping business in Europe."

"Why do you think he got kicked out of the universities?"

"I found him at two different schools he doesn't list on his biography."

"Maybe he just switched schools."

"Nope. I did a search and found him listed on a French site called 'Girl Beware.' Girls post about guys they think other girls should watch out for. The site got closed down, but you should read the posts about him."

"If the site was closed down, how can you still see the posts?" Jack hopped up.

"Nothing is ever removed once it goes on the web. Nothing." She clicked a few buttons and a page appeared. "There are plenty of sites that capture the data, but the Internet Archive is the best. It's all about a free and open Internet. It allows anyone to upload and download anything digital to its data cluster, but the bulk of the data gets collected automatically by web crawlers. The bots work to preserve as much of the public web as possible. It's got a web archive, the 'Wayback Machine,' that has over one hundred fifty billion web captures. Here it is."

Jack looked at the screen.

"Like I said, the translation sucks, but the bottom line is a few girls accused him of getting them drunk and having S&M sex: tying them down, that kind of stuff."

Jack read over the accounts. "That's not sex. It's rape. Nothing happened to him?"

"Like I said, he left the schools right after, so I'm guessing he got thrown out. And then something else happened."

She clicked, and a French newspaper article appeared. It showed a picture of a house with crime scene tape across it.

"At a party at his father's summer house, a girl drowned in the pool. She was only seventeen. It was eventually ruled an accidental drowning, although the girl's family kept pushing the police to reopen the case. They said he got off because he was rich. That was five years ago, and that's when he came to America."

Jack knitted his brow. "Why would Marisa date a man like that?"

There was a knock at the door. Replacement hopped up, but Jack was already moving and held up his hand to stop her. He looked through the keyhole and saw a shadow of someone standing next to the door.

He took a step back and to the right. "Who is it?"

"Hello, Officer," Kiku answered.

He opened the door, and she walked in carrying a brown shopping bag. "I did not expect you both to wait up for me." She glided over to the kitchen counter and set the bag down.

Jack locked the door. "What did you find out?"

Kiku sauntered back over to him. "I know you are an American, and I do not want to be rude, but you really need to work on your etiquette." She took off her short winter jacket and handed it to him.

"You know what?" Replacement stepped forward. "Our friend is missing, so save the Miss Manners speech and tell us if the scumbag had anything to do with it."

A small smile spread across Kiku's lips. "Well said." She walked back to the bag on the counter. "I had to wait until Arber fell asleep. He was quite animated after you left, and made several phone calls. I don't know who he spoke with."

She removed a bottle of vodka, a bottle of triple sec, and two limes from the bag.

"Kamikazes?" Jack said.

"You know your drinks." Kiku opened the vodka.

"Did you get anything else?" Replacement huffed.

"He had a guest. Veronica Martin. She is married, but I assume her husband is away. She lives here in Darrington. I did not find anything suspicious."

Replacement bit her bottom lip. "Did you just walk around the house?"

"They were asleep. It was nothing." Kiku opened a cabinet and took out three glasses.

Jack put one of them back. "She's not having one."

Replacement frowned.

"But you will be joining me, will you not?" Kiku asked.

Jack nodded.

Replacement pouted. "That's not fair."

"Never said it was," Jack replied.

Kiku laughed, which caught Jack off guard. It wasn't a reserved laugh; it felt real.

As Kiku poured the drinks, her lips slowly pressed together. "We need to talk." She handed Jack a drink and then walked over to the recliner. "My employer has heard nothing. Do you know if the Mancinis have heard anything?"

Jack resisted the urge to check his phone and shook his head.

Kiku frowned. "The Mancinis will be coming to town. It will not be good when they start looking for her too. They will not be as subtle." She said the words with precision.

"Do you know for certain they're coming here?" Replacement asked.

Kiku swirled her drink, then took a large sip. "What I know is irrelevant. What I do *not* know, however, is important. Time is running out, Jack. What would you suggest?"

Jack took a swig of the Kamikaze as he walked over to the window. "I don't want to shock anyone, but I'm just winging it here. If I had something—anything—I would go to Prescott and get the FBI involved."

"What do they have that we don't?" Replacement said, crossing her arms.

Kiku settled back in her chair. "You have an inflated sense of self."

"Screw you," Replacement snapped. She stomped over to Jack. "You took classes in kidnapping, right? What would the police do?"

"I took *one seminar*. That doesn't make me capable of handling this."

Kiku chuckled. "Think of it like landing a burning plane in a action movie. You've had a look at the cockpit, so you're our best shot at a pilot."

I wish I had a parachute. "Okay, the first thing the police would do is tap Severino's phone. That way, when someone calls, you can trace it."

"Then let's do that," Replacement said.

"They've already done it. Prescott may hate me, but I think he'd let me know if someone reached out."

Kiku smiled. "That is something in our favor."

"But I figure," Jack said, "that if someone did kidnap her, they wouldn't just call. They would have to know the phones are tapped and he's under surveillance."

"Even I would know that," Replacement said.

Jack stretched. "The next thing I'd do is pull her credit card and phone records. But we need the FBI to get those. I mean… you can't hack her bank account—can you?"

Replacement shook her head. "No, but I bet I don't have to. Does she have a computer at home?"

"Yes."

"Odds are she caches her passwords or writes them down nearby. Most people do, even though it's stupid. I just need to get on her computer."

"Your assistant is smart," Kiku said.

"I'm not his assistant," Replacement shot back.

Kiku slowly raised one eyebrow.

"What?" Replacement snapped.

"I was just thinking about the relationship you and Jack have. I do not wish to be mean, but clearly you're an accessory," Kiku said, rising from the chair.

"*What?*" Replacement's hands clenched into fists.

"You've got it wrong, Kiku." Jack downed the rest of the drink and grabbed his jacket. "But now's not—"

A ringing phone cut him off. It was the burner. Jack rushed over to it and picked it up.

"Hello?"

"They're coming," Ilario whispered. "I can't talk. They're on their way to Darrington. I'll try to find you when we get there."

"Who's coming?"

There was a long pause. "Everyone."

28

BROMANCE

Jack, Replacement, and Kiku silently slipped into Marisa's apartment. Jack motioned for Replacement to wait while he and Kiku fanned out to sweep through the rooms, making sure nothing new was missing.

"Besides the broom, everything's the same," Jack said.

Kiku picked up the broom and set it against the wall. "You're a fast man who can take a good punch."

"Me?" Jack tilted his head. "I didn't think you'd be walking after I hit you with that shipping pallet."

"Actually, the bottle hurt more. It connected with bone."

Jack pointed at his jaw. "What about this?"

Replacement groaned. "Can you two continue your bromance and who-can-get-hurt-more-and-not-cry conversation later? We have work to do."

Jack and Kiku exchanged a grin.

They headed back to the art studio, where Replacement sat down in the swivel chair by the computer and wiggled the mouse. The screen lit up; the computer was already on.

"Most stuff is web-based now," Replacement said, searching, "and… bingo. She keeps her history. I'll check her mail first."

She pulled up a complete listing of Marisa's emails and scanned them. "Huh. Her spam filter blows, but other than that, it looks like she doesn't get many emails."

Jack leaned in. "I don't get much email either, and I'd imagine she gets less, but I figured she'd have something."

"Well, she got a few," Replacement said. "Here. Subject is WHERE R U???"

"Read it."

"MARISA. WHERE R U??? THE COP KEEPS COMIN AROUND LOOKING 4 U. U R WORRYING US. SHAWN."

"That must be Shawn Miller," Jack said.

"Who?"

Kiku answered, "He's the tall guy at the tattoo parlor."

Jack and Replacement both looked at her quizzically.

"It was the second place I looked."

"He sent a few messages," Replacement said.

"Read them," said Jack. "And look for any from Arber de Lorme, too. And—"

"I know what I'm doing," Replacement said. "Just let me concentrate and I'll let you know what I find." She sat slightly forward with her ankles crossed under the chair. All of her focus was on the computer monitor.

Jack and Kiku idly explored the studio while Replacement worked. At one point, Kiku tipped up a sketchpad to reveal a charcoal sketch of Jack standing in a doorway, his hands above his head, holding on to the frame. He wore a crooked smile on his face and nothing else.

"When we find her, I'm ordering a copy of this one," Kiku said. Her eyes traveled up Jack's body before she put it back down.

Jack blushed.

"Okay," said Replacement. "I uploaded all her email to another account so I can sift through it later. But I've found a few things already."

"What did you get?" Jack cracked his wrist.

"She broke it off with Arber and didn't really have anything to do with him except when it came to festivals and a couple paintings she sold. He sent a few groveling emails asking her out, but she blew him off. He did want to buy her work, and she did sell some stuff to him."

"A lot of art? Big money?" Jack asked.

"Nothing crazy expensive—a few thousand. And she turned down a lot of them. He did offer a lot for the piece she has in the festival, though. It's called *Girl*. Ten grand."

"It's worth more," Jack said.

"Well, her response was, 'I'm not selling. Don't ask me again.'"

"Did he?" Kiku asked.

"Oh yeah." Replacement pulled up Marisa's response and turned the screen so Kiku could see.

Kiku grinned. "I like her style."

"One more thing." Replacement opened another email. "It's from Shawn, about three months ago. He offered to buy the tattoo parlor if she ever wanted to sell."

"Was she thinking about selling?" Jack asked.

Replacement shrugged. "It's only one email. Marisa wrote back to say if she ever did, he'd be the first in line."

Jack looked at Kiku. "It's worth a conversation." He turned back to Replacement. "Anything else?"

"That's it for the email," Replacement said. "She saved her password for her phone account, so I logged in no problem. The billing page is up to date as far as this morning. She hasn't used her phone since the afternoon she went missing."

"What about her credit cards?" Jack asked.

"Looks like she just has one credit card, issued through her bank. I could check it if I could log in to her bank account, but I'd need her PIN, which I don't have."

"I thought you said it would be cached," Jack said.

"I had hoped, but some sites don't let you." Replacement pointed to a notebook. "She wrote down her password in here, but not the PIN. People don't usually write that down. I can try to guess, but the chances are next to zip."

"And if you guess wrong three times, you'll lock the account," Kiku added.

"Pull up the login screen," Jack said.

"You really want me to guess?"

"No. Just pull it up and enter the password. I might know the PIN."

Replacement brought up the bank login page and entered everything but the PIN. Jack then leaned forward, typed in 2614, and clicked the login button.

Marisa's bank account information appeared on the screen.

Replacement's mouth fell open. "How did you know her PIN?"

Jack looked over at a sketch on the wall. It was in pencil and just an outline, but he recognized the mountains from when Marisa and he had taken a vacation together. She had drawn the view from their bed.

"It's my badge number," he said.

29

FAILED TO FOLLOW

Kiku lay down on Jack's couch while Replacement did more research on the computer. Jack watched the traffic below.

The apartment was quiet except for the sound of Replacement's clicking and typing.

"Do you know if Marisa kept cash on hand?" Kiku asked Jack.

Jack thought for a minute. "I don't think so. Not on her, anyway. She usually used the credit card she kept in her phone case. She didn't like to carry a purse."

"In that case, since we now know that Marisa has not accessed her credit card or recently withdrawn cash from her bank account, I believe that eliminates the possibility that she went somewhere voluntarily. Staying anywhere takes money."

"She hasn't used her phone either," Replacement added.

Kiku met Jack's dark stare. Jack understood.

No activity on any of her accounts... It's confirmation that she's been kidnapped—or worse. She's not safe.

Kiku shut her eyes and rolled onto her side.

After a while, Replacement let go of the mouse. "I think I found something out about Arber that might be worth following up on."

"Oh yeah? Let me see it." Jack massaged her shoulders as he looked at the screen. Replacement brought up the police database, and with a few clicks, a report appeared.

Jack leaned forward.

"It's labeled a preliminary report," she said. "By a Detective Joe Davenport. It says he received a phone complaint regarding Arber. It's regarding a Skylar Boyce and was filed by Tina Boyce. There's a note sheet attached as the next doc."

Replacement clicked to the next page. The image was of a handwritten notepad page that Joe had torn off and scanned. Five words were circled in red: *Alcohol. Drugged. Incapacitated. Sexual Assault.*

"Tina Boyce accused Arber of drugging and raping Skylar," Replacement continued. "The report is classified as F2F. What does F2F mean?"

"Failed to Follow. It means Joe contacted the people, but they didn't want him to follow up. It happens. People call the police in the heat of the moment but then decide against it later on."

"How the hell was that not followed up on?"

"It doesn't mean Joe didn't actually follow up. Most likely he tried, but the victim was unwilling to cooperate. It fits the pattern of what Archer was accused of in France, though. And we know that Marisa was in communication with Arber." Jack considered. "It might be worthwhile to go talk to Joe Davenport about this. See what shakes loose. I'd also like to go back over to the tattoo parlor, ask Shawn about his offer to buy it from Marisa, and see his reaction."

Jack could see the tension in Replacement's shoulders. He started to rub the back of her neck. "How are you holding up?" Jack asked.

"Better now."

Jack's hands gently kneaded her shoulders. Her muscles relaxed beneath his touch. Replacement moaned.

As Jack massaged Replacement's temples, she let her head hang forward. "Oh, I love that," she purred.

"Should I leave you two alone?" Kiku said from the couch.

Replacement popped up a little in her seat and turned crimson.

"Sorry. We were trying to be quiet," Jack said, turning around.

Kiku laughed. "Hardly. But your plan is sound. Would you mind if I took a quick shower before we go?"

Jack shrugged. "Sure. We have time."

As Kiku slipped off the couch, she grinned wickedly. "And when Alice takes her shower, I, too, would like a back rub."

Replacement huffed, Jack blushed, and Kiku strolled into the bedroom.

30

LIKE A PUPPY WITH A SHOTGUN

As Jack parked in front of Joe Davenport's two-story colonial, he smiled at the collection of boats in the side yard. They were all freshwater vessels, ranging from two beauties on trailers to a one-man, flat-bottomed canoe. Joe was an avid fisherman, and the closer he came to retirement, the more time he spent with a rod in his hand.

Jack walked up the flagstone walkway to the white front door. As he reached for the bell, Joe's wife, Bonnie, opened the door. Bonnie Davenport was in her early sixties, with short gray hair. She had beautiful, welcoming eyes, and her thick glasses made them even bigger. Today she wore a flowered dress with an apron tied around her waist. She gave Jack a hug, then leaned back and squeezed his shoulders, looking him up and down like a mother inspecting a child. After a moment, seeming satisfied with her appraisal, she said in a light, high voice, "How have you been, Jack?"

"I'm good, Bonnie."

Jack had only met the woman a few times at police functions, but she always greeted him like a friend.

"Joe's fishing." She smiled and tilted her head to the side. "Canada again. His brother called and told him the fish were jumping into the boat. He practically ran out the door."

That guy has more vacation time than anyone I know, Jack thought.

"Do you know when he'll be back?"

"Tonight. It shouldn't be too late." She leaned in and whispered, "I'm making him a pecan pie."

Jack whispered back, "I won't tell him," and winked. He wanted to add, "If he's in Canada, we don't have to whisper," but Bonnie's smile was so sweet it derailed his sarcasm.

She clapped her hands together. "It's been his favorite since he was a little boy. Should I give him a message?"

"No. Thanks, Bonnie. I'll just call."

She hugged him again, and Jack hurried back to the car, already dialing Joe's cell.

"I knew it," he muttered when Joe's voicemail kicked in. "You'd think a guy who goes to Canada to fish would get a phone that gets reception up there."

"Are you kidding?" Replacement put her feet on the dashboard. "He probably went out of his way to get the phone plan that had the worst reception in Canada."

"She is correct." Kiku leaned forward from the back seat. "What fisherman wants to be interrupted?"

Jack pulled away from the curb. "Well, it would be nice if he was a detective first and a fisherman second."

Replacement picked up her smartphone. "The report said that Skylar Boyce lives at 18 Winston. We could go talk to her."

"Good idea. I know where that is."

As Jack drove, he regularly checked the rearview mirror.

"You do not need to worry," Kiku said. "We are not being followed."

"What are you, some kind of ninja spy?" Replacement turned to look at Kiku. "Do they teach you that in the Yakuza?"

"I am mostly self-taught."

"Were you born in Japan?"

"No. I am half Korean. I was born in Korea and raised in an orphanage."

"Did you move to Japan when you were adopted?"

Kiku exhaled and looked down at her hands. "In a manner of speaking. But that would be the sterilized version. A truer telling would be that the couple who ran the orphanage were beaten nearly to death because they couldn't pay the bribes necessary to stay open. They were driven out of the country. As a result, I was sold and shipped to Japan for delivery, like cattle."

Jack had angled the rearview mirror so he could look at Kiku, but she didn't even flinch as she revealed all this. If anything, her eyes became brighter and wider. And Jack knew well the emotions behind the look. He didn't run from pain, and neither did she. They both ran forward and embraced it.

"*Sold?*" Replacement's voice was a mixture of puzzlement and anger.

Kiku gave a slight, stiff nod. "I did not make it to my destination, fortunately. I was meant to be a prostitute, but instead I was selected to... work imports and exports."

Jack could see Replacement was confused. "They used her as a mule," he explained, his voice low. "They like to use women and kids to smuggle things."

"I prefer 'courier,'" Kiku said. "My demeanor was a good fit for transporting items through customs. There was a need, and I was capable. I excelled and was rewarded."

"What's that pay?" Replacement now knelt on the seat, completely turned around.

Jack shot Replacement a look. "Not enough. Turn around."

"I'm just curious." She rolled her eyes and stayed where she was.

Jack deliberately tapped the brakes, and Replacement had to grab the headrest to keep from sliding into the dash.

"Hello!" She glared at Jack.

"We're almost there. Sit down."

"We can discuss this at another time, Alice," Kiku said.

"No, she can't," Jack said, pulling onto Winston.

"I'm not talking about joining the Yakuza, Jack. I just had some questions," Replacement snapped.

"She's right, Jack," Kiku said. "You have to stop treating her like a child. She's a grown woman."

Jack shook his head as he parked in front of 18 Winston. The small yellow house had been split into two units, and the taste of the renters on each side was evident in the upkeep. On the right side of the house, the grass was mowed and the walkway was swept. On the left side, the grass was long and a harvest wreath still hung on the door. Both driveways were empty.

"Did the address say the A side or the B?" Jack asked Replacement.

"Neither. It just said 18."

Just then a bright red convertible pulled in on the left. "Well, now we can ask," Kiku said.

"Wow." Replacement whistled. "That car sure doesn't go with this house."

A woman in her mid-thirties, with shoulder-length brown hair, got out of the car. Her tan skirt was short and too tight for her, and her high-heeled boots went up past her knees. She had a cropped jacket that did little to flatter her wide waist. She carried a bag of groceries on one arm and a big bag of dog food on the other.

"Someone's compensating," Replacement said. But her sarcastic grin vanished when she saw Jack's confused face. "What? That's what you said about Arber and his boat, right?"

Kiku chuckled, leaned forward, and whispered something in Replacement's ear.

Replacement turned bright red.

Jack opened the door. "Stay in the car."

They all got out.

Jack waved at the woman, who was headed for the house. She didn't wave back.

"Good morning!" Jack shouted. "I'm sorry to bother you, but I'm looking for Skylar Boyce."

"At least let me put this crap down," the woman called back. She dropped the dog food bag on the front brick steps and set the grocery bag next to it. Then she turned around. "What did that little tramp do now?"

"She hasn't done anything wrong," Jack said. He walked closer, but left her plenty of space. "We just need to ask her a few questions."

The woman looked Jack up and down, and a smile spread across her face. "I'm sorry." Her voice softened. "I'm Tina. Pleased to meet you." She daintily held out a gloved hand.

Jack flashed a smile. "Jack Stratton. It's nice to meet you, too."

Kiku started to raise her own hand, but Tina stepped right up to Jack. "Someone like you…" Tina looked him over and made a face. "You're not with youth services, are you?" she asked. She now stood uncomfortably close.

"Actually," Kiku smiled, "we just need to do a routine check on Skylar. Is she here?"

Tina didn't take her eyes off Jack. "No. She moved in with a friend. Now it's just me."

"She moved?" Replacement asked.

Tina exhaled. "Not legally. This is still her house, and I can still declare her. She'll be back. You know how teenage girls are. I can't do anything right, and the little wench can't be wrong. She'll come back around. It's no big deal. Who called you?"

"We can't say." Replacement pressed her lips together.

"I already know who." Tina turned to face Replacement. "It was that busybody Carol Bartlet. She's sticking her fat nose in because we went to high school together, and she doesn't like me."

"We just need to speak to Skylar and ask her a couple of questions about a report that was filed," Jack said.

"A report? What report?" The color left her cheeks. "Are you with youth services?"

Jack started to open his mouth, but Kiku spoke first. "Yes, miss, we are. If you could just give us Skylar's address, we'll be on our way."

Tina rubbed her hands on her skirt. "Well, she's staying at Carol's. Just temporarily." She quickly added, "It's only a couple of streets over. Juniper. 57 Juniper."

"Thank you," Jack said.

"This doesn't have anything to do with…? It's just a request with youth services, right?"

Jack cleared his throat. "Actually, Miss Boyce…"

Tina let out a fake chuckle. "I thought I cleared that report up. It wasn't Skylar; it was me it was about. I had a little too much to drink, and I got in a fight with my boyfriend." She flashed a forced smile and raised her hands in front of her. "It's all set now. It was nothing, really."

Jack glanced over at her car. "Your boyfriend? Arber?"

"We're not together anymore. I need to go." Tina turned and picked up the bags.

"Miss Boyce—" Jack started, but she cut him off.

"I'm sorry. I have to go. You can go talk to Skylar. She's not my problem anymore." She opened the door and disappeared inside. The door slammed shut with a loud bang.

Jack shot a look at Replacement and Kiku before striding back to the car.

"What was that look for?" Replacement grumbled as they pulled away from the house.

"I told you both to stay in the car."

"*She* should have." Replacement pointed at Kiku.

"I'm not a dog," Kiku snapped.

"Oh, you're not? Is a Kiku a bird, then?" Replacement said.

Kiku's lips pressed together. "It means chrysanthemum. And with a name like Replacement, you are in no position to make jokes."

"I didn't say I didn't like it. I do," Replacement shot back.

Jack held up a hand. "Listen. I didn't mean any disrespect when I asked you to stay in the car. You two need to think. How is a woman going to react if three people get out of a car and walk up to her house?"

"You're right, Officer." Kiku crossed her arms. "You should have stayed in the car."

"Ha," Replacement added.

"Ha, yourself." Jack opened his window an inch. "I'm the best person to talk to her."

"Are you?" Kiku raised an eyebrow. "You said yourself she'd be intimidated."

"By three people coming to her door."

"One big guy is better than two little girls?" Replacement scrunched up her face.

"Look. I shouldn't have to explain it, but…" He shot a look at Replacement. "Kiku is just as scary as me."

"Excuse me?" Kiku growled.

"No offense, but you give off a vibe."

"A *vibe*?" Kiku looked poised to leap into the front seat.

Jack swung the rearview mirror around so she could see herself. "Look at yourself. You're scary."

Kiku's eyes smoldered and her canines flashed, even while she tried to force a polite smile. "Normally people think I'm harmless."

Replacement scoffed.

"They do." Kiku's wolf face was back.

"Oh, yeah. Real harmless," Replacement said. "Like a puppy with a shotgun."

"You want the person slightly intimidated," Jack said. "Slightly, but not freaked out. That's why I bring Replacement when I need to talk to a girl. It takes the edge off."

"See?" Kiku smiled at Replacement. "You're an accessory."

Replacement glared at Jack.

"No—" Jack stuttered. "You're a tool."

"Oh, that's *so* much better," Replacement spat.

"I'm just trying to get the job done. You're helping me…"

Just shut up, Jack.

They rode in silence until Jack pulled into the driveway at 57 Juniper. It was a medium-sized garrison-style house with a big back yard. Two older cars were parked in the driveway.

"I'm staying in the car," Replacement said coldly.

"Me, too." Kiku looked straight ahead.

"Fine," Jack said.

He shut off the engine, but before he could get out of the car, a tall, thin woman in jeans and a baggy sweatshirt opened the door of the house and looked out. She eyed the car, then started walking over.

"Great," Jack muttered. Instead of getting out, he rolled down his window. *Let her see all of us waiting harmlessly in the car. Slightly better than three people hopping out.*

As the woman approached, Jack gave her a big smile and a little wave. "Carol Bartlet?"

The woman stopped a few feet away from the car. She had waist-length, slightly graying dirty-blond hair. She was a homely woman, but her smile was big and genuine. "I'm Carol. Can I help you?"

"Yes. I have a couple questions concerning Skylar Boyce. Do you mind if we get out of the car?" Jack asked.

"Please do." Carol stepped aside.

All three got out, and Jack shook Carol's hand. "I'm Jack Stratton, and I'll only need a minute. Would it be possible for me to speak with Skylar?"

"May I ask what this is regarding?" She leaned away from him a little.

"It's regarding a police report that was filed."

"Are you a policeman?"

Jack inhaled. He could see both Kiku and Replacement preparing to answer. "No. I'm a private investigator. I'm looking into Arber de Lorme."

Carol's lips pressed together, and her expression hardened. "The police couldn't do anything about it. The complaint was dropped."

"That's why I want to speak with Skylar. I need to understand why she dropped it. A friend of mine is missing, and I need to know if Arber has anything to do with it."

Carol deflated. Her shoulders slumped, and she looked from face to face. "I'm so sorry. Certainly. How can I help?"

"It would be best if I could speak to Skylar."

"She's at my sister's with my daughter for school break. I'll write down the number."

Replacement handed Carol her phone. "Here. You can just type it in the notepad app."

"My sister's name is Janice," Carol said. "I'll call her and let her know you're going to call, but…" She looked up at the sky. "I don't know if Skylar will say anything."

"Do you know why Skylar dropped the report?"

By her pinched expression, Jack knew Carol was holding something back.

"Carol. I wouldn't ask if I wasn't looking for my friend. I know Arber had a sordid past in France—"

"You found out about that?" Carol's eyes locked on his. "I looked him up when Skylar came here, but…"

Give her space. Don't try to convince her. Let her decide on her own. She took Skylar in. She cares about her. She wants to help.

Carol squeezed her arm as she continued. "Skylar refused to file the report. She changed her story and insisted to the police it wasn't her."

Jack softened his voice. "Her mother, Tina, said she was dating Arber and got mad at him when she was drunk. Tina said *she* made it all up, not Skylar."

"Tina made *that* all up," Carol replied. "Tina lied. Skylar told my daughter what really happened, and my daughter told me." Her chin lowered and her mouth pulled down on one side. "I went to the police, but with Tina 'confessing' and Skylar refusing to say anything, what could they do?"

"What did your daughter say happened?"

Carol crossed her arms. "Skylar was only seventeen, and that man preyed on her. Arber was dating Tina, that was true, but I think he was really after Skylar all along."

"Why didn't her mother do anything?" Replacement asked.

"Skylar asked if I'd go with her to talk to her mother, and I did. I knew Tina in high school, but I never imagined she'd turn out like that. At first Tina said she was going to"—she inhaled—"nail him to the wall, but after she called the police… well, Tina got a phone call from Arber. He said Skylar had a crush on him and made the whole thing up."

"Tina *bought* that?" Replacement looked disgusted.

"No. Arber bought *her*," Carol said. "To clear up the 'misunderstanding,' he gave her a vacation, money, and did you see her car? The red convertible?"

"You can't miss it," Jack said.

"For some people it's thirty pieces of silver. For Tina… she sold her daughter for that car. I hate that damn car." Carol looked down. "Excuse my language, but it just kills me. Skylar is the nicest girl, and she has to live with not only what happened to her but… she knows. She knows Arber gave her mother that car to buy her silence. Now she's reminded of it every time she sees her mother driving around town."

"I'm sorry."

"If I can do anything to help, please let me know."

"You already have," Jack said. "Thank you for your time."

***

Kiku ran her finger along the window as they drove away from Carol's. "I will go take a closer look at Arber tonight."

"Not you," Jack said. "I'll call Joe Davenport and make sure he pays Arber a visit. That'll keep Arber in line until I can deal with him."

"But what if he had something to do with Marisa?" Replacement protested.

"He didn't. He's a serial rapist; Marisa doesn't fit his MO." Jack gripped the steering wheel. "He goes after young girls. The girl in France, and now Skylar. He probably only dates women his age as a cover. Like that lady he had over."

"A lady?" Replacement spat. "She was cheating on her husband. I'd use a different word to refer to her."

"Don't worry, I'm going to deal with Arber. But after we find Marisa. Meanwhile, Joe will shake him up enough that he won't try anything."

"I do not like the justice system in this country, Officer." Kiku stared out the window. "It is slow."

"So, where to next?" Replacement asked.

"I want to hit the tattoo parlor and talk to Shawn. It's fishing, but it's better than waiting around."

"Why even consider him? Just because he asked Marisa about buying the tattoo parlor?"

"Yeah, it's thin, so we don't need to lean on him hard. I just want to see his reaction."

Kiku leaned forward. "I think in this case, perhaps I am better prepared to ask him questions. Do you mind? How do you Americans say it—giving me a turn at bat?"

"Better prepared?" Jack asked. "In what way?"

"You have spoken with him a few times with no results. I have many methods of enticement. Give me fifteen minutes?"

Begrudgingly, Jack nodded. "Okay."

Replacement looked wide-eyed at him, but closed her mouth with a huff.

It was still early when they pulled up in front of the tattoo parlor, but already six people sat around the tables. Shawn stood behind the counter.

"How do you want to play this?" Jack said.

"You start the conversation. Then follow my lead," Kiku said. Her smile fired up his curiosity.

Together, they headed inside. Shawn stood up straight as they approached the counter. "She hasn't called or nothing," he said to Jack.

"No one has?" Jack put both hands on the counter, and Replacement swung over to his left side.

Shawn gestured to the customers and shrugged. "Nobody has seen her. Total radio silence. I'm starting to get a little freaked out."

Kiku stepped forward. "Perhaps you can be of some assistance to me, then."

Shawn looked her up and down, gulped, then shrugged. "Sure. How?"

"I do not plan to return to Japan in the foreseeable future, but I want to add to my Irezumi." Kiku pulled down the shoulder of her shirt to reveal part of an elaborate tattoo.

Shawn's mouth made a popping sound as it fell open. His hand shot out and hovered just above her skin. "Is that Tebori? Real Tebori?"

Kiku smiled. "You know your craft. It is."

A couple of the customers craned their necks to get a look at whatever Shawn was so excited about, but Kiku pulled her shirt back up.

"They use bamboo, right?" Shawn asked.

Kiku grinned. "Sometimes. Mine was done with steel. Do you have a moment to hear my proposition and see?"

"See?" Shawn almost danced from one foot to the other. "Can I see the whole thing?"

Kiku nodded.

Shawn hurried over to the curtain to the back rooms and held it open. As Kiku sauntered past, he looked desperately back at Jack. "Can you just… tell people I'll be back?"

"Sure will."

Damn, she's good.

Replacement whispered, "I think he's more excited about seeing her tattoo than seeing her naked."

Jack followed Kiku with his eyes. "He's an idiot."

Replacement stepped on his foot.

***

Fifteen minutes later, Kiku pulled aside the curtain and walked out. Shawn hurried after her, hovering just behind.

"Marisa is the only one who could touch that tat. Seriously." His hands went up. "That's just… wow. I've never seen… That was freakin' unbelievable."

Kiku's head dipped in a polite bow. "Thank you." She looked at Jack and shifted her eyes toward the door.

Jack walked over to the exit. He called back to Shawn, "If she calls, you call me."

Shawn was already moving toward the guys hanging out at the tables. "I will."

As they walked out the door, Jack could hear Shawn talking to his friends. "Dude, she has a real freakin' Tebori. They did it with steel. That's one tough chick! But her skin was so perfect…"

As soon as they got in the car, Replacement spun around to face Kiku. "Did you find out anything?"

Kiku sat forward. "Shawn said that Arber has come to the studio several times."

Replacement raised an eyebrow. "How did you get that out of him?"

"I have my ways." She smiled. "He said Arber wanted to buy Marisa's painting but she would not sell."

Replacement scoffed, "We knew that from the emails."

"But Shawn also said that the last time Arber came to the studio, they had a loud argument and Marisa threw him out. That was the day she went missing."

"Arber didn't come back in? He must have called," Jack said.

"Very perceptive. Arber called the studio yesterday and left a message for Marisa to call him."

"That rules Arber out of Marisa's disappearance." Replacement said. "If he had something to do with it, why would he call looking for her? But are you sure about Shawn?"

"Shawn is very nice, but not bright. I doubt he had anything to do with it."

Replacement, who was still kneeling, put her head down on the seat. "Just because he's stupid doesn't mean he's a good guy."

"Shawn is very excitable, and he went on and on about wanting to start his own tattoo parlor. It was not even his idea. It was his girlfriend's. Then Marisa gave him a raise last month, and he has practically given up the idea already anyway. It's a dead end."

Jack gripped the steering wheel.

Poor choice of words.

31

IT COULD HAVE BEEN WORSE

Jack paced back and forth across the living room floor, regretting ever letting Kiku and Replacement go for some takeout. He stomped into the bedroom and looked at the clock: 6:15 p.m.

Where the hell are they?

He plodded back into the living room and dialed Replacement's number. Again, he went straight to voicemail. "When you headed out, you said you were coming right back," Jack barked into the phone. "With all the crap going on, you'd think you'd give me a flippin' call back."

Just then, his police scanner crackled. He kept it turned on 24/7.

The dispatcher's voice came over the radio. "Car 63?"

"Copy," a man's voice responded.

"We've got a 10-70 in progress at 18 Winston."

"10-4."

Jack gawked at the scanner. *10-70. No. There's no way they called a 10-70 at 18 Winston.*

As Jack turned to head out the front door, it flew open. Replacement raced inside and headed straight for the bathroom.

"Wait a second," he called out.

"One minute." She made it to the bathroom and closed the door before he got there.

"Are you kidding me? I've been calling you for over an hour." He tried to turn the handle, but she'd locked the door.

"Sorry, I shut my phone off," she yelled. He heard the water turn on.

Jack straightened up and sniffed.

Gasoline.

The odor was strong and distinct. He reached up to the top of the doorframe and pushed down the little rod that unlocked the door. His hand shook in anger as he jiggled the handle until the door opened.

Replacement shrieked. She stood in the shower, fully dressed, with the water soaking her clothes.

"I'm in the shower!" she pleaded.

"With your clothes on." Jack stomped in and slammed the door shut.

"I'm going to take them off, so you have to leave."

"Where were you?" Jack's body shook.

"We… Kiku and I… we had to do stuff."

"Stuff? *Stuff?* I just heard a 10-70 over the scanner at 18 Winston."

Replacement's shoulders slumped. "Is a 10-70 a car fire?"

"Yes. Yes it is. And since you wouldn't know a radio code if it bit you on your butt… Did you torch that car?"

She lowered her head.

"That's arson! Do you realize that?"

"I didn't do it." She held her hands up.

"*Kiku* set the car on fire? Damn it. Damn it!" Jack pounded the sink, and everything on it jumped. His hands balled into fists and he pressed them against his forehead. "You drove my car. My Impala. You drove my car to go… commit *arson*."

"I didn't know she was going to do that." Replacement rubbed her hands together. "At first we headed over to Arber's. She said she was going to pay him a visit, but he wasn't home. So we headed over to Skylar's mother's house."

"Why? Do you realize what a huge mistake that was?"

"It would have been worse if I *didn't* go," Replacement said, sticking her chin out.

"Worse? How could it *possibly* be worse?" Jack threw his hands up.

"Because if I wasn't there, Kiku would have put Tina *in* the car and *then* lit it on fire." Replacement's voice broke, and her lip started to tremble.

Jack reached out for her. "Don't cry. Please don't."

She burst into tears.

"Stop. Stop." Jack shut off the water and wrapped his arms around her.

She pulled him close, her wet clothes instantly clinging to his. She buried her face in his chest, and he rubbed her back.

After a couple minutes, he leaned back and lifted her chin. "You okay?"

She nodded.

"You should get out of those clothes."

"I will. You have to get out of here first."

Jack let go of her and walked to the door. "Why did you jump in the shower with your clothes on?"

"I got gas all over them. I didn't know what to do. I was afraid to just leave them on the floor."

"They're not gonna burst into flames." Jack exhaled. "Where's Kiku?"

"She said she needed to go back to her hotel room."

Jack shut the door quietly, but then stormed into the kitchen to grab his phone—only to realize he didn't have Kiku's number. He went back to the bathroom and knocked on the door.

"Stay out," Replacement answered.

"I know," Jack said, trying not to let his anger creep into his voice. "Do you have Kiku's number?"

"It's in my phone."

"Where's your phone?"

"Kitchen counter."

Jack thundered back into the kitchen, found Replacement's phone, and used it to dial Kiku. The phone rang once, then Kiku picked up.

"How mad was he?" Kiku answered.

"*Was?*" Jack growled. "I'm *beyond* mad."

"Oh. I am sorry, Officer."

"You made her an arsonist."

"Accomplice. She just drove."

"Not funny. Not funny at all," Jack snarled.

"I respect you, Officer, but you are not my keeper."

Jack hung up and tossed the phone on the counter.

32

WATCH YOUR BACK

Jack paced while Replacement sat at the computer. Every few minutes, the police scanner would click on, and Jack would stop and listen. Afterward, he'd resume his pacing. He periodically checked both phones again before setting them back down on the counter.

Finally, he started opening and closing the kitchen cabinets. *Where the hell is that bottle of vodka?*

"What're you looking for?" Replacement asked.

"The vodka Kiku brought by. I want a Kamikaze."

"No."

"Excuse me?" Jack let another cabinet close with a thump.

"I need your head in the game. You drank last night. No."

"You don't get to dictate if I drink or not."

Replacement swung around in the chair. "What if something happens and we need to go out? Do you want to be one hundred percent, or sloppy?"

Jack glared at her. "Where is it?" he persisted.

Replacement turned back to the computer. "I drank it."

Jack laughed. "Shut up. There was more than half a bottle. You'd be—"

The police scanner kicked on. "Car 17. Code 13 at the Imperial."

"10-4," a man's voice responded.

Replacement looked up. "What's that in English?" she asked.

"Suspicious activity at the Imperial Motor Lodge. I think it was Tom Kempy."

Jack walked over to his phone, but before he could pick it up, it started to ring.

"Jack?" Kendra asked as he answered.

"What's up?"

"Are you anywhere near the Imperial? Just got a 911 from a guy who saw an Asian woman being chased by three big guys. He described all three as looking Italian."

No. What now?

"On my way."

Replacement was already moving for the door. Jack snagged his jacket and flew down the hallway, out the door, and into the Impala. Replacement leapt in on the passenger side, and the tires squealed as Jack sped away.

"The Imperial is on the west side of town," he said. "If I head around downtown and cut by the graveyard… six minutes."

"What's going on, Jack?"

"That was Kendra. The suspicious activity was an Asian woman being chased by three big Italians."

"Do you think it's Kiku?"

"Has to be. I should have had her stay."

The roads Jack selected were deserted, but they also had some sharp curves. The Impala could fly, although she tended to slide into the corners, so Jack frantically worked the gas and brakes as he barreled forward.

He hit redial as he drove.

"Jack?" Kendra answered. "Tom's driving around, but he's seen nothing. They're ghosts."

"He get any description of the car? Direction?"

"No."

Jack drew a mental map in his head and picked the faster route to the Imperial. He turned the Impala into the Old Meeting House graveyard. A single-lane road twisted through hills cut into terraces. The Impala shrieked as Jack struggled to keep it on the pavement.

"There." Replacement pointed to the right. Jack saw the sweep of headlights briefly gleam behind one of the hills.

He'd driven through the cemetery on a hundred patrols, scaring off teenagers who used the solitude of the graveyard to hide from prying adult eyes. He gritted his teeth as the wheels slid along the edge of the road, skimming a ten-foot drop. Replacement clung to the ceiling handle, and he could see the color drain from her cheeks.

As he rounded the corner, he saw a large sedan coming from the other direction, and he slammed on the brakes. The Impala growled in protest as it tried to grip the pavement, its nose dipping so low the front bumper scraped the ground and sparks flew. Replacement gasped and braced for impact, and Jack gripped the wheel with both hands—but the car finally stopped.

As the car settled back, bouncing off the shock absorbers, Jack looked into the terrified faces of the two men in the car in front of him. Fat Man was driving, and Big Nose was in the passenger's seat.

The Mancinis are in town.

"Move over to the driver's seat," Jack said quickly. "If anything happens, get the hell out of here."

Replacement looked at him. Her face was still pale, but he knew from her expression that there was no way she'd leave without him.

He got out of the car, and noticed there was less than three inches between the Impala and the Mancinis' car. *I cut that a little close.*

Paolo stepped out of the rear door, closed it behind him, and stepped off to the side of the road. Fat Man let the car roll back as Paolo walked forward. The car stopped after ten feet, but no one else got out.

Paolo folded his hands in front of himself.

Jack waited.

Shut up and wait for him to talk.

Paolo tilted his head. His weathered face looked even older than it had only a few days ago. "Have you found anything?"

"She hasn't used her credit card or phone, and she hasn't withdrawn any cash."

"Is that all you've got?"

"Has anyone contacted you?"

Paolo just stared back at him.

"I'm looking for her, too, Paolo. It's not about Omerta."

Paolo laughed. "I can't stand those movies. I'll give you some free advice. If you don't know about something, you shouldn't talk about it. It makes you look stupid."

"I know you don't talk to cops, but—"

"That's what it means. Omerta. We're men. We handle it ourselves. You're a cop, so I'm not going to you or anyone else."

"I'm not a cop. Not anymore. I'm suspended."

Paolo's bushy eyebrows knit together, and he clenched his jaw. It made him appear bear-like.

I see why Marisa called him Orsacchiotto, but he looks like the kind of bear that rips your head off.

"We got a call," Paolo admitted at last. "One word. Darrington."

Why would—? No, don't think about it now. Just get Kiku.

"I need a favor, Paolo."

Paolo raised an eyebrow.

"You have a woman with you, and I need her."

Paolo took one step forward, and Jack was surprised the ground didn't shake when he stomped down.

"Why would you ask for her?" The low challenge echoed in the darkness.

Fat Man and Big Nose got out of the car and positioned themselves in front of the hood.

"I don't think she—"

"You don't *think?*" Paolo held up a trembling finger.

"I need her to find Angelica."

"So do I." Paolo looked him up and down. "She's with them. She's Yakuza."

"I know. But she doesn't have anything to do with it."

Paolo walked right up to him. Jack may have been a lot taller, but he felt smaller before the barrel-chested man.

"You don't know jack. Do you know why she's here? Her name is Kiku Inuzuka. She's Takeo's pit bull." He stuck his finger in Jack's face. "You went to see Takeo. We know."

Damn.

"You must have alarmed him, because he sent his best. When you went to Takeo, you put him on notice: if anything happens to Angelica, he expects you're going to come after him for revenge."

The realization of what he had done hit Jack like diving into ice water. His chest tightened, he tilted his head back, and his eyes narrowed.

Paolo tapped his temple. "Think. Do you believe Takeo's just going to sit there, waiting to see if you kill him? That's not the kind of man Takeo is. He doesn't wait to see how someone will act; he acts first." Paolo thrust his hand back at the car. "I'm saving your life. She's an assassin. She's *your* killer. She was sent for your head."

Jack could see Kiku's outline in the back of the car. She was slumped forward, sitting in the middle of the seat. He could also make out the shadow of another person next to her.

Paolo glared. "Now get the hell out of the way."

Jack cleared his throat. "I need her, Paolo."

The old man froze. Jack knew there would be no more words. No screaming, no "Did you not understand me?" speech.

"She can help me find Angelica," Jack said. "But if you take her now, the war begins."

"It already has. We can use her for bargaining."

"What do you think Takeo will give for her?" Jack asked. "If Takeo has Angelica, which I don't think he does, would he really trade her for Kiku?"

Jack heard sirens, and looked toward the entrance of the cemetery, behind the Mancinis' car. Over the hills, he saw the flashing lights of a cruiser.

He looked back at Paolo. "I'm on Angelica's side."

The cruiser skidded to a stop behind the sedan. Kendra and Donald opened their doors, weapons drawn. Kendra's shotgun was a welcome sight.

Donald called out, "You good, Jack?"

Thanks for telling them my name.

"We're good. We're all good," Jack called out.

He looked at Paolo, and he could almost see the debate rage in the old man's eyes. "Paolo. I vouch for her."

Paolo spit. "Before you can vouch for anyone, I have to trust *you* first."

Jack's fists tightened at his sides. "Angelica didn't really talk about her family," he said, "but I asked her one day when she started to love art. She said when she was little, her uncle took her to the Metropolitan Museum of Art. He showed her the works of Michelangelo and Da Vinci. He told her she had greatness in her. I know *you* don't trust me—but Angelica did."

Donald shifted, and Kendra pulled the shotgun tighter into her shoulder. Fat Man glanced at Big Nose, and they both looked at Paolo. Paolo stood motionless, staring at Jack. Jack had played his cards, and now he waited to see what would happen. Over the sound of the engines, he could hear his heart thumping in his chest.

Paolo spit again. "I hold you responsible. In this whole thing." He jabbed his finger at the Impala and Replacement. "You and her."

He stalked back to his car and yanked the door open. Kiku stepped out. Paolo turned to glare back at Jack one last time before he got in the car. Big Nose and Fat Man followed. The sedan moved forward slowly, driving right onto the grass to get around the Impala.

Kiku walked toward Jack with her head down. He could tell from her posture she'd taken quite a beating.

"Keep walking and get in the car," Jack whispered to her, and then he walked over to Kendra and Donald.

"Thanks for the save," he said.

"You always said this was the way someone would go if they rabbited from the Imperial," Kendra said. "Guess you were right."

Donald rubbed the back of his neck. "So... What just happened here? No—don't tell me. Just tell me what we're supposed to say to Collins."

"Don't say anything. You guys didn't see anything. You got a 911, checked it out, everything was fine."

"She okay?" Kendra asked.

"She's fine. You'd better get going."

Kendra nodded. "Watch your back, Jack."

33

CAN YOU LOVE?

"The couch is fine." Kiku's voice was soft.

Jack led her into his bedroom.

Kiku stopped. "I can't. Thank you, but—"

"I'd save arguing," Replacement called out from the bathroom, where she was going through the medicine cabinet. "He's stubborn."

"Do you want to take a shower?" Jack offered.

Kiku started to shake her head, then winced. "No, thank you." Her eye was swollen shut, and the skin from her cheekbone to her jaw looked like one giant bruise.

Replacement returned and put a hand on Jack's arm. "I'll help her."

Jack left the two of them alone, and shut the door behind him.

He headed to the kitchen and opened the refrigerator. The ingredients for the Kamikaze were still there, but no vodka.

Where would she put it?

He scanned the apartment. His eyes stopped on the oven he never used.

That's where she hid the girly comforter before.

He opened the stove; the vodka bottle was there. He made a large Kamikaze, filled up a plastic bag with ice, then knocked on the bedroom door.

"Come in," Replacement called.

He entered. Kiku lifted herself up on her elbow and graced him with a lopsided grin.

He walked over to the bed and handed her the drink. "Thought you could use this."

"Thank you." She took a huge gulp.

He gave her the ice bag. "I'll be out in the living room if you need anything."

"Thank you." Kiku set the drink on the side table and lay back down.

Jack returned to the living room. Replacement exited behind him and quietly closed the door. She looked at Jack and made a face. "She's going to have one heck of a headache. Do you want to sleep in my room?" she offered.

Jack sat down and kicked off his shoes. "I'm good on the couch."

Replacement scrunched up her face and went into her bedroom. She came back with a pillow and blankets. "I can tell by looking at you there's no point in arguing," she said.

"Thanks." Jack rubbed his head. "If Kiku is settled in, why don't you go get some sleep too? I know neither of us has slept much lately. We'll get up early and start afresh."

Replacement pouted, but Jack could see dark circles under her eyes.

"Go on," he said. "Go to sleep."

"Are you sure you don't want to sleep with me?" Replacement asked.

Jack knew she meant *sleep and sleep only*, but the question made a warmth spread out in his chest. "I'm good. Go to bed."

"Well… okay then." And with a little wave, she went off to bed.

Jack stripped down to his boxers, pulled the back cushions off the couch to make a little more room, then lay down and stared at the ceiling.

Someone has her. Marisa must be going out of her mind.

Jack thought he'd never sleep, but as he closed his eyes and tried to drive the images from his mind, he eventually nodded off.

***

Hot desert sand whipped in the wind. Chandler shoved Jack's shoulder. He opened his eyes. A glance at his watch told him what his mind already knew—it had been over fifty-two hours since he'd slept.

"May I have the attention of the infidels?" a man with a thick Arabic accent shouted from a balcony across the street.

Jack, along with seventy-three other soldiers, perked up his ears. He was on the third floor of what was left of a motel. Directly across from him, in what used to be an office building, insurgents held Private E2 Jeremy Billings hostage.

Jeremy stood on the balcony beside the man with the accent. He had his arms tied behind his back, and blood and tears ran down his face. He looked as if he could barely stand on his own. It had been fifty-two hours of hell for him. Jack was surprised at how well he was holding up.

And throughout those entire fifty-two hours, the soldiers who surrounded the building, including Jack, had begged for permission to go in and rescue their comrade—but all requests had been denied. Some new negotiator was en route.

Every couple of hours, they would drag Jeremy out, and the same man would yell out something about Jeremy's life. The beginning was always the same—he'd call for their attention—and then he'd state something new about Jeremy. They had no doubt found some of the information from the letters Jeremy had on him when he was captured. The other information they had tortured out of him.

Fifty-two hours ago, Jack had never even heard of Jeremy Billings. Now he knew his father's name was Carl and his mother's was Wendy. He got his first kiss in the sixth grade and was recently married to a girl named Angie. She had a birthmark on her cheek and her hair smelled like strawberries. She liked to walk in the woods and paint. Jeremy wrote to her every day, and they were expecting their first child.

"Occupiers!" the man called out again. "You have our demands. We call for an immediate withdrawal of all troops. If not, the blood of this man is on your hands, and his memory will haunt you to the gates of hell."

Chandler gripped his gun and Jack could hear his teeth grinding. Jack knew how he felt, because he felt the same way. Billings was a soldier doing his duty, not some bargaining chip.

"Jeremy Billings just wants to go home to his beloved childhood sweetheart," the man shouted. "He longs to hold his unborn child. Shall I read you the end of his sweetheart's letter?"

Jack slammed his fist into the concrete. *Jeremy's captors are surrounded. They have no way out. They know they're going to die. And that makes men do unthinkable things.* He wanted to move, to do something. But like all the other soldiers, he had been ordered to stand down.

The terrorist shouted again. *"Baby. I can't wait to see you."* He was obviously reading the letter. *"Two more weeks. I love you. I'm blessed that you'd marry me. You're my best friend, and I know you'll be the best father. I can't wait to hold you."*

It turned Jack's stomach to hear the guy twist the girl's words.

Jeremy's head sagged forward. A man stepped up behind him, grabbed him by the shirt collar, and yanked him back into the shadows.

"I gave you forty-eight hours," the accented man called out. "It has been fifty-two. His wife will be a widow and his child an orphan, and it's because of you."

A gunshot rang out, and for a moment, silence descended upon the street.

Jeremy's body was tossed over the balcony.

Jack and the other seventy-three soldiers opened fire before the body even hit the ground. Chandler's massive light machine gun spewed casings in a wide arc. Jack unloaded his assault rifle into the three murderers, who went down in a hail of bullets. He kept firing until his gun was empty, and then reloaded and fired again. When those bullets were gone, he unloaded his pistol.

Jack looked at Chandler. His gaze was fixed on Jeremy's body, which now lay in the street. Jack looked at the body, and then quickly turned away.

A little girl stood in front of him. A little girl with red hair and freckles.

I'm dreaming. Wake the hell up.

"I'm sorry," he whispered.

"No parties and no birthdays," she sang. "No tuck-ins and no play days. No hugs and no kisses. Just a bunch of lost wishes."

Jack slumped down against the wall and turned back to Chandler. But it wasn't Chandler; now it was Jeremy. The little girl was gone.

Jeremy took his helmet off. "Hey."

Jack swallowed and tried to close his eyes, but he couldn't.

"Can I ask you one question?" Jeremy ran his fingers through his hair. "Can you check in on my wife?"

"I did." Jack rubbed his hands on his pants; the sand scraped his skin. "When I got back, I went to see her."

Jeremy smiled. "Thanks."

***

Jack fought for air. He felt as though he'd been bench-pressing three hundred pounds for hours, and now his muscles had gone limp.

Someone lifted the blanket and slid over him. Tender hands skimmed his skin, and supple yet strong arms held him close. He relaxed into them. The soft body slid into the space between him and the back of the couch. He shifted over. With his eyes still closed, he let his head fall back, and he felt the warmth of the body next to him.

When Jack opened his eyes, it wasn't Replacement's arms he found himself in; it was Kiku who was partly on top of him, wrapped in a thin sheet and a T-shirt, holding him. Her right eye was almost swollen shut and a deep bruise ran from her cheek to her jaw, but she cradled his body against hers. Jack wanted to say something, but instead his eyes just locked on hers. There was an understanding there. He could tell she saw it, too. They shared a bond.

Pain. We've both been broken.

Jack slumped back, and she laid her head on his chest. He could hear her heartbeat. The warmth of her skin radiated through the thin sheet into his. There was no shame about lying there, but there was nothing sexual about it, either. He let go.

"You were an orphan, Officer?" She spoke softly.

"Yeah."

"Your mother was a prostitute?"

Jack nodded.

"Mine was, too. My father was Japanese. She was Korean."

"Is that how you ended up in the Yakuza?"

"Yes. They took me in. They protected me."

Funny what she considers protection.

Kiku was quiet for a moment. "Officer, can you love?"

It was an unusual question. Jack thought about it, but didn't answer.

They lay there awhile. Jack didn't to move. His whole body felt weak. After the nightmares, he could barely move, and the last thing he wanted to do was think. He just wanted to feel.

"I see love in Marisa's sketches of you," Kiku said. "She loves you. I see it in the way Alice looks at you. But you... you hold back, so I wonder: Can you love?"

Jack closed his eyes. Kiku's arms tightened slightly.

She continued. "I don't know if I can." Her sigh ran across his chest. "I have been with men, but I have never loved."

Jack breathed in deeply. Her head rose and fell with his chest.

"When life has beaten a person down, one withdraws," she said.

Jack understood that.

"Do you know how to grow tomato plants?" she asked.

Jack's brows pulled together. Her mind worked in such tangents. "No."

Kiku's fingers traced a figure on his chest. "I grew some plants on my balcony when I first came here. There was a frost, and I thought they'd died. I started five plants. Four died. But the plant that lived, it started with three leaves. When the frost came, the plant pulled back all its nutrients from its leaves so the plant itself would live. It survived, but those leaves died."

He stroked her hair.

She lifted her head to look at him. "Is that what happened to us?" Jack could hear a slight tremor in her voice. "Did we cut off our feelings to survive? Is that why we can't love?"

He could feel her breath on his neck.

"I watched you in the restaurant, and you intrigued me," Kiku said. "I could see you knew the danger, but you still went ahead. That is the kind of man women love."

"What kind?"

"The kind of man who would journey into hell to get them back." Her fingers ran down along his jaw, and she lifted his chin. "Why did you tell the Mancinis to let me go?"

Jack closed his eyes. "I need you to find Marisa."

Her hand moved up to the side of his face. "You still lie to me."

Jack debated. "You didn't take her. You don't think the Yakuza did, either."

"They didn't." She laid her head back down. "You know what the old Italian said is true."

"I do."

"Do you know who Damocles was?"

"No."

"Damocles worked for King Dionysius. One day, Damocles told Dionysius he was lucky to be king. And Dionysius answered, 'If you think I am lucky, how about you try out my life?' Damocles agreed. He enjoyed his position until he noticed a huge sword hanging by a horsehair over his head. He saw then what the true price of being king is."

"Uneasy lies the head that wears the crown."

"When you went to see Takeo and threatened him with harm if something happened to Severino's daughter, you put a sword over his head. Because you are a police officer, he did not kill you—but he will not let you leave that sword dangling long."

Jack looked up at the ceiling. Their breathing fell into sync, helping him relax even more.

"Paolo told you I was sent to kill you," said Kiku, "but you still asked for me back. Why?"

Jack touched her arm. "Something you said. You and me. We're a lot alike." His mind flashed back to the soldier. "I followed orders blindly once. I should have done something, but I didn't, and a good man died. I don't do that anymore. I couldn't just let you die."

"If Marisa dies," she whispered, "you will die, too."

Jack closed his eyes.

"And it will be me who must kill you."

"You'll have to get in line." Replacement's voice was just below a growl.

Jack sat up quickly and dropped Kiku onto the couch. Kiku lay there, loosely wrapped in the sheet.

Replacement stood with her hands at her sides and her feet spread apart. She almost looked menacing.

Jack held up a hand. "Nothing happened."

"It is not what it appears." Kiku stood. "Jack had a nightmare, and I came out to check on him. There was nothing sexual about it."

"Nothing sexual about lying on top of a man?" Replacement glared at Jack.

Kiku smiled.

Replacement scowled at her.

Kiku pulled the sheet a little tighter around herself. "I honestly did come out to check on him, but I agree, you cannot lie with someone like that and have it not be sexual."

"Oh, thanks," Jack said to her. Then he turned back to Replacement. "Nothing happened."

Wrapped in the sheet, Kiku walked back to the bedroom. She gazed over her shoulder at Jack. "I am sorry to say, that is also true." She shut the door.

Jack and Replacement stared at each other. Replacement's face scrunched up. "It's my fault, I suppose," she muttered as she sat down.

"Why?" he blurted out.

Shut up, you idiot.

"I just… never mind." Replacement pointed toward her door. "Go sleep in my room."

"No. I got the couch—"

"Yeah, right." She rolled her eyes. "I'm not leaving you out here alone. Go."

34

DAMOCLES

Jack opened his eyes and stared at the ceiling. When they had moved downstairs, Replacement had picked out a single bed for herself, and naturally, she'd gone for the cheapest one available. But he'd gotten her the super-comfortable one instead, and after sleeping on it himself now, he didn't want to get up. He was exhausted.

But he knew he couldn't just lie there. *I got that one call from Ilario and then, nothing. Where is she? Paolo was only told to come to Darrington.*

Jack tossed the comforter off and leaped out of bed—then realized that his clothes were out in the living room, in front of the couch. *Great.*

He opened the door and peeked out. Kiku was in the kitchen, and Replacement was at the computer. He grabbed a blanket off the bed, wrapped it around himself, and headed out to get his clothes. Kiku looked up from the kitchen. Replacement spun around in her chair, and a satisfied grin spread across her lips.

"Morning," he mumbled. He grabbed his clothes and shuffled back into the bedroom. *I should have just sprung for her own apartment.*

Fully dressed, he came back out. He walked over to Kiku in the kitchen. The swelling around her eye had gone down considerably, but the extensive bruising was painful even to look at. "How are you feeling?" he asked.

"I feel well. Would you care for some breakfast?"

"Love some."

Jack glanced at the clock on the stove; it was practically noon. *I guess I really needed the sleep.*

"Don't worry, we both slept in too," Kiku said.

"I didn't," Replacement called over her shoulder.

"Have you eaten?" Jack asked.

"Yup," Replacement snapped.

Kiku smiled. "I waited for you."

Replacement's mouse banged against the desk.

I'm surrounded by way too much estrogen.

After Kiku had scrambled some eggs and dished up a couple of plates, they sat down at the counter to eat. Jack bowed his head, and just as his eyes began to close, he saw Kiku do the same. With one eye open, he stared at her. After a moment, she opened her eyes to look questioningly at him.

"Would you like for me to say grace, Officer?"

"Sure… I didn't know you—I say grace, but I didn't want to force you."

She closed her eyes. "God, I thank you for this food, and I ask that it make our bodies and minds strong. Give us the grace to accept the trials that come our way. In Christ, I ask this."

Replacement spun around in her chair. "That was nice."

Jack leaned closer to Kiku. "She rates prayers. That was actually a big compliment."

"Thank you. I spent two years in a Christian orphanage in Korea."

Replacement's face softened. "How old were you?"

"Nine."

"I guess we're more alike than I realized," Replacement said.

Jack watched both women. There was something about the way they carried themselves that was similar. Jack had always chalked up the feeling that Replacement looked ready to bolt to her boundless energy, but now that he was getting the same impression from Kiku, he realized he was wrong. Like a fox that had been hurt and hunted, they were both always on guard. Ready to fight or flee at the slightest sound.

You can say that again, Jack thought.

The police scanner coming to life interrupted his thoughts.

"Unit seven, we have a code three. One hundred and two Highland Avenue."

"Copy. Responding," a man replied.

Jack ran for his keys. "That's an emergency call for an ambulance. One-oh-two Highland is the address of the tattoo parlor."

All three raced to put their shoes on and get their jackets.

"I'll drive," Jack said as they rushed out the door.

***

When they got to the tattoo parlor, an ambulance and a police cruiser were parked out front. A small crowd of people had gathered outside, and Tom Kempy was trying to keep control.

"The paramedics are coming out, and we need to clear this doorway," Tom tried to explain to the crowd.

One look at the people's faces told Jack that Tom's approach wouldn't work. Half of them looked concerned, but the others were just along for the ride, eager to see what was going on.

Jack bellowed in his most commanding voice, *"Move back!"* He didn't have his uniform on, but he was still all cop. He marched straight to the door, gently pushing the crowd back. "Move back!" he shouted again. "Give them space." By the time he'd made it to Tom, he'd cleared a wide path on the sidewalk.

Two EMTs came out of the tattoo parlor, wheeling a stretcher with Shawn Miller on it. It was clear he was unconscious, and he'd really been worked over. Black eyes, broken jaw, nose, arm…

Jack looked up at one of the EMTs, struggling to remember the man's name. "Hey, boss," he said, deciding on a nickname that flattered, "did he say anything?"

"No. A girl inside found him. She's still pretty upset. How've you been?"

Jack shook his hand. "Been better, thanks. I'm going to head in to talk to her."

The EMTs loaded Shawn into the ambulance and headed off, siren wailing. Jack turned once again to the crowd, which was starting to close back in. "All right, everyone, let's move back. Let's keep the sidewalk clear."

A voice chimed in from behind him. "How can you set such a fine example of working police procedures and yet be a poster boy for how to infuriate Sheriff Collins?"

Jack turned to see Robert Morrison walking over from his cruiser. Morrison was a tall African-American man in his late fifties. He wore the tan uniform of the sheriff's department, without the hat, and his curly black hair was short and graying at the temples. And even though he had a smile on his face, Jack could see the look of disappointment in his eyes.

Jack came to attention. "Undersheriff."

"Don't do that, son." He stretched out his hand. "I appreciate the show of respect, but save it for Collins. Actually, just stay away from the man for now. Why the hell didn't you call me?"

"What was I going to say? Collins had already made up his mind. Why drag you into a fight I can't win?"

"Because I can try to talk some sense into him." He looked up at the sign over Marisa's shop. "The girl you think is missing owns this place?"

"Yes, sir. The guy they just took out is the assistant manager, Shawn Miller."

"Can he give a statement?"

"Not right now. Unconscious. EMT said a girl found him. I'd like to talk to her."

Morrison gave him a look. "You're going to let me handle that. Collins is out of town, but I keep expecting him to jump out of the floor and start yelling at me for even breathing the same air as you."

"Sir, I—"

"Bring me up to speed after we talk to the girl."

As they walked inside, Jack realized he didn't see Kiku or Replacement anywhere. *They'd better be behaving themselves.*

Tom was talking to a crying girl at one of the tables, and he snapped to attention as they approached. "Undersheriff. I have the scene under control, and I'm taking statements now."

"Good job, Tom," Morrison said. "Miss? Can I ask you a few questions?"

The girl sobbed into a handful of tissues but nodded.

Morrison leaned down. "Can you please tell me what happened?"

She sniffled. "When I came to work, there was no one here. I thought Shawn was in the back, so I called for him, but he didn't answer. I thought maybe he went into the alley for a smoke. I walked back there, and Marisa's office door was open. He was"—she sobbed—"Shawn was lying on the floor. And there was—blood everywhere."

"Was he conscious?" Morrison asked. "Did he say anything to you?"

"He was just moaning. I called 911."

"You did the right thing. I know this was difficult."

As Morrison patted the girl on the shoulder, Jack spotted movement in the back hallway. His jaw dropped when he saw that it was Replacement, standing just outside Marisa's office door. She saw him, turned, and whispered to someone inside. A second later, Kiku walked out of the office. Kiku grinned at Jack, and he glowered back. Then the two women walked out the rear entrance.

"Jack," Morrison said. "Do you know if this place has surveillance?"

Jack tried to regain his composure. "None, sir."

"Figures. I'll start a canvass of the neighborhood after I've checked out the office."

Sheriff Collins's voice crackled over the radio. "Morrison? Are you on scene?"

Morrison looked wide-eyed at Jack. "Yes, sir, I am."

"I'm en route. Five minutes," Collins snapped. "If Stratton shows up, keep him the hell out of it."

"Yes, sir." Morrison clicked his radio off. "That's your cue to make for the exit."

"Of course. I'm just going to go out the back way," Jack said. He started down the hallway.

Morrison followed. "Jack! Do you have any idea what he'll do if he finds you here?"

"I'll just take a quick look. Two seconds. I know the office; it will *help* you."

"Lately *you* and *help* seem to go together like peanut butter and bullets."

Jack looked into the office from the doorway. The tattoo table in the corner was covered in blood, and there was more blood splattered on the walls. *Damn. Someone really worked that guy over.* But the rest of the office looked undisturbed.

Jack walked over to Marisa's desk and examined the papers stacked in neat piles. *The desk was not that neat when I left. And Shawn said no one but Marisa ever came in here.*

Jack walked back out.

"Well?" Morrison asked. "Do you have an opinion?"

"Yeah, but I have about one minute before Collins gets here."

"Go." Morrison angled his head toward the exit. "Fill me in when you can."

"Thanks." Jack hurried out the back door.

Jack reached the end of the alley just as Collins's Crown Vic pulled up in front of the tattoo parlor. Jack scanned the street, but the Impala was gone. *Replacement got the car out of here. That was smart.* He walked off in the opposite direction. *Except now I don't have a car.*

An unmarked car pulled up beside him, and Jennifer Rivers stuck her head out. "Need a ride?"

Jack stuck his hands in his pockets and rocked back on his heels. "I was just out for a walk."

"I only have a minute, Stratton. Get in."

Jack hopped in the back seat. Jennifer glared at him in the rearview mirror. "Is there a reason you want me to look like a chauffeur?"

"Yeah. I'm trying to have Collins not see me."

Jennifer pulled away from the curb. "I may have a hit."

Jack sat up straight. "What? What do you have?"

Jennifer sighed. "If Walter knew I was talking to you, he'd have my head examined. You know that, right?"

"Well then, let's not tell Walter." Jack grinned. "What have you got?"

She shook her head. "We intercepted another call. It wasn't part of our wiretaps, it was during a separate NSA investigation. They received it a day ago and just now pushed it over to us. Walter thinks that you just peeved everyone off and led them here on a wild goose chase. But—"

Jack grabbed the back of the seat and pulled himself forward. "What did you get?"

She pulled into a doughnut shop drive-through.

Jack's hands went up. "You have a doughnut craving now?"

"Hey, I'm helping you out here. When Walter and I got to the tattoo parlor, I saw you slinking away down the street, and I suggested donuts so I'd have an excuse to get away from him and come talk to you." She turned to the speaker. "Three medium coffees, regular, and an assorted half-dozen." She pulled forward without waiting for an answer. "Our wiretap intercepted a call made to Severino. The caller was a man. He just said 'Darrington.' The NSA shared with us that they intercepted a separate call from a different phone that was made to Takeo. We're working on identifying the caller, a woman. They spoke in code and we're trying to crack it."

"If it was code, why do you think it's related?"

"They traced the sending cell to a tower in Darrington." She grabbed some bills from her purse.

"Did they understand any of the call?"

"One word was Greek. Damocles. It's part—"

"I know the story," Jack said.

"Do you know what it means, then?" She looked back at him.

Yeah, I'm letting my executioner sleep in my bed.

Jack shook his head.

Jennifer handed the teenage girl some cash and took the coffee and doughnuts.

"I know you can really tick people off, Stratton." Jennifer pulled away from the window, then pulled over by the curb across the street. "But for this much activity, there has to be something more than that going on. Let me work on Walter."

Jack's brain was already trying to process the information he'd just gotten, and he didn't care whether Prescott was on board or not.

"I need to show him that the tattoo parlor and everything else is connected... I know you two didn't hit it off, but he's a great investigator. We'll find her, Jack."

"Thanks for the heads-up." Jack opened the door and got out.

He stood on the sidewalk and watched her drive down the street. *Damocles. I'm not the only one with a sword over my head, though. Marisa has one, too. They called the Mancinis to town because the exchange is coming. And it's coming soon.*

35

LIVE OR DIE?

Once again, Jack was rescued from a long walk home. The Impala pulled up beside him, and Jack slid into the driver's seat, nudging Replacement over next to Kiku. All three now sat in the front on the bench seat.

"This is a little awkward," Kiku said, shifting closer to the window.

"If it's too close, hop in the back," Replacement suggested dryly.

Jack drove away from downtown. "Did you guys touch anything in the office?"

Both women shook their heads. "Someone beat the tar out of that guy," Replacement said. "Did you see his face?"

Jack gripped the steering wheel. "It was Paolo."

"That is what I would assume, but how can you be sure?" Kiku asked.

She's not asking because she doesn't believe me; she just wants to know how I figured it out. I like it when someone believes in me.

"Besides the blood, the office was neater than when I left. Paolo loves Marisa and would be respectful of her things. Stuff was knocked off the desk and was then put back… carefully."

Replacement turned to Kiku. "He's good."

"Very." Kiku turned to look out the window, and Jack couldn't help his chest puffing up a bit.

Replacement tilted her head. "Why did Paolo beat him up so badly? He didn't know anything."

"The Mancinis wanted to be absolutely sure of that." Kiku's voice lowered. "They can be very brutal."

Jack's throat tightened as he remembered Kiku in the back of Paolo's car. "Rivers picked me up."

Replacement shifted in her seat. "The FBI lady? Why?"

"She wanted to give me a heads-up. They intercepted a phone call to Severino. They know the Mancinis are in town."

Jack didn't say anything about the call to Takeo. He knew Kiku had to be the one who had placed it. He watched her out of the corner of his eye, but her face betrayed nothing.

That's her tell. She hardens up. She called Takeo, but she's not going to tell me why.

"Where are we going, and why are you driving like a bat out of hell?" Replacement looked around, and Jack knew she was looking for something to hold on to.

"Arber's." Jack pumped the brakes and turned right.

"Why?" both women asked in unison.

"The Mancinis are headed there."

"How do you know?" Once again, they spoke at the same time.

"That's creepy," Replacement said. "Stop it."

"Paolo worked on Shawn for a while," Jack said. "Shawn's tough, but he must have told him everything about Marisa."

"Including Arber," Kiku added.

"And if Shawn told them that Marisa got in an argument with Arber and threw him out, I have no doubt they'll go to Arber's next."

Replacement looked at Jack. "Let's go."

***

"The lights are off," Kiku noted as they approached Arber's house.

"Do you think he's out?" Replacement asked.

"No. The garden lights are out, too," Jack said. "I think someone cut the power to disable the alarm."

Jack pulled into the driveway. There wasn't another car in sight. "Stay in the car," he ordered, and both women got out.

That worked.

"I'll go in the back," Kiku said. "There's a slider in the walkout basement." She disappeared into the darkness.

Jack and Replacement headed for the front door. Jack knocked and waited. He rang the bell and beat on the door.

No response.

Jack tried the door, and it opened. The alarm panel's lights were off. *Of course. No power.*

In the moonlight from outside, Jack could see ceramic shards on the floor of the entryway. Something had been shattered here. He drew his pistol and motioned Replacement to get behind him.

"Mr. de Lorme, this is the police. We are entering the premises," Jack called out.

Silence greeted them.

He moved left, through a huge study, and entered an even bigger kitchen. Everything looked new and expensive. Jack held up his hand, and Replacement bumped into him.

Jack turned and glared.

She mouthed, "Sorry," and moved against the wall.

They stepped through the kitchen into a hallway, and Jack saw a doorknob turning. He put one hand on Replacement's chest and held his finger up to his lips.

The door opened, and Kiku appeared. She motioned them over.

"He's in the basement," she whispered. "It's bad."

I wonder what her definition of bad is.

"Is he alive?"

"Sort of."

That's bad.

She started back down the stairs, gesturing for Jack to follow. Jack looked at Replacement and held out his hand to indicate that she should stay here. Her eyes blazed.

"Listen, Alice, I—I don't want some hideous image burned into your head." Jack whispered, but it was still a growl. "I have so many in mine, one more doesn't matter to me. I don't want you—I don't want you to have to be like me. Just—please don't argue."

To Jack's surprise, Replacement nodded.

Jack turned and headed down the steps, and he was very glad he'd had Replacement stay upstairs. Arber lay in a bloody heap on the floor. Two baseball bats and a chain splattered with blood lay around him. Jack could only recognize this bloody pulp as Arber by his hair and build. He was still breathing, though, and groaning softly.

Kiku was standing by the wall, next to a laundry rack. She caught Jack's eye, then pulled on the rack, swinging back a section of the wall and revealing a hidden room. "It's a recording room," she said. "Looks like he has cameras in the bedrooms and bathrooms. They're... not for security."

Anger suddenly coursed through Jack, his pulse raced, and his teeth ground together. *Marisa would have come here. Did he video her?*

"Live or die?" Kiku asked.

"What?" Jack asked.

Kiku looked puzzled. "Should I finish him off, or should we go?"

Just then Replacement came thundering down the stairs. "We don't kill people," she said. Jack saw her staring at Arber and gagging, but as he moved toward her, she held up a hand.

Kiku pointed to the hidden room. "The TV in there is paused on a scene of him raping an unconscious girl."

"We don't kill people," Replacement repeated.

"He may not survive," Kiku said. "Besides, Paolo ensured that Arber will not be hurting any more girls. It appears he used that bazooka he carries to shoot Arbor in the groin."

Jack winced.

They headed back upstairs. Jack used the kitchen phone to dial 911, then wiped it down. He waited until he heard the operator come on, said nothing, and motioned for them to go. He wiped down the door handle as they left the house.

They flew down the driveway. Kiku now sat in the back seat, and Replacement was in the front. Jack noticed that all the color had left her face, and he knew what image was burned into her mind. *I wish you hadn't seen that.*

They were just pulling away when Jack saw the flashing lights ahead and heard the sirens.

"Police," Kiku whispered.

"Ambulance," Jack corrected.

Its sirens blaring, an ambulance rounded the corner, sped past them, and turned into Arber's driveway.

Jack frowned.

"What's wrong?" Kiku asked.

"That's way too fast for a response time. Someone else must have called them."

A police cruiser came flying past next. Jack angled his head away and kept going.

Jack looked over at Replacement. She was getting even whiter, and he was starting to worry about her getting carsick. "You okay?"

"I'm all right." Her voice sounded shaky. "Do you think that guy did something to Marisa?"

"No. If Arber had done something to Marisa, Paolo would have skinned him."

Replacement's throat tightened, and she held up a hand. "Didn't need that."

"Sorry."

"What's our next move?" Kiku sat up between them and squeezed Replacement's shoulder with one hand.

"Regroup," Jack said. "I have to think. Let's go back to my apartment."

36

NORMALLY IT JUST HURTS LIKE HELL

Jack parked the Impala and hopped out. As they walked toward his apartment, he noticed Ilario sitting in a car across the street.

Jack didn't turn his head. "Don't look at me," he said to the two women. His voice was clear and clipped. "Both of you head in."

Kiku took Replacement by the elbow and started to speak animatedly to her as they walked up the steps of the building.

Jack crossed the street and got into the passenger seat of Ilario's car.

"How'd you find me?" he asked.

"Paolo looked you up. He said some cop said your name. You're the only one named Jack in the sheriff's department."

Thanks again, Donald.

"Did you get anything?" Jack asked.

Deep circles stood out under Ilario's red eyes, and his skin was pale. He slumped in the seat. "I called. Paolo's been… He's been… looking."

The kid hasn't seen this side of the family business before.

"You were with him at the tattoo parlor."

Ilario nodded.

"Did Shawn say anything?"

Tears formed in Ilario's eyes, and his lips trembled. "Is he okay?"

Jack stopped himself from merely saying yes. "I'll check."

"Paolo—I've seen him mad, but…" Ilario suddenly looked up. "I don't have much time. Shawn didn't do it. But he talked back, and Paolo got mad. Shawn told us about you and another guy."

"Arber."

"Yes. We went there next, and Arber slammed the door in Paolo's face. My uncle didn't care for that. They started asking Arber questions, and Paolo kept looking at this mirror. All of a sudden he grabbed the guy and just smashed his head into it." He swallowed. "There was a camera behind the mirror. I don't know how Paolo knew, but he went crazy. The guy had this room—"

"I know about the room."

Ilario's voice sounded distant. "Arber told us everything. He'd get girls drunk and drug them and…"

Jack pushed down the disgust that churned inside him.

"But Arber said he never touched Angelica. He said she didn't like him. They only dated a couple of times, and Angelica dumped him."

"Paolo believed that?"

"Yeah. After what they did to Arber, I do, too."

"Did Arber say anything else? Anything about her paintings?"

"He said he buys her paintings. Gives her top dollar. Paolo broke his hands then. He said a scumbag like him wouldn't do that. Arber admitted going to her apartment to try to talk to her about a new painting, but he said she wasn't there."

"Did he say he went inside her apartment?"

"Yes. He went on and on. He was begging. I think he thought if he told the truth they'd let him live. He told Paolo he wanted to steal her painting, so he used a key he took from her to get in, but the painting wasn't there."

That must have been when he took the business card back. Dead end. Nothing.

"Paolo shot him in the groin and left him to die. I just couldn't…"

"You called the ambulance?" Jack asked.

"No matter what someone's done, I couldn't leave him like that."

"Have you heard anything else?"

"No. My father's going crazy. He's getting more men, and he's going after the Yakuza."

"I don't think they had anything to do with it."

"Do you *know* that?" He grabbed the steering wheel and glared at Jack.

"Ilario, I'll find her. You have to let me know the minute you hear anything, okay? Angelica's counting on us."

Ilario nodded. "I have to get back."

Jack started to get out of the car, and Ilario grabbed his wrist.

"I saw the pictures she's drawn of you in her apartment. Angelica trusts you. You have to find her."

***

Jack paced and listened to the police scanner. There was a constant stream of police officers radioing in their positions. Detectives were now at Arber's house, and Collins must have called out half the force.

"Well, we can rule out the two people who may have had a local angle to grab her," Jack said.

"You suspected Arber and Shawn?" Replacement was once again working at the computer.

"I didn't suspect them, but I didn't rule them out either. Shawn wanted to buy her business, and Arber was a scumbag ex-boyfriend."

"We can rule out the Yakuza and the Mancinis too," Kiku said, not looking away from the window. She held a cup of tea with both hands.

Jack was silent.

Kiku turned around and lifted an eyebrow. "You still distrust me, Officer?"

"You checked in with Takeo."

The wolf-like smile spread across her lips.

Replacement shot to her feet so fast her chair tipped over behind her. "You ratted us out? And now you're *smiling?*"

Jack saw Kiku go rigid, and he tensed.

"I didn't tell him anything he did not already know." Kiku sighed. "But I had to check in."

"What did you tell him?" Jack asked.

"Why did you even have to talk to him?" Replacement demanded.

Kiku looked from Replacement to Jack and back again. Then she turned back to the window. "If I didn't call him, he would send more men, and I would face repercussions."

"What did you tell him?" Jack asked again.

"That we have heard nothing. I let him know that I am following you... closely."

"Did he say anything?"

She looked down into her teacup. "He's going to send men if there is not progress soon. He would rather fight a war someplace other than his front steps."

"Anything else?"

"He wanted to know if Angelica lived someplace else before coming here."

"Why?" Replacement asked.

"If we did not take her, it must be someone else," Kiku explained. "He has men looking at our enemies, but that has not been fruitful."

"So you're going to say you're being framed?" Replacement sneered.

Kiku glared.

"Anything else?" Jack asked again.

Kiku looked back at him, and her lips pressed together. "I did not inform him of your suspension... yet."

Jack's heart sped up, but he nodded and forced his face to remain expressionless.

Replacement turned to look at him, and Jack could see the fear growing in her eyes. *She's smart. She's figuring it out.*

Replacement spun around to face Kiku. "Because Jack's a cop, Takeo didn't kill him."

Kiku nodded.

"So if you tell Takeo Jack is suspended..." Replacement's eyes narrowed. "I'll do more than take your pinky if you even *think* about hurting Jack."

Kiku folded her arms across her chest. "I've been nothing but honest. Would you like me to lie?"

"I'd like you to die." Replacement grabbed a pen off the desk.

"Alice!" Jack grabbed her arm.

"Seriously, Jack?" Replacement spun around. "She's sent to kill you, and you go on like it's nothing. You let her sleep here. We still don't know she's not the one who took Marisa and is just pulling the strings behind the scenes."

"She didn't do that."

"No." The gold flecks in Replacement's green eyes blazed. "You have to give me more than your BS detector on this one. Give me a fact. It's your life. How do we know she didn't come and take Marisa?"

Jack hesitated.

Replacement tapped her foot. "Answer me, Jack."

Jack walked past her to Kiku. "You first saw me at the Golden Blossom restaurant, right?"

"That is correct."

"Did Takeo tell you to come here, or did you follow me?"

"I told you. Takeo sent me, and two men, to follow you. They lost you when you changed in the store, but I did not."

Jack cracked his neck. "The Yakuza didn't know where Marisa was. Neither did the Mancinis. The Mancinis didn't come here until they got the anonymous phone call telling them Marisa was in Darrington."

Kiku and Replacement exchanged a look to see whether the other understood what he was saying. Both shrugged.

"And you said Takeo asked if Marisa lived someplace else," Jack continued, pacing.

Replacement threw her hands up. "Jack, if you're figuring something out, can you clue me in?"

Jack exhaled. "Do you know that program you wrote?"

"The one for the cars at the tollbooth?"

"Yes. I need you—"

The police scanner crackled. "All available units. 10-31 on West and Newton. 10-31 Handle's parking lot."

Jack ran for the door. Kiku and Replacement scrambled after him.

"Shots fired. Two blocks away," Jack explained as he pulled on his jacket.

They raced down the stairs, and the Impala's tires were spinning in seconds.

***

"Handle's Liquors." Jack tried to picture the storefront as the Impala slid around the corner and he punched it. "Large parking lot. Small apartment building next door. Three floors. There's an Italian restaurant next door."

Replacement held on to the ceiling handle as the Impala raced down the street.

Jack let the wheel spin as he straightened out on the last turn.

"There." Kiku pointed to a car in the parking lot with both doors open.

Jack could see Paolo lying on the ground and Ilario kneeling beside him. Whoever was in the driver's seat was slumped over the wheel.

"You two stay in the car," he said.

Replacement started to jump out, but Kiku grabbed her arm.

Gun in hand, Jack raced over to Paolo. Ilario had his hands pressed against Paolo's thigh.

"Get the boy out of here," Paolo growled at Jack.

"No!" Ilario shook his head.

"Go, boy. I'm dead."

Jack looked Paolo over and counted at least five bullet wounds. Paolo's face was ashen, and blood ran out of his mouth. "Ilario," Jack said. "An ambulance is on the way. Go."

Paolo pressed his huge gun into Ilario's hand, then grabbed Ilario by the back of his neck. "You're a good man. Become a great one." Paolo pushed him away and coughed.

"Go to my car now," Jack ordered. "And tell them to drive you away from here."

Ilario ran and got in the Impala, and Jack waved at Replacement to take off. He could hear the sirens getting closer. Replacement cast a worried frown his way, but she did as she was told.

As the Impala pulled away, Jack knelt down next to Paolo. "Who did it?"

Paolo glared at Jack. "You'll never learn."

"Forget your stupid code. You won't go to the cops even if they kill you, I get it. Do you get that they'll kill Angelica? They'll kill her, Paolo."

Paolo started to gag, and blood sprayed upward. His head rolled to the side.

Sirens filled the air.

"Paolo, damn it. Tell me. Who?"

Paolo's mouth opened and closed.

"Hands on your head!" ordered a voice behind Jack.

"Who?" Jack pleaded.

"Hands on your head!"

Paolo looked at Jack and mumbled, "Traditore." Then he closed his eyes.

"*Gun!*" the voice behind Jack screamed.

I have my gun in my hand—

Jack convulsed as the Taser's charge coursed through his body. He fell sideways onto the bloody pavement and writhed in pain.

They're just doing their jobs. If I were them, I'd probably have shot me.

He couldn't see who'd Tasered him, but he felt at least three policemen swarming him and putting the cuffs on. Everything began to spin, and he knew he was blacking out.

That's a first. Normally it just hurts like hell.

Everything went dark.

37

WHAT YOU DO BEST

Jack sat at the metal interrogation table and didn't look up at the two-way mirror. "Sheriff, can you come in so I can explain?" he called out.

From the sound of the muffled thud behind the wall, he was sure Collins had heard him.

"Can you at least send in Rivers or Prescott?"

A minute later, the door swung open, and both of them walked through.

Prescott had a snarl on his face, and his rock-crushing voice was even lower than usual. "Way to go, smartass. Now we have two dead Mancinis. Why don't we start with what you were doing at Handle's?"

"I heard it on the scanner, so I went—"

The soft thud against the wall caused all three to turn and look at the two-way mirror.

Jennifer leaned forward and whispered, "You have no idea how mad he is."

"Okay. So the cowboy runs out on his own again when he hears a 911 call?" Prescott said. "Boy, you must have been real close. What was the response time of the officers on the scene, Rivers?"

Jennifer looked down at her clipboard. "Seven minutes."

"I heard you were fast, Stratton, but that's just a little too much of a coincidence for me."

Jack leaned back in his chair and did his best to imitate Walter's gravelly voice. "How far away is my apartment, Rivers?"

Walter slammed his hands on the table. "You caused all this, and it's a joke to you."

Jack cracked his neck. "First off, the whole slamming the table and getting in my face business won't help. Secondly, you know I didn't start this. Marisa was kidnapped. The Mancinis got a call."

"I *know* they got a call! We have their phones tapped! Did you forget that part, Jack? Did you forget you're one of us? Did you forget about being a cop?"

"Since I'm the one looking in the right direction, ask *yourself* that question, Walter."

"We're supposed to be working together, and what do you do? You break into Marisa's apartment. You contact not only the Mancinis but Takeo Ishikawa too. Now you're running around with a known Yakuza enforcer. You talked with Shawn Miller, and now he's in intensive care with a broken jaw and ruptured spleen. Arber de Lorme is also in the ICU, and we have a witness placing a big blue boat of a car on his road."

A thump from behind the wall made the whole mirror shake.

Prescott's face turned beet red, and he stormed out of the room. Jennifer looked down at Jack and shrugged.

"This is my damn town!" Jack heard Collins yell from the hallway.

"Don't even try to pull jurisdiction on me, Collins." Prescott was even louder. "Stay the hell out of that room. Put someone else in there to witness if you can't keep it on an even keel."

Walter stormed back into the interrogation room and slammed the door.

Keep it calm and get him talking.

"I need you to work with us, Jack." Jennifer held up a hand when Walter opened his mouth. "Save it, Walter."

Jack smirked.

"You too, Jack." She glared at him. "I'm not doing the whole good cop/bad cop thing. We know the Mancinis got a phone call. One word: Darrington. Man's voice."

Jack raised an eyebrow. "Is that all you have?"

Walter slammed his hands on the table again. "No. We know you talked to the tattoo kid, but you're not the one who bashed his teeth in. That was Paolo. We know you went to de Lorme's house."

Let that go. Don't even comment.

"Now de Lorme's in ICU, but I'm not particularly sympathetic there. We found his tapes. We know what he was accused of in France, too. I know you didn't neuter him. That appears to be the handiwork of the Mancinis too."

Jack stared at Prescott but it was Jennifer's expression he was trying to read.

She didn't mention the other phone call to Takeo, and neither did Prescott.

"What about Marisa?" Jack tried to put his hand calmly on the table, but the metal still rang when his fist hit it. "Have you found anything on her?"

"No phone calls on any of her lines. No bank activity of any kind. Nothing."

No news then. Damn it.

Jack looked at the ceiling.

Walter kicked the chair. "Screw you, Stratton."

"I thought you were going to help us." Jennifer pressed her hands together.

"*Help* us?" Walter jeered. "He's about as helpful as high wind in a prairie fire. Just ask his flunkies how 'helpful' he is." Walter's finger jabbed the air.

"What are you talking about?" Jack asked.

"They didn't tell you? Wow, they're either real upset or real loyal. Collins suspended Donald Pugh and Kendra Darcey for not reporting their run-in with you in the cemetery."

Damn it.

"Like you give a damn, Stratton. You're a wrecking ball that doesn't care. What's the count on careers flushed down the toilet because of you, including your own?"

Jennifer stepped forward. "What did Paolo say?"

"He's not going to tell us." Prescott jammed a finger in Jack's face. "But we got a BOLO on the shooter's car. Turns out it clipped a telephone pole on the way out of the parking lot. Witnesses said the engine was smoking like a chimney. They couldn't have gotten far."

"Jack, did Paolo say anything?" Jennifer asked again.

"He's not gonna tell you anything," Prescott scoffed. "Sure, he'll go back and tell it to his new bang. How's that working for you, Jack? What's it, a nightly three-way?"

Shake your head and close your mouth. Let him talk.

Jennifer leaned closer. "Maybe we can talk to Collins. Tell him you're cooperating. You help us, we help you."

"Are you falling for his bull? Seriously?" Walter glared at Jennifer. "He ain't that good-looking." He turned back to Jack. "I don't think you *want* to find her."

Jack stretched his legs out and crossed his arms. "Me? I'm the guy who's looking. What have you been doing, Wally?"

Prescott marched over to a side table and picked up a folder. He walked back over and dropped it on the table in front of Jack. "Read it. Why don't you find out all about the girl you know nothing about?"

Jack flipped open the folder. On top was the mug shot of a teenage girl with deep circles under her eyes. It took him a moment to recognize Marisa.

Walter jabbed a finger at the photo. "That's her. Hard to believe, huh? That's how I met her, and *I* helped her. She was seventeen and scared as hell. Did she tell you why she came into the program? Did she, Jack, or did you not care to ask because you just wanted to get laid?"

"Walter—" Jennifer tried to cut in.

He glared at Jennifer and continued. "She came to us about a boy. What was his name?" He flipped through the file to an autopsy picture of a dead teenager. "Anthony Marinetti. Marisa said they went to school together. He was seventeen, too. Do you know what he did to Severino? His big sin was he liked a mobster's daughter. Look at him." He poked the photo. "Kinda screws up a little girl's head when her father puts a bullet in her boyfriend because he snuck a kiss."

Jack looked down at the photo. He'd seen the boy's face before. Marisa had drawn him. He'd seen the sketch in her apartment. The emotion behind the drawing had haunted him, and now he knew why.

"I never thought that scared little girl was gonna straighten out, but I got her set up in this small town and I thought, yeah, here she might have a chance. But along comes Jack Stratton, and everything I tried to do for her goes out the window."

"Yeah. You did a great job keeping her safe," Jack snarled.

"You're an idiot, Stratton. You don't know how many times over the years I thought about checking in to see how she was doing, but we *can't*. No contact. It's what keeps their secret safe. This is on *your* head, Stratton, not mine."

Jennifer stepped forward. "If you two will stop this pissing match, we may still be able to find her. Jack, did Paolo say anything about who shot him?"

Jack looked up at her, but his internal debate lasted only a second; there was no way he was telling either of them. "He was dead."

Jennifer sighed. "Was anyone else there?"

Anyone who saw Ilario will say yes, but I can't put him there.

"No."

"That's bull, Jack." Prescott kicked the chair over, and it skittered across the floor. "Total bull. We have a witness who put another Italian at the scene. Do you know what I think?"

"You think?"

"Screw you, Stratton. You know what I *really* think? I think it's you. From what I've been reading in your evaluations, you're a nutcase who never should've been a cop. Son of a murdered kid and a hooker. Abandoned by a whore, you spent a few years in the system. That screws with your head. You go into the Army, and not surprisingly, you get out with checkered results. One of your commanding officers said you had a…" Walter looked up at the ceiling and stuck his tongue in his cheek, "… a 'death wish.' I think he said not only are you not afraid of death, but you court it. And now all this latest crap. You're as out there as the crazy homeless guy you dragged in here who started all this."

Jack sat stoically.

"You know what I think? I think this is some lover's quarrel, and you're using all this as camouflage. You killed her and dumped the body. But to cover your tracks you created this missing person case and spun the tale. You were ticked off at Marisa, and now she's missing. Pretty good cover, Stratton. How much is she worth, huh? Or are you playing both sides of the fence now? You're banging a Yakuza and meeting the Mancinis in a parking lot? I think Marisa was stupid and naïve enough to fall hard for your bad boy crap and get your badge tattooed on her back, but you? You either killed her or sold her out. Tell me I'm wrong. Go ahead and—"

Jennifer slammed her hands down on the table. "*Shut up!* Just shut up, Walter!" she screamed. She rubbed her palms and turned to Jack. "Jack, we have witnesses who placed another person next to Paolo. They also said you talked to him."

You can't tell them about Ilario.

Jack looked right at her. "I didn't see anyone else."

"So if I run a check on all the credit cards from that Italian restaurant, nobody else's number is gonna come up?"

Walter spun around and walked to the corner of the room.

Shut up now, Jack, and end it. Give them something so they think you're going along, and get out of here.

Jack lifted his hands. "You're right. Paolo did say something. I asked who shot him, but he was bleeding out. He could barely talk and it didn't make sense."

"Did he say who? Did he describe them?" Jennifer asked.

"It was hard to understand him. He just said 'Orsacchiotto.'"

Jennifer looked to Prescott, who shrugged.

"It's Italian," Jack continued. "I have no idea what it means."

"Did he have a gun?"

Tilt your head. Look down. Open your mouth like you're going to say something. Shake your head.

"No. I didn't see one."

"He didn't see anyone else either. Come on, Jennifer, he's a lying bastard," Walter spat as he marched back.

"Then you're done with me, right?" Jack stood.

"Sit your ass down, Stratton."

"Make me."

"I *can* make you. You ever want to wear a badge again?" Prescott gave a snide grin. "Sit down and keep talking."

"Charge me or call a lawyer. I'm done talking."

Jennifer's mouth fell open.

Prescott looked truly surprised. "Seriously? You lawyer up, and your career's over."

"As you said, it already is. Right now Marisa is out there, and I'm the only one looking for her."

"You're an idiot, Stratton." Prescott rolled his eyes. "You'd rather throw your career away along with any hope of finding Marisa?"

"No, I'm going to *find* her. But not by sitting here and talking to you about it. Are you going to charge me?"

Prescott looked at the two-way mirror, then back at Jack.

"I didn't think so."

Jack walked out the door.

38

LIKE A BABY?

Jack sat outside the processing office for fifteen minutes before the door finally opened. He marched inside to the desk and looked down at a thin middle-aged woman with shoulder-length brown hair: Shelia Hardy. Jack didn't exactly know Shelia, but she always gave him a friendly wave in the hallway.

"Officer Stratton." She didn't look up as she pushed a small package of papers toward him. "Please sign."

Jack had to force himself to keep from hanging his head. He signed the papers, set down the pen, and looked up.

Shelia's shoulders slumped, and she mumbled, "Thank you."

Jack marched out of the office. He could feel everyone's eyes on him as he stormed down the corridor. His nostrils flared and his lips pressed into a thin line.

He headed straight to Evidence to get his belongings. Stopping in front of a counter with a glass slider, he rang the bell.

Bill walked up with a manila envelope. "I went and checked on your gun, but they took it to Ballistics."

Jack knew Bill. Jack had given him tips at the shooting range. He had helped fix Bill's car. Jack had even helped him move. But right now, Jack glared at his friend.

"It's my gun, Bill."

Bill raised his hands innocently. "Jack, it's not here. They took it to Ballistics."

Drop it. It's not Bill's fault.

Jack took the manila envelope and looked inside. "Where's my phone?"

"Information Services. They have to review it."

Jack removed his wallet and put the empty envelope down on the counter.

Bill gulped. "Sorry."

"Not your fault, Bill."

Jack headed to the first floor entrance. The big double doors swooshed open, and the cold air slapped him in the face. He inhaled deeply.

"Jack? Jack." It was Jennifer's voice.

Jack didn't turn around, he just kept going.

"Jackass," she growled as she ran up next to him.

Jack glared at her.

"I'm not your enemy. Can I remind you I tried to help out?"

"What do you want?"

"How about we start with, do you need a ride home?" She smiled.

Jack took a deep breath. "I'd have called for a ride if you hadn't taken my phone."

"Your phone's at IT and your gun's at Ballistics. You should be glad Collins let *you* go."

Jack cracked his neck. *Glad I left the burner in the Impala.* "I don't need a ride, and I don't need the good cop/bad cop routine."

"Jack, I'm not playing you or doing that. Listen, I think Walter can help. Really."

Jack raised an eyebrow. "Are you serious?"

"I have an idea. Can I drive you home, and we can talk on the way? Please?"

Jack searched her face. Jennifer's lips pressed together, and she tilted her head. "Fine."

"I'm in the garage."

They walked to the three-story parking garage across the street. Jennifer's heels clicked on the cement, and Jack waited for her to do the talking.

"If someone called the Mancinis, they're going to call again. We have Severino under constant surveillance. Paolo was his enforcer. His death is going to shake things up." She smiled hopefully.

"Shake things up, or apart?" Jack grabbed the railing and took the stairs two at a time.

Jennifer had to hurry to keep up. At the top of the stairs, she huffed, "If you'd give me a second, I can explain."

Jack waited. She grabbed the railing and stood there panting, trying to catch her breath. "We've been monitoring..."

Her voice trailed off, and Jack saw all the color drain from her face.

Jack's head whipped around to see what had her so spooked. He immediately noticed a man standing between two cars.

Asian. Medium build. Spiky hair.

"*Gun!*" Jennifer screamed.

Jack instinctively reached for his own weapon.

Damn. I'm unarmed.

Jack moved to get out of Jennifer's way to give her a clear shot, but she grabbed Jack by his shoulders and yanked him backward. As Jack pitched toward the stairs, Jennifer wrapped her arms around his waist.

"*Get down!*" she screamed as they were launched headfirst down the steps.

Jack landed hard on his shoulder; he pulled Jennifer against him, trying to cushion her fall. They slid down the remaining concrete steps and crashed into the landing.

Jack struggled to pull himself free and grab her gun from her holster.

"Give me your gun!" Jack roared as Jennifer rolled in the other direction.

"I have it," she snarled as she stood up. She took one step, cried out in pain, and fell forward.

Jack grabbed her shoulder, flipped her onto her back, and yanked her gun out of the holster. He aimed at the top of the stairs and tried to steady his breathing.

Tires squealed from the top level, and Jack jumped over Jennifer and raced up the stairs. He only saw the rear end of a sedan turning the corner and heading for the exit.

Public garage. Two exits. One is automated.

He sprinted left. When he reached the edge of the building, he grabbed the ledge and peered over. He could hear the echo of the car fade and realized he had picked the wrong side.

No!

Jack let fly a string of obscenities. He raced back over to the staircase, where Jennifer was limping into view. Her face said it all. She was fighting back tears, and he was sure they weren't just from pain.

"Come on." Jack ran over and put his arm around her waist.

"We need to call it in," she said.

"No." Jack's voice was cold, and Jennifer froze.

He practically had to drag her across the cement toward her car. When they reached it, she leaned heavily against it. "Jack, we need to call this in."

"You can't. You need to trust me. Give me your keys." Jack held his hand out.

Jennifer glanced around, and her eyebrows squeezed together. She swallowed and stared at Jack. She dropped the keys into his hand. "Are you going to clue me in?"

"Yeah. Later. Get in."

Jack moved over to the driver's seat and slid it back as Jennifer got in the car. He backed up, headed down to the manager's office on the north side, and hopped out. Through the window, he could see a teenager and a guy in his late fifties having a conversation.

Jack rapped on the window, and they both jumped.

"What?" the older man snarled as he slid the window open.

"I need to see your security cameras."

"I told you so," the teenager said.

"Shut up," the older man growled and then turned to Jack. "I wish we could see them, too, so you could nail that jerk that just hauled ass out of here."

"None of the cameras work?"

"None of them," the teenager said.

Damn.

"Did you get a look at the car or the driver?"

The older man shook his head. "I was back in the office."

The teenager shrugged.

"How could you not see it?" the old man growled. "You had your face stuffed into that stupid phone. I don't pay you to sit on your ass and play games. You were supposed to be watching the gate."

The teenager's shoulders slumped a bit. "I wasn't on my phone."

"Then why was your phone in your hand?"

The teenager blanched. "I... I was... I had it out because..."

Jack put his hand on the window. "So, your cameras aren't working, and neither of you got a look at the car or the driver? How did they pay?"

"They didn't," the old man grumbled. "The gate's busted, so Junior here is supposed to be watching it. *Outside.*"

"I got cold. I came in for, like, a minute."

Jack stormed back to the car and pulled through the broken gate.

"Who was that guy?" Jennifer asked. She leaned forward and scanned the street.

"You're asking the wrong question." Jack turned left and headed for his apartment. "You should be asking: Why did he come for you?"

"What? I thought he was after you…" Her voice trailed off, and she swallowed.

"No. He was waiting for you. He didn't know you would offer me a ride home, so he had no reason to be at the parking garage for me."

"Why? That makes no sense."

Jack turned right and stopped at a light. When it turned green, he took a left.

"Where are we going?"

Jack adjusted the rearview mirror. "Right now I don't think it would be a good idea for you to go back to your hotel."

"You really think they're after me?" Jennifer sat up straighter.

"Just… I need to get some things from my apartment, and we'll go someplace."

"Hold on. I don't answer to you. You answer to me."

Jack pulled over to the curb and turned to stare at her. "You want to be on your own? Fine. You're on your own. No offense, but I don't know how you got out of the Academy."

"I'm perfectly capable—"

"This isn't a game, and it's not pushing reports. Quiet down for a couple minutes and let me think, or get out."

Jennifer shifted in her seat, then winced.

"Besides," Jack continued, "you wouldn't get far on that ankle."

"It's my car."

Jack raised an eyebrow.

"You wouldn't just leave me on the side of the road?" She leaned away from him.

Jack pulled back out onto the road. "Theoretically, no."

His apartment was only a couple minutes away, and they rode in silence. He parked in the back and ran around to the passenger door.

Jennifer patted the pockets of her jacket. "Crap, I lost my phone. Must have been when you threw me down a flight of stairs."

"Well, we're not going back for it now," Jack said. "Come on, I'll help you."

Jennifer got out of the car and held up a hand. "I can walk."

Jack stepped out of the way and swung his arm in a wide arc. "After you."

Jennifer took four halting steps and stopped. She grimaced, and her eyes fluttered. "I just need to ice it."

"Okay." Jack folded his arms and waited.

She looked back at him, glared, took two more steps, and then put all her weight on her left leg. She closed her eyes. "Can you help me inside?"

"Well, I can give you a shoulder to lean on, and we can awkwardly lurch up a couple flights of stairs like some weird three-legged race… or you can suck up your pride and let me carry you."

"Carry me? Like a baby?"

"No."

Don't smile. Don't smile.

He smiled.

"You male chauvinist p—"

"Hey, it has nothing to do with you being a girl."

"If I was a guy would you carry me?" She crossed her arms and wobbled on her one leg.

"I'd do a fireman's carry if you were a guy. So yeah, there would be a difference. You decide. I carry you like a baby or ass in the air over my shoulder. Your pick."

The color rose in her cheeks. "Fine."

Jack debated asking Jennifer her choice, but instead he just scooped her up in his arms and headed for the door. Jennifer put one arm around his shoulder, and Jack tried not to smile as she looked everywhere but at him.

"Are you going to be okay carrying me all the way to the third floor?" she asked.

"I'm fine." Jack turned sideways as he navigated the stairwell. "And we only have to go to the second floor."

Jennifer huffed and bit her lip.

When Jack reached his door, he used his foot to bang on it.

Jennifer held up a hand. "I could have knocked."

"Next time." Jack grinned.

Kiku opened the door and took a step back. But her look of surprise quickly changed to anger, and her wolf-like features were accentuated.

As Jack strode through the door, Replacement looked over her shoulder and almost fell out of the computer chair. "Who's she?"

"Jennifer Rivers, FBI." Jack carried her to the couch. "Jennifer, this is Alice and…" He glanced at Kiku, whose face had now relaxed into a neutral mask. He hesitated to say Kiku's name.

"I am Kiku." She bowed her head slightly as she introduced herself.

"What happened?" Replacement asked.

Jack set Jennifer down on the couch and stood up. "She sprained her ankle. At least I hope it's a sprain."

Replacement headed for the kitchen.

Jennifer grimaced and adjusted herself on the couch. "It's not that bad."

Jack hurried over to Replacement at the freezer. "Where's Ilario?" he whispered.

"We dropped him off at the Colonial Motel. He was upset but okay." Replacement scooped ice into a plastic bag. "What happened to you?"

"Don't ask."

"Why did you bring her here, Officer?" Kiku moved over to the window and peered out into the darkened street below.

"Someone tried to ambush her."

Replacement slammed the freezer and spun around with the bag of ice in her hand. "Where?"

"They were waiting for me at my car." Jennifer put her face in her hands.

"Why would the Mancinis come after her?" Kiku directed the question at Jack.

"It wasn't the Mancinis," Jack said.

Kiku's lips pressed together, and he noticed her weight shift to her back leg. Replacement moved to stand beside Jack. Jennifer sat up on the couch and looked at Kiku.

Jack lifted his hands waist high. "Everyone settle down."

"Were they Japanese or Korean?" The muscles in Kiku's neck stood out.

"He matched the description of the man who took Marisa."

"Asian." Kiku didn't ask; it was a statement.

"Before you draw on me," Jack said, "I know you and the Yakuza didn't have anything to do with it."

"How do you know that?" Replacement demanded.

"I'll explain everything, but we need to get out of here," Jack said.

"What?" all three women asked.

"The guy was waiting for Jennifer," Jack explained. "The drop must be getting close, and I need to get you guys someplace safe." He looked at Replacement and swallowed, seeing the disapproving look on her face. "So, you can... keep an eye on Jennifer." He looked at Jennifer, who sat up and scowled. "Because... of your ankle."

"If you think I'm going to just sit on—" Replacement began, but Jack cut her off.

"No. You're the most important piece of this. I need you to grab your stuff. Bring your laptop and grab the GPS device." He turned to Kiku. "Kiku, grab your bag."

Jennifer patted the pockets of her jacket. "Crap, I lost my phone." She pulled off her jacket and sat up.

Kiku frowned. "Now would be a good time to explain that I don't just follow orders, Officer."

Jack heard the door to the apartment above them smash open. He froze and held up his hand. All four of them looked toward the ceiling.

"Wha—" Jennifer started, but Jack held his finger to his mouth and motioned with his other hand.

"Give me your gun."

Jennifer drew her pistol and shook her head.

Kiku's gun was already out, and she was moving silently toward the door. She stopped, pulled a five-shot .380 from her boot, and handed it to Jack.

Jack slid next to the door and waved Replacement back. He held up a fist, opened his hand, turned the knob, and peeked out.

Anyone upstairs is going to realize their mistake right away when they see my old apartment is empty. Question is, do they rabbit, or look for another apartment?

He could hear someone approaching the stairs.

Jennifer moved behind him and leaned forward; she inhaled sharply and reached out for the wall to steady herself. Her hand pressed against the door, and it started to open.

Jack's hand shot out and grabbed the handle, but the door had already moved a few inches. He fought the urge to glare back at her, and instead kept his focus down the hallway.

He didn't have long to look as bullets ripped through the thin walls and into his apartment.

Jack spun around, pushed Jennifer down, and lunged for Replacement. Kiku had already dived to the floor and flipped over the hallway table for cover. Jack grabbed Replacement, and they slid behind the counter.

Kiku's eyes followed the bullet trail in the wall. She fired two shots through the wall before Jack cut her off.

"Cease fire! You could hit one of my neighbors." Jack held up his hand and listened. His ears strained to hear through the ringing in his head, and he heard the old front door of the apartment building crash open into the wall.

He pointed at Replacement and then at Jennifer. "Watch her. Stay here."

He flew out the door with Kiku right behind him. Jumping down the steps, he used the railing to cover the first staircase in a leap. His chest tightened when he saw Mrs. Stevens lying face down in the hallway. *No.*

He ran over to her, while Kiku kept moving and sprinted out the door. As he looked for a wound, Mrs. Stevens's eyes flew open, and she started to scream.

"Mrs. Stevens, Mrs. Stevens!" He held her by the upper arms. "Are you hit?"

Her red hair wobbled as she shook her head, and then she burst into tears.

Replacement came rushing down the stairs.

"She's not hit. Go get the stuff now," Jack barked. "Mrs. Stevens, the police are coming. You're going to be okay. I'm sorry."

She looked like a plump koi as her mouth opened and closed, gulping for air. Jack helped her to her feet.

Kiku ran back in. "They were long gone. I didn't even see the make of the car."

"We have to leave."

Kiku headed out back.

Jack turned to Mrs. Stevens. "You need to tell the police you need an ambulance, okay? Everything is fine."

Her eyes went wide, and she started to gulp air again.

"Not fine but… okay," Jack added. "It will be okay. I'll make it up to you."

"Go." She waved one hand at the door and fanned herself with the other.

Jack spun around and rushed back to his apartment. Replacement was coming out with a duffel bag. Jennifer hobbled behind her, putting her weight on one leg.

Replacement patted the bag. "I got everything."

Jack looked at Jennifer's leg and muttered, "Sorry. Ass in the air." He tossed her over his shoulder before she could complain. "Move."

They hurried down the stairs and across the little parking lot to the Impala, where Kiku was already waiting. They all piled in, and Jack gunned the Impala and raced out of the parking lot. He took the first right and pressed the gas pedal down.

Slow down. Drive normally.

Jack tapped the brake and felt something slide forward and hit his foot. He looked down. Paolo's Magnum stuck out from under the seat.

"You left his gun in the car?" he said.

"Whose gun?" Jennifer leaned forward.

Jack kicked the gun back under the seat. "A friend of mine."

"Why are we leaving the scene of a shooting?" Jennifer's jaw quivered, but she glared at Jack.

"So you don't end up dead, stupid." Replacement shifted in her seat, and Jack slowed down as a cruiser flew past them.

"We can't go to the police right now," Jack muttered.

"Where are we going?" Kiku began to reload her gun.

Jack handed her back the .380. "I fired two shots."

"Got it." She reloaded that gun too.

"Where are we going, Jack?" Replacement put her hand on his shoulder.

"The Imperial."

39

THE IMPERIAL

The Imperial Motor Lodge was a popular stop for prostitutes and drug addicts. You could pay in cash and get a room by the hour. All three women looked relieved when Jack slipped the housekeeper twenty dollars for clean sheets and blankets. They got what would be considered a suite by Imperial standards: separate bathroom, king-sized bed, a short couch, round table, and four chairs.

Jack got the women set up in the room and headed for the door. "I'll be right back."

"I'm coming," Replacement said.

"No."

Replacement huffed and flopped onto the bed.

Kiku followed Jack to the door.

"She goes, I go." Replacement hopped back up.

"Just me. Five minutes." Jack walked out and shut the door.

He drove a block east to a small ranch house with a detached garage. Jack pulled up and hopped out.

A man in his sixties opened the front door and peered out. He was dressed in an untucked flannel shirt that did little to cover his large belly. Round cheeks popped out from a bushy beard that matched his thick eyebrows.

"Jack?" he called in a deep voice.

"Hey, Carl. I have a huge favor to ask. I need to park in your garage for a couple days."

"World must have gone to hell if you're hiding the Impala in my garage." He laughed. "Zombie apocalypse?"

Jack chuckled. He didn't have many people he considered friends, and Carl was on the fringe edge of the list, but he was a good guy who kept his mouth shut.

"Something like that. Can I pull her in?"

"Sure, it's empty. I finished the Ford I was working on. Need a hand?"

"I've got it." Jack ran over and pushed the door open.

"I'll need it free again at the end of the week, though."

"I only need it for a day or two. I appreciate it."

Jack pulled the Impala in. As he got out, he saw Paolo's gun sticking out from under the seat. He popped the door panel and dropped the gun in, took the burner phone out, and sealed the panel back up. Then he walked back out and shut the garage doors.

"I owe you. Thanks," Jack called out as he jogged down the driveway.

"You gonna run home? I'll give you a ride if you give me a minute."

"No, I need the exercise."

Jack's smile vanished as he ran back to the Imperial. He checked the burner phone as he went.

Still nothing. Something has to break… soon.

***

All three women peppered him with questions as soon as he walked in the door.

"Wait a second. Listen." Jack held his hands up. "Alice, is your laptop set up?"

"Yes, but how about you start with what we're doing."

"Or where you went," Jennifer added.

"Or where we're going." Kiku leaned against the wall and folded her arms.

Jack put his hands on his hips and tried to catch his breath. "First things first. That cut opened up on my leg. Can you take a look at it?" he asked Replacement. He headed for the bathroom.

She followed him in. "Darn it, Jack. I didn't bring any bandages, and I doubt this place has any."

Jack shut the bathroom door, turned the water on, and held his finger to his lips. "Listen. My leg is fine. I needed to talk to you alone. You're the only one I totally trust. I need you to run that program for me. The one for the cars going through the tolls. How long will it take?"

She bit her lower lip. "Depends on the connection, but I'm just pulling data, not images, and doing the processing on the laptop, so… hopefully I'll have something in an hour or two."

There was a knock on the door, and Kiku opened it a crack. "You need to hear this, Officer."

They hurried back into the main room. The police dispatcher was speaking on the scanner. "No rain or snow is forecast. ME is still an hour out. The wrecker is on standby."

"10-4. Thank you, Bev." The other voice belonged to Tom Kempy, the world's most polite cop.

Medical examiner?

"Can you turn that up?" Jack walked over to the table.

"Shoot," Replacement blurted out. "While you were detained, they found a car on fire out on… I forget the—"

"That's what I was going to tell you before you pigheadedly stormed off and we ran into that guy." Jennifer stood up. "They found a car on Woodlawn. A jogger called it in. When the fire department got there, they found a body in the back."

"The county ME isn't there yet?" Jack asked.

"No. The ME was at some family thing upstate," Jennifer said. "He's on his way back, and they taped off the car."

"A dead guy in a burned-out car." Jack looked at Kiku. "I bet that's the guy Paolo shot."

She walked over and picked up her jacket.

"Wait a minute." Replacement looked for her own coat.

"You need to stay," Jack said.

"*I'm* not staying." Jennifer limped over to get her coat. "I'm not going to be used as an excuse for babysitting."

"You're the one who needs a babysitter, you clueless—" Replacement snapped.

"Knock it off." Jack held up his hand. "I need to check this out. Your ankle is in no shape to go anywhere right now. Ice it, because I'm going to need you."

Jack walked over to Replacement's bag and rummaged inside. When he pulled out the GPS device and slipped it into his pocket, Replacement's eyes narrowed, but she didn't say anything.

Good girl.

"We'll be back within an hour."

Jack looked at Kiku, and she gave a sharp nod. They headed out.

"Transportation?" Kiku looked at the parking lot, which was now lacking the Impala.

Jack stopped. "We'll have to get creative. We can't use my car for this one—I can't risk it being recognized. But we need to get to Woodlawn, which is over toward Big Blue, and then to Hometown Suites near the police station."

"Come on," Kiku said. She headed for the garage across the street, and Jack followed.

I can't believe I'm doing this.

"The cars on the left should be the ones they finished working on but haven't been picked up yet," Kiku said. "You stay on the passenger side and talk naturally. Give me a minute."

"I know how to steal a car," Jack said.

Kiku raised an eyebrow.

"I learned. I figured if I knew, it would help me catch car thieves."

"If it makes you feel better, Officer, I plan to bring it back."

"Great. Now I feel just fine."

Kiku walked past the first two cars and stopped at the third. In a flash she opened the door, slipped in, leaned over, and started the car.

Jack yanked his door open and jumped in. "How did you do that so fast? That was…" His voice trailed off when he saw the keys dangling out of the ignition.

"When they work on the cars, sometimes people pay by credit card, and the mechanics just leave the key under the seat so the guy can come get his car after hours." She grinned. "You tend to overcomplicate things, Officer."

"And here I thought you were some master car thief."

"I am." She pulled out.

Jack pointed. "Woodlawn is east. It's also heading out of town. I'll have Replacement check if there were any cars stolen out there."

Kiku kept her eyes on the road. "You think they only had the one car?"

"Yeah. And they're not the kind of guys to wait around for a ride. Ditch the car with the fatally wounded guy and steal another. It's what I'd do."

"If you were that kind of man." Kiku smiled. "You *are* a dangerous man, Officer. It would be a scary thing if you were not caged in by your principles."

"Letting something out of a cage sometimes isn't the best idea." Jack pulled out his phone and dialed Replacement. "Hey. Can you check for a stolen car for me while that thing is running? Great. Check if anything was reported out near Woodlawn and call me. Thanks."

"You keep her at a safe distance." Kiku checked her mirrors as she sped up.
"What?"

"Having her stay with Jennifer."

"I want her to be safe."

"She doesn't want that."

Jack leaned against the door. "Really?"

"Alice likes the danger. Did you see her face during the shootout? She had a hard time keeping her head down. I like that."

"I'm not keeping her at a distance. Just safe."

"If you build a cage, it won't keep her."

Jack opened and closed his mouth. He was about to argue the point, but Woodlawn Avenue was approaching quickly. He pointed to the left, and his phone rang.

"Hey. Did you find out anything?" He looked out the window.

"No cars reported stolen today at all. I'm running the report on the cars from the tollbooth, too. Where are you?"

"Pulling onto Woodlawn. I'll call back. Thanks."

Kiku tipped her head up, but Jack had already seen the cruiser on the side of the road.

"Pull up behind it," Jack said.

Kiku put her hazard lights on and stopped behind the cruiser.

"This time I'm not asking: stay in the car," Jack said. He grabbed a flashlight from the glove compartment and hopped out.

"As you wish, Officer."

As Jack approached the cruiser, Tom Kempy walked over to him. "Hey, Jack."

"Hi, Tom. Looks like you're babysitting until the ME arrives."

"Listen, Jack…" Tom looked uneasy. "Sheriff Collins gave me one order. One direct order."

"I'm pretty sure I know what that was. But I just need a quick look." Jack held up his hand with his index finger and thumb close together.

"I can't, Jack. Did you hear about Donald and Kendra?"

"I'll be one second. Just look the other way." Without waiting for an answer, Jack hurried around Tom and the cruiser.

The car was parked at an angle just off the road. It was now just a shell, after being completely engulfed by fire. Even the trees nearby were blackened from the flames. Jack pulled back the tarp that had been draped over the rear of the car, flicked on his flashlight, and shone it on the corpse in the back seat.

The fire must have been intense. It was hard to see where the corpse left off and the remains of the back seat started. The acrid smell was terrible. Jack tried to breathe as little as possible. He looked at the man's shoulder and the broken teeth in his mouth.

As Jack focused the light on the man's chest, a golden twinkle flashed. His eyes narrowed. *Jewelry. It melted.*

Just above the glob of gold was a two-inch piece of white ivory shaped like a curled horn. Jack held the light on the man's chest. "Italian," he muttered.

Flicking off the light, he pulled the tarp down and walked back.

Tom Kempy shuffled over to him with his hands in his pockets. "Sorry about your suspension." He cleared his throat. "If you need anything, just ask."

"Thanks, Tom." Jack patted his shoulder as he passed. "I appreciate it."

"See you around, Jack." Tom waved.

Kiku looked up as Jack jumped in. He didn't say anything as she started the car and turned it around. As the flashing lights from the cruiser faded in the distance, Jack turned to her.

"It must be the guy Paolo shot. It looks like the shot almost took off his shoulder. Someone smashed his teeth out. They wanted to delay identification."

"Could you determine anything else?"

"The body was in really bad shape, but he was Italian."

Kiku's lips pouted and one eyebrow went up. "I saw the car. With a fire that hot, even *you* couldn't tell if he was Italian."

"He was wearing an Italian horn. It was gold plated. The gold melted, but the ivory didn't."

Her eyes widened, and he knew she understood. "A cornicello."

"The guy's not Swedish."

At the main road, Jack turned north. "The way back to town is south. North is Big Blue. It's a huge hiking mountain with a single ski run. There are plenty of houses and cabins all over it. They could have taken her anywhere around here but it has to be close."

"How can you be sure?"

"I think Paolo ran into the kidnappers. I think it was by chance, and Replacement may have been right."

"About what?" Kiku interrupted.

Jack exhaled. "The Italian restaurant."

"You think they went and got something to eat?" Kiku scoffed.

"We're not dealing with soldiers. I don't know why they went into town, but Paolo must have run into someone he knew and realized they were the kidnappers. It's too much of a coincidence for an ex-Mancini crew to be here."

"That explains why they got into a shootout," Kiku said.

"Paolo hit the guy with that cannon of a gun, and the kidnappers took off. When people are scared, they run toward where they know. They headed north, so their base must be in this direction."

"But why ditch the car here?"

"Prescott said the car clipped a telephone pole and was overheating. The car made it this far then broke down. They probably burned it to dispose of any evidence."

Kiku nodded. "I would have too. They could have used the windshield washer hose to siphon out the gas. It's the fastest way."

"I'm not asking how you know that."

Kiku grinned. "Then they could have stolen a car from any of those homes over there."

Jack looked up into the mountains. "I think they're holed up someplace close."

Kiku nodded. "There are many places to hide. Lots of cabins."

"That's the problem. Too many. But we won't have to check them all. We're going to Hometown Suites."

"Can you clue me in as to why?"

He held up the GPS device. "I need to plant this. We'll stick to the back roads. We'll be—"

"Stop!" Kiku shouted.

Jack hit the brakes. His headlights reflected off the eyes of a deer on the side of the road.

Kiku opened the door and jumped out.

"What the hell? Kiku?" He pulled the car to the side of the road and got out to join her.

There was a bright moon, and the deer stood clearly before them. It didn't run; in fact it wobbled as it stood in the grass. An arrow had pierced it low in the neck, and its side was matted in blood.

"Whoever winged it should have put it down," Jack said. He turned back toward the car. "I don't think it'll make it. Maybe I can—"

Jack didn't flinch when the shot rang out from Kiku's gun, but the sound seemed to pass straight through his chest. He looked down at the dead leaves as he listened to the echo fade. Slowly, he turned around.

Kiku walked over to the deer, knelt down, and pulled the arrow out. She bowed her head. After a moment, she stood and came back to Jack.

"I couldn't let it suffer."

I'm glad she's on my side.

***

They rode in silence toward Hometown Suites. Jack drove. He tried to keep his eyes on the road but found himself glancing repeatedly at Kiku. She kept her head on a swivel, constantly scanning.

Finally, she spoke. "I admire that you serve a purpose rather than a cause."

"I'm not quite following you." Jack looked at the speedometer and slowed down.

"You are an officer, but you disobey for a greater purpose. Most men of your character are driven by adhering to a mold and not following an unscripted path. It is a very rare quality you have. I find it truly... Virile." She smiled. "Masculine."

He remembered the heat of her body. The toned muscles under her soft skin. He shifted in his seat. As he looked at her, her eyes smoldered, and he swallowed.

"I am tempted to lie," she said, "but I can't. I find you very desirable. You appeal to me, but I will not let that interfere with my job."

I appeal to you?

"Thanks," Jack said, "for not letting it interfere with finding Marisa."

"I know you are a man heatedly in love, but I still have not figured out whether it is with Alice or Marisa."

Jack turned away from her probing gaze.

Kiku laughed. "I do enjoy seeing you blush, too. In some ways you are very... innocent."

"Me?" Jack blinked rapidly.

Kiku settled back into her seat. "Innocent is a poor word choice. I mean pure."

Jack cocked his head. "If you knew what I've been thinking, you wouldn't have picked that word, either."

"I would. I do." Kiku crossed her ankles. "It actually makes you even more desirable. I am going to have to work at not forcibly taking you."

Jack turned different shades of red as he ran Kiku's words through his mind. But before he could dwell on them too long, the Hometown Suites came up on the right.

It was a small hotel complex, three stories high and split into suites. It was very popular with families during foliage season, but even now the front parking lot was full.

Jack drove around back, looking for a specific car he hoped would be there. He found the car he was looking for, parked in the corner, near the dumpster.

He handed Kiku the GPS device. "I'll pull up alongside. Make it look like you're throwing something out. It's magnetic. Tuck it under the back bumper."

She leaned over and pulled an empty soda bottle from under the seat. "This will do for a prop."

Jack swung into the empty space next to the car, and Kiku hopped out and left the door open. She tossed a bottle in the trash and shook her hands like they were wet. A moment later, she got back in and shut the door.

"There's a warehouse near the Imperial where we can ditch the car," he said as he backed out.

She leaned closer.

Jack felt the color rush to his cheeks, and he moved in his seat.

As they pulled onto the road, Kiku put her mouth next to his ear and whispered, "I don't know if even *you* could teach me how to love. But it would be very nice trying."

She kissed his cheek, leaned back in her seat, and grinned wolfishly.

40

DEAD MAN'S HAND

As Jack walked into the hotel room, Replacement jumped up and rushed over to him. But Jennifer, seated on the bed, just looked at Jack with red, puffy eyes and a downturned mouth. It was evident she'd been crying.

"Did you tell her?" Jack asked.

"No." Replacement crossed her arms. "It's a tiny room." She pointed at the computer. "She saw."

Jack and Kiku walked over to the computer. The image on the screen was from a tollbooth camera. It was the same car they had just tagged at the Hometown Suites.

Walter Prescott's car.

And in the driver's seat, clearly visible, was Walter Prescott.

"Prescott came over on the day Marisa was taken," Replacement said. "I expanded the search, and found he's come to Darrington at least three times in the past month."

"How did you know?" Jennifer asked.

"Prescott told me."

"What?" all three women said.

"When I first met him, Prescott said only three people knew Marisa was in Darrington: him, her, and his supervisor. I've been asking myself who kidnapped Marisa, but that was the wrong question. Whoever took her knew that Marisa Vitagliano was Angelica Mancini and that she had moved to Darrington. They knew where she was."

"She never told her family where she was?" Replacement sat on the bed next to Jennifer and put her hand on her shoulder.

"No," Jack said. "No one. The Yakuza didn't know where she was, either."

"But if Prescott is behind the kidnapping, who are those men working for him?" Kiku asked.

"They're Yakuza and Mancinis," Jack answered dryly.

"Huh?" Replacement's face scrunched up. "You just said they didn't have anything to do with it."

"Well—they *used* to be Yakuza and Mancinis. Paolo said *traditore*. It means traitor. A rat. Paolo recognized the man who shot him. I'm guessing it was someone who turned on the family, went into the witness protection program, and—"

"Prescott is using men *he* placed in witness protection as his own gang! That is brilliant," Kiku remarked. "They already know how to operate."

"That son of a bitch." Jennifer pounded her leg. "Prescott has access to them all."

Jack and Kiku exchanged a glance. The difficulty level just went up. They were facing a hand-picked, experienced crew.

"So is he setting her up?" Replacement jerked her thumb at Jennifer.

"Looks that way." Jack sighed. "Prescott needed someone naïve and inexperienced to ride shotgun while he made his plan."

Jennifer shook her head and glowered at the floor. "Jack, how long have you known?"

"Since the interrogation room. Walter said he hasn't seen her in years. But when he was trying to get under my skin, he said something about Marisa having my badge number tattooed on her back. Well, that's a new tattoo—which means he's seen her recently," Jack explained.

"We need to call someone. I can go to my supervisors," Jennifer offered.

"No. What do we have on him? They pick him up, and Marisa's dead. Someone tips him off, she's dead." Jack cracked his neck. "I have a plan."

Jennifer folded her hands. "No offense, but I think I know more about handling a kidnapping than you. What are you planning to do?"

Jack walked over to the round table and sat down. "We can't do anything until Prescott calls the Mancinis for the money drop, but that exchange has to happen soon. They shot up my apartment, and one of them is dead. The heat is on, so Prescott will want it finished."

"What do we do in the meantime?" Replacement asked.

"We wait."

***

Jack paced the floor while Replacement surfed the Internet. Jennifer lay on the bed and stared at the wall, and Kiku stared at her phone after finally giving up on trying to get the TV to work.

"Can you get something to watch on your laptop?" Kiku asked Replacement. "My phone reception keeps cutting out."

"Yeah, but the download speed I'm getting blows. It would take me an hour to download a commercial." Replacement made a face. "It's because of the mountain—reception out here sucks."

Kiku grabbed her backpack and pulled out a deck of cards. "Anyone up for a game?" She sat down and started to shuffle.

"I'm in." Jack spun his chair around so he could lean into the back.

Jennifer shook her head.

Replacement shrugged and sat down at the table.

"Poker?" Kiku offered.

"I know how to play." Replacement grinned.

Jack scratched his face to cover his smirk.

Kiku looked up at Jennifer. "It will help take your mind off things if you join us."

"I just want to lie down and die," Jennifer said.

Kiku reached back into her backpack and pulled out a fifth of whiskey. "Do you need a little antidepressant?"

With a sigh, Jennifer got up and limped into the bathroom. She came back with four paper cups.

"Rules?" Jack asked.

"Five card draw. Jacks are wild." Kiku winked. "Ante is two cents. Max bet is a dime raise, or it'll be a fast game."

Jennifer took the bottle and poured.

"What do we bet?" Replacement asked.

"Hold on." Jennifer handed Kiku the bottle and reached for her purse. She fished around inside and came up with a handful of coins. She and Replacement divvied up the pile, and Kiku dealt. Once everyone was ready, Kiku raised her plastic cup.

"To my victory." She smiled, tossed in her ante, and took a swig.

As everyone else did the same, Jack's eyes widened. "Wait, Alice." He warned her a second too late.

Replacement's eyes crossed, and she launched into a coughing fit.

Kiku looked up at the ceiling and laughed long and hard.

Replacement was unable to speak, but she waggled her finger at Kiku. Finally she coughed out, "It just went down the wrong way."

"*Any* way is the wrong way. You're nineteen," Jack growled.

Kiku grinned. "That's the legal age in Panama."

"We're not in Panama," Jack said. "Don't give her another."

Kiku held out the bottle to Replacement, and Jack grabbed it.

"We could get the call any time. One-drink limit tonight, ladies." Jack set the bottle at his feet. "Besides, these cups are huge."

Replacement held up her cup and winked at Kiku.

"She's old enough." Kiku picked up her cards. Her smile vanished when she looked at them.

She can't be that obvious.

Replacement huffed.

She can. *What a poker face.*

Jennifer slid in a nickel. She looked over at Jack. "Is there any chance you're wrong?"

"No."

Jennifer turned her hands flat on the table and looked at the ceiling. "Why would Walter do it? Money?"

"Money makes people switch loyalties," Kiku said.

Jack tossed in a nickel. "It's more. Prescott spent years trying to catch these guys. He's about to retire. It was his whole life's work, and not one conviction stuck. That can drive you over the edge."

"I think it's for revenge." Replacement rolled a nickel in.

"For what?" Jennifer downed the rest of her cup.

"One of the Mancinis put his first partner in a wheelchair," Replacement said.

"That could be it," Kiku added as she put in her nickel.

Jennifer muttered, "Karl Weaver. He's dead. He died last year. They had a ceremony for him at the Bureau. They dedicated some conference room to him." She searched their faces. "Walter wants revenge."

Jack cracked his neck. "Now we know the why."

"Have you ever kidnapped anyone?" Replacement asked Kiku.

She nodded, but didn't look up from her cards.

"How many people did you bring?" Replacement asked.

"Three cards," Jennifer said.

"Four men." Kiku dealt Jennifer her cards. "Not including me."

Jack held up two fingers, and Kiku effortlessly flicked two cards his way.

Replacement took two cards too. "Is that typical?" She looked around the table.

Jack thought for a second. "I was guessing four, not including Walter. Two guys grabbed her. Paolo killed one. Three guys at the apartment, though… and I wouldn't figure they'd leave Marisa alone, so ad one to watch her. I'm thinking there were five, one's dead, leaving us four to still deal with."

Kiku only took one card.

"How do you get three guys at the apartment?" Jennifer asked. "I thought it was only two."

"Two shooters," Jack explained. "They split so fast they had to have a driver waiting."

"They did," Kiku said.

"So it might be four guys and Walter." Jennifer looked at the ceiling. "I was starting to think you weren't crazy, Jack, but now I'm not sure. It sounds like you're planning on taking them all on by yourself." She tossed her cards down. "Fold."

Jack grinned and flicked a dime onto the pile.

Replacement's dime landed at almost the same time.

Kiku tossed out her own dime. She flipped her cards over, and Jack laughed.

"A pair of nines? And you said I shouldn't play poker." He turned over his three queens. "Come to Daddy." He reached out for the pot, but Replacement swatted his hand.

"Read 'em and weep." She put down her cards and fanned them out. Black aces and eights with a jack of hearts. "Full house. Jacks are wild, right?" She giggled. "I bet it means you'll be lucky tomorrow, Jack." She held up the jack of hearts. "See? That's you."

Kiku looked at Jack but didn't say anything. She didn't have to. Jack knew the cards. It was the dead man's hand.

41

FACE-SUCKING VAMPIRE

They played poker for another two hours, redistributing the coins every time someone won the table. Jack cut everyone off at one drink, but the damage was already done to Replacement. She made a huge deal out of every round and bet wildly, but she only won the first hand. Jack was sure Kiku even tried to throw a few her way, and so did he, but she still ended up losing badly.

Suddenly, she got up and stumbled. "Jack, I just thought of something. I need to talk to you… privately."

She took him by the hand and headed for the bathroom. He had to steady her twice, afraid she was about to take a header into the wall.

Jack shut the door, and she leaned heavily against the sink. "I'm not second-guessing you… because you're always right." She slurred a few of her words. "But, shouldn't you call for backup?" She wrinkled her nose.

He smiled. She was even cuter when she was a little tipsy. "I have it covered. We'll get the proof, and then I'll call for backup. Okay?"

"On cop shows they always call for backup *before* they go in." She waved her finger.

"If I call anyone, they're going to arrest me."

Replacement frowned and looked at the floor.

Jack lifted her chin and smiled. "Trust me."

She looked up at him and started to grin, but then her eyes zeroed in on him. Her hand shot out, grabbed his head, and tilted it to the side. "What's that?" She snapped as she peered at his cheek.

"Uh…" He looked in the mirror and saw the tiny spot of lipstick on his cheek. "Paint?"

Replacement's eyes blazed. "Red black-cherry lipstick?"

Damn.

"It was Kiku?"

"No…"

Replacement yanked open the door. Jack tried to block her, but she ducked under his arm.

"*Seriously?*" she yelled as she charged into the room.

Kiku jumped up from her chair.

"Listen, you little face-sucking vampire. Keep your stinking hands *and lips* off my guy." She stuck her finger right in Kiku's face.

Kiku didn't blink. "My apologies. I am sorry to have upset you."

The apology seemed to bring Replacement up short. She scratched her head and looked back and forth between Kiku and Jack.

It's like she's playing eeny, meeny, miney…

Her head stopped, and she glared at Jack.

Damn it, I'm moe.

"It's his fault." She pointed at Jack. "He does that to you. Gets you all—" She moved her hands rapidly in front of herself. Her head swung back and she eyed Kiku suspiciously. "On the cheek? Nothing else?"

"Nothing. But again, Alice, you are right. It *was* his fault, but *I* apologize to you." Kiku winked quickly at Jack when Replacement looked away.

He rolled his eyes and mouthed, "Thanks."

Jennifer walked over to Replacement. "Why don't you and I take the first shift?"

"Yeah." Replacement snarled at Jack. "We'll take the first shift."

Jennifer smiled and led her over to the bed. Replacement looked at her, confused.

"That means that we sleep first." Jennifer helped Replacement lie down, pulled the blanket over her, then lay down beside her.

Replacement huffed once or twice, but slowly the alcohol began to win the war. She was asleep in minutes.

Kiku headed over to the couch and whispered, "If no one has an objection, I need some sleep, too."

Jack noticed the circles under her eyes. He sat at the table. "I'll take first watch."

He picked up the deck and shuffled. He dealt out a game of solitaire, but before he started, Jennifer propped herself up on her elbows and looked at him. Jack nodded over to the chair, and she slipped out of bed.

"You wanna play?" he asked, but she shook her head as she sat down.

"What're we going to do?" Her forehead creased with worry.

"I planted a GPS device on Walter's car. I have an idea to get him to take us to Marisa, but it has to wait until the Mancinis get a call."

"What if they don't call?"

Then Marisa's dead.

"They'll call. Then we'll follow Walter. Once we get our proof, we call for backup."

Jennifer inhaled deeply. "There are a lot of loose ends."

Jack sat back. "It's all I've got. You can write up that I came to you with the information on Walter."

"Your career is done then."

"It's done anyway. That email killed me."

"She wrote it?" Jennifer pointed at Replacement.

Jack nodded and smiled.

"You're pretty laid-back considering she cost you your job."

Jack shrugged. "Collins could use anything. It's my attitude that cost me my job."

"You can't follow the rules?"

"I follow rules fine until I don't anymore. I'd rather be wrong and look stupid than do nothing and have someone get hurt." He looked down at the cards. "I remember I heard this story when I was in the Academy. Some guy took this little kid from a shopping mall. All these people saw it, but no one stepped up and confronted the guy. The kid was calling for help, but no one did anything. Officers interviewed them afterward, and they all said they didn't want to get embarrassed if they were wrong, and maybe it was just that the kid was throwing a temper tantrum."

"Well, this isn't about getting embarrassed. Now it's not even about your job. You could get killed, Jack."

He shrugged. "None of us make it out of here alive. Besides, there are worse things than dying."

"Like what?" Jennifer sat back.

"That guy at that mall? He killed the little kid. Before the kid went through hell, he begged for help, and everyone turned his back on him. I'd rather die than live with myself if I did nothing."

"Would you trade your life for hers?"

"I don't think the Reaper offers deals." Jack tapped the deck of cards on the table. "But if he did, it would be a fool's bargain, trading me for Marisa."

Jennifer's lips pressed together in a thin smile. "I trust you, Jack." She patted his shoulder and got up. "I didn't expect you to back down."

She slipped back into bed as Jack started his game.

42

A FAVOR

The burner phone danced on the table like water dropped in a hot skillet. Jack flipped it open before the second ring.

"Yeah?" He walked into the bathroom and closed the door.

"Jack, they called." Ilario sounded out of breath. "They want twenty million dollars by two o'clock this afternoon."

"Where?"

"The base of Big Blue. The parking lot of a walking trail."

"Anything else?"

"No. It sounded recorded. I wrote it down. Twenty million dollars. Two p.m. Base of Big Blue. South side. Parking lot. Then—they hung up."

He's holding back.

"Ilario. There's something else. What happened?"

"They… they put Angelica on. She was crying."

Jack wanted to put his fist through the wall. "Did she say anything?"

Ilario sobbed. "Just my name. Twice."

"Listen closely, Ilario." Jack looked at his watch: 6:30 a.m. *Big Blue is a twenty-minute drive.* "I need you guys to be there at nine thirty. Got it?"

"Why? I don't—"

"You have to do this, Ilario. Nine thirty."

"I don't know if we can get the money by then. We only have five million cash with us."

"Bring that. You need to make a big show of it. Three cars minimum. SUVs. Big ones."

"Okay," Ilario replied.

"You have to be strong for Angelica. Repeat it back, what time?"

"Nine thirty. Base of Big Blue."

"Right. If you hear anything else, call me."

Jack hung up the phone and stepped out of the bathroom. All three women were watching him.

"Get ready," he announced.

Replacement jumped out of bed, groaned, wobbled, and headed for the bathroom. Jack picked up the five-shot .380 and frowned at the five-round chamber.

Kiku walked over to her backpack, reached inside, and pulled out a seventeen-round Glock.

Jack assessed the guns. "One of them has a semi-automatic. We're outgunned, but the plan isn't to get into a shootout. We're going to follow Prescott there and call in the cavalry."

Kiku lifted out the fifth, took a swig from the bottle, wiped her mouth with the back of her hand, and smiled roguishly.

Jack shook his head. "Just wait here. I'm getting the car."

He headed out the door and broke into a jog. The cold air felt good on his face. His lungs took in huge gulps of air, and he smiled as he felt the power of his own muscles.

He broke into a sprint and let go. He stopped thinking, stopped hurting, and just ran. Carl's garage came into view too soon, and he slowed to a trot and then to a walk until he caught his breath.

He pulled out his phone and dialed.

"Undersheriff Morrison." Morrison's voice was still groggy with sleep.

"Sir, I need to ask a favor."

There was a long pause. "You can ask, Jack."

"Sir, according to regulations, you have the authority to schedule emergency response drills."

"What?"

"You have the—"

"I heard you, but I don't understand where you're going with this. Actually, I do understand where you're going, but I don't know why."

"Sir, I need you to call out a drill… this morning."

"This *morning*?" Something fell to the floor in the background.

"Right now, actually." Jack tipped his head. "Everyone in full tactical. Vests, masks—"

"Full tactical? What are you prepping for? War?"

"Yes, sir."

There was a long pause.

"Did you find her?"

"Not yet, sir. But we will this morning. I need only our men on this, sir. That's why I need everyone in personal cars. No cruisers. No police radios. The gather point is Westbrook School. Oh eight hundred."

"Westbrook?"

"Yes, sir." *It's five minutes from Big Blue, but far enough not to attract attention.*

"Not to sound selfish, Jack, but I just left my wife sleeping in our bed, and I'm not going to throw away a career unless you give me something."

"Walter Prescott's the one behind Marisa's kidnapping, sir. He placed her here. He came to Darrington the day she was taken, and he's using guys from witness protection as his crew. I have photo evidence from the tolls. If I'm wrong, you're just running a drill. If I'm right, then your career might take a hit because you helped me."

"Hold up, Jack. I need to think."

Jack walked over to the garage doors and undid the chain.

Undersheriff Morrison cleared his throat. "All right." He sighed. "I'll call the drill. And I'll make sure Prescott doesn't know. But Jack—don't be a hero."

"Yes, sir."

43

THAT'S AMORE

Jack parked the Impala down the street from the Hometown Suites. Replacement was in the passenger seat, Kiku behind her, and Jennifer in the back next to her. Jack looked at Replacement and the laptop in her hands. "Is it working?"

"I have a strong signal. His car is still there."

Jack held up his hand for quiet, then dialed Prescott.

"Prescott," Walter answered.

"It's Jack."

"Stratton? Where the hell are you? You've got half the police force looking for you after—"

"Shut up, Prescott. The Mancinis got a call."

"So *now* you want to try cooperating? I haven't heard anything about a call."

"They called me afterward. Listen. It's going down at ten o'clock."

There was a brief pause. "Ten?"

"Ten o'clock this morning. The caller told the Mancinis to bring ten million dollars to the base of Big Blue. It's right—"

"I know where the hell Big Blue is. Who told you this?"

Jack exhaled.

Wait. Let him stew.

"Marisa's little brother."

There was a long pause.

"It's seven twenty now," Prescott said. "I need to... get a team together."

"I'm going to be there," Jack said coldly.

"Yeah, sure. I'll... I'll keep you informed."

Jack hung up.

"Brilliantly played, Officer." Kiku grinned in the back seat. "He'll think they're double-crossing him. But why do you think he'll go there?"

Jack pulled down the rearview mirror. "If you thought someone was going to rip you off for millions, would you just call and ask, or would you go there?"

"Good point," Jennifer said. "But why did you say ten million when they want twenty million?"

Kiku answered. "Lies work best in layers. Now he thinks they're changing the time to cut him out *and* taking a smaller cut because it would take the Mancinis time to raise twenty million. It adds credibility. That was a nice touch." Kiku leaned forward and put her hand on Jack's shoulder.

"Jack's very good at lying," Replacement said. She looked at Kiku's hand and shot Jack a dirty look. "Most of the time. Except when he's caught with his pants—"

"Not the time."

"When would be the right—?" She looked down at the screen. "He's moving."

"That was fast." Jack put the Impala in gear and pulled away from the curb.

"Can I ask why we're trying to follow him in this big boat of a car that everyone knows?" Jennifer said.

"I know my girl, and I'm not taking some unknown car on this."

"This car is your *girl?*" Jennifer's eyebrow arched.

Replacement kept her eyes on the laptop. "Don't go there," she said. "Trust me. It's a no-win. Left onto Wellington."

Jack grinned. "Took the bait. He's heading out of town. Strap your seat belts on, ladies."

"He's pulling away," Replacement announced. "Jack, step on it."

Jack punched the gas and settled back into the seat. "This is the plan. We follow him to wherever they're holding Marisa, and I call the cavalry."

"I don't think your ruse will fool them for long," Kiku pointed out.

"It doesn't have to. Once I confirm where Prescott's going, fifty cops can be there in five minutes."

"How?" Jennifer asked.

"They're running an emergency drill at a school five minutes down the road from Big Blue."

Jennifer flopped back in the seat, and her mouth fell open. She laughed. "How the hell did you pull that off?"

"That's Jack." Replacement gave him a quick smile and then focused again on the laptop.

The peak of Big Blue rose up in the distance. The winter had been unseasonably warm, so Jack didn't know whether they had even opened the one ski slope that ran down its face. Prescott was headed up the west side, which was dotted with houses and cabins. Forest spread out on either side of them, and the sight distance dropped off as they wound their way up the curving road.

"You can ease back a little," Replacement said.

The Impala swung up the heavily wooded road. At least this road was paved; a lot of the roads around here were little better than wide bike paths. After a bit, Replacement pointed to take the right, and Jack complied.

Damn. We're going farther than I thought. These roads are going to increase the response time, too.

"Slow down." Replacement angled the screen. "He stopped."

"I see him. Cabin." Kiku leaned forward and pointed to the right.

Between the trees, Jack saw a small cabin and the glow of brake lights. He stopped the car.

"Do you have a map of the area?" Jack asked.

Replacement pressed a few buttons, and a map appeared.

He studied the road layout, then scowled. "I'd rather come around from the back, but this road doesn't loop around. I don't want to stop here and have Prescott come right back into us either."

"He's going to know you set him up," Jennifer said. "He'll figure it out soon." She pulled out her pistol.

"Then it's time for the cavalry," Jack said. But he froze when he looked at his phone. "Oh, no. No signal."

Kiku and Replacement checked their own phones, and shook their heads.

Jack reached for the door handle and looked at Replacement. "Drive back until you get a signal, then call Undersheriff Morrison."

"I'm not leaving you," Replacement said.

Jack held up his hand. "I need someone to go."

"I'll go." Jennifer climbed over the front seat. "With my ankle I'm not much good anyway. I need a phone."

Jack handed her the burner phone as he, Replacement, and Kiku jumped out.

"Morrison?" Jennifer asked as she put the Impala into reverse.

"Just hit redial. It's the last call I made."

Jack watched her back up on the road. He took a few steps toward the woods that separated them from the cabin. "Prescott won't trust them," he said. "He may move Marisa, and if he does, we can get him on the road."

"This isn't the best spot for an ambush, Officer. As you said, they have the firepower in their favor."

"I'm going up," Jack said.

"*We're* going up." Replacement started after him.

"No. You're last line," he snapped. He handed her the little five-shot .380. "Pull the trigger. Five shots. That's it." He gave her a stern look. "They know how to shoot, Alice. Stay here. Seriously. I'll shoot you in the leg if you try to follow."

Replacement's jaw clamped shut.

Jack hurried into the woods, and Kiku followed. They moved fast and low as they approached the cabin.

Prescott's car was parked out front, and there was another sedan parked on the left. Judging by the size of the cabin and the window placements, Jack estimated it had one large living room and a couple of side rooms.

"How long do you think it will take for your ruse to be discovered?" Kiku asked.

Jack made a fist. "I'm hoping it screws them up for at least fifteen minutes. They'll argue. They'll deny it, and then Prescott will figure it out. That's when it gets interesting."

"You think they'll move her?"

"He still won't trust them. He'll want—"

They both spun around at the sound of a breaking branch.

Jack's throat tightened, and he slowly lowered his gun, which was pointed at Replacement's head. She was crouched over, and her hands were up. Her eyes were wide as she gave a little wave.

"That's *amore*," Kiku whispered.

Love? I wonder how you say "I'm going to kill her" in Italian.

Replacement quietly crept the last few feet. "Sorry," she whispered. "Are you going to shoot me in the leg?"

Jack scowled, but before he could respond, a yell from the cabin drew their attention.

"Sounds like it's getting interesting," Kiku said.

Jack heard the Impala coming back up the road. "Jennifer's back."

"That was fast," Replacement said.

They waited in position while Jennifer parked and then hurried through the woods to join them, limping heavily. When she reached them, her eyes were wide and her face was ashen. "They're coming," she panted. "But—" She gulped air.

"What?" Jack asked.

"Walter sent me a text message, and it was strange. I think he's losing it. I've known Walter for years and I'm worried he's at the end of his rope. If his plan is falling apart, he may try to get revenge on Severino by killing Marisa."

Jack started to stand, and both Kiku and Replacement put a hand on his shoulder. "I *have* to do something," he said.

"Jack's right," Jennifer said. "We need to go now. Surprise him. If he hears the police coming, she's dead."

Jack looked at the cabin and the layout. "Kiku, go east. Jennifer, go west. I'm going through the front door."

"We don't need a dead hero, Jack," Jennifer said.

"I'm not charging in, just planning on drawing their fire. I'll kick the door, then get out of the way. That's your signal. Once you open up, I'll pop back out, and I'll drop anyone left."

They nodded, and Kiku sprinted wide to the right. She had the most ground to cover, and she disappeared quickly into the woods. Jennifer moved low and fast, and Jack turned to Replacement.

"Stay here. Wait for Morrison."

She nodded.

She has no intention of doing what I say.

Jack moved to the edge of the forest.

Woodpile. Car. Cabin.

He quickly ascertained the best route to the house. He covered the short span to the woodpile and crouched low. He looked for Kiku but saw nothing. Jennifer had headed a bit wide, but she moved fast.

Jack dashed to the rear wheel of Prescott's sedan and did his best to crouch down behind the tire. He leaned his shoulder against the cold metal of the car, looked back, and almost cursed aloud. Replacement's head popped out from the edge of the woods.

Damn it! I should have shot her in the leg.

He waved her back and made a cutting motion over his throat.

Move, Jack.

He covered the fifteen feet to the cabin in the blink of an eye, but it felt like forever. His muscles groaned in protest as he went from full speed to full stop and silently reached the side of the cabin.

Kiku was still nowhere to be seen, and Jennifer was out of sight now, too. But he knew they should be in place in a minute. He pressed his back against the wood next to the door and shut his eyes.

Please, God.

When he opened his eyes again, he saw that Replacement had moved up to the woodpile and was about to sprint to the car, following his route. Her small frame was an asset as she got low, and she was a blur as she covered the distance.

Jack held up his hand for her to stay, and she nodded. *I really hope she means it this time.*

He listened. Men were yelling inside, and their voices blended together. *Minimum: three. Max: six.*

Jack knew he was supposed to bust the door open, take cover, and let Kiku and Jennifer open fire. That would give all of them the best survivability rate. Kiku was faster than Jennifer, so she'd open up first. And that meant she'd draw their fire. The chances of her surviving were slim.

No way. It's not her day to die.

Jack knew what he'd do before he even started for the cabin. He had run most of the scenarios over in his head already. And every way he crunched the numbers, odds were he died.

But odds are they die, too.

He stepped back and kicked the door open. *"Freeze!"*

Everything slowed. There were three men plus Prescott in the living room. They all turned to look at him, and he saw the guns in their hands.

He also saw their guns start to rise.

Two rounds apiece.

Jack zippered Prescott first. One in the gut and one center mass.

The spiky-haired Asian had a submachine gun. Jack put one in his chest and one in his head. Kiku's pistol grip was small for his hand, but the gun shot straight.

The second man got a shot off that hit the doorframe next to Jack's head before Kiku opened up. She fired three-round bursts, and they all looked to have hit their mark. Prescott took three in the back. The third guy could have killed Jack if he'd followed through, but instead of firing on Jack he started to turn toward Kiku, and bullets from three sides cut him down.

Prescott fell to his knees and looked at Jack with a mixture of hate and pleading. It was an expression Jack had seen too many times.

He knows he's dead. He hates my guts, but he's still thinking he may have a chance to live. Now he's begging.

Three guys and Prescott.

Prescott pitched forward, dead.

Jennifer stepped into the cabin from the door on the left. Her hands trembled slightly but she kept her gun aimed at the bodies on the floor.

Replacement stepped up behind Jack with the little .380 held at arm's length. She looked nervous.

She's scared out of her mind, but she had my back.

Jack swept the room. Kiku climbed in through the window. Jennifer leaned against the doorframe and stared at Prescott on the floor.

"Are you hit?" Jack whispered.

Jennifer kept looking down and shook her head. He heard her gag.

Besides the room Jennifer came in through, there was only one other room off the main area, and the door was closed. Jack held up his hand and hurried over to it.

Instinctively, he scanned the frame for booby traps, but quickly dismissed the thought.

He opened the door.

It was a bedroom, with only one occupant.

Marisa.

She was tied onto a bed with her head turned toward the door. Her eyes locked on Jack's, and he could see the mix of hope and disbelief in her eyes. She closed her eyes tightly and opened them again. The truth appeared on her face like a sunrise; the doubt faded, and her eyes widened and gleamed.

She lost it. Her chest heaved with sobs, and she strained against her bonds.

Oh, Angel...

A surge of emotions washed over him. His chest tightened, and he could feel the rush of adrenaline course through his body. Instantly, he was at the side of the bed. His palm smashed the headboard, and pieces of wood flew against the wall. He pulled her wrists free. Marisa wrapped her arms around him and buried her face in his neck.

"Jack. Jack," she sobbed.

"I'm here, Angel. I'm right here. I've gotcha." He held her tightly.

She clung to him.

Kiku was suddenly beside him, a knife in her hands. She cut Marisa's ropes and then patted her down, looking her over. "She is uninjured."

Replacement appeared in the doorway, and Jennifer stood behind her. "Jack, Morrison will be here any minute," Jennifer said. "Alice and Kiku have to go. If they're found here..."

Jack turned to Replacement and Kiku. "The town isn't that far. Can you make it to the base and catch a ride back to the hotel? Cut down the trails so no one coming from town will see you. We'll meet you back at the Imperial as soon as we're done."

Replacement shook her head. "I stay with you."

Kiku leaned in and whispered something in her ear.

Replacement clenched her teeth and gave a curt nod. She spoke to Jack. "Okay. We'll meet you back at the Imperial. How long?"

"It could be a while."

"How will you explain this?" Kiku asked.

Jack shrugged. "I'll figure out something. I'm thinking about going with the man-in-the-cape angle."

"Wipe down your gun and leave it here," Jennifer told Kiku.

"She's right," said Jack. "If not, Ballistics will start looking for you and your gun."

Reluctantly, Kiku complied.

Marisa continued to cry, and Jack just held on to her. Replacement's hand reached out for Marisa and hovered just above her shoulder. She left it there briefly before turning and leaving the room.

Kiku winked at Jack before following. "I'll keep an eye on her."

Jennifer slipped out of the room too.

Marisa wept, and Jack gently rocked her. He could only imagine what she'd gone through, and right now he just wanted to get her to the hospital.

"Angel?" he whispered.

Marisa looked up at him. Deep black circles stood out under her eyes, and the right side of her face was swollen. She searched his face, and a brief smile flashed across her lips before she buried her face in his neck and pulled him close.

"Jack, please get me out of here."

Jack rubbed her back. "The police will be here in a minute."

"Please? Get me out of this room." She continued to cry.

"I will. I'm going to take you out to the car, but I'm going to carry you, okay?"

She nodded.

Jack lifted her up in his arms and carried her out of the room. He pressed her face into his shoulder so she wouldn't see the carnage inside the cabin. He cradled her gently as he stepped outside. Marisa gulped in deep breaths of cool air and blinked rapidly. He could feel her long lashes against his neck.

The Impala was still parked way down the road, so Jack carried Marisa to Prescott's car. He yanked open the rear door with one hand and gently set her inside. He pulled the seat belt around her and clicked it into place. "I'll call Ilario and tell him you're safe as soon as I have a signal."

She smiled up at him.

Where's Morrison? He should have been here by now.

As he reached into his pocket for his phone, he remembered Jennifer had taken it. Then several thoughts sped through his mind.

She screamed at Prescott when he mentioned Marisa's tattoo. She thought I lived on the third floor. She ran toward the cabin—she didn't limp.

He stood up and looked at the spot where the four of them had crouched before they came to the house. Her words replayed in his head.

Walter sent me a text... He may try to get revenge against Severino by killing Marisa.

Jack froze. *He sent her a text? But Jennifer lost her phone in the parking garage.*

Oh no.

A bullet tore into his side. He stumbled against the car, twisted around, and pitched forward. All of the wind was knocked out of him as he landed face first in the dirt.

"Jack!" Marisa screamed.

Jennifer ran up and pistol-whipped Marisa in the side of the head. Her head snapped back, and she fell onto her side on the seat. Jack blinked rapidly, trying to get his breath, but he felt as though someone had a foot on his throat. He coughed and tasted blood. He couldn't breathe.

He fumbled for his gun, but his muscles weren't cooperating. The slightest motion made pain sear through him.

Jennifer picked up his pistol and heaved it toward the house. "I tried to get you to stop, Jack," she growled.

Jack lay there helplessly, struggling to breathe. He could only take in the slightest bit of air before he had to exhale. His vision blurred.

Jennifer squatted down. "I'm sorry about having to shoot you, Jack. I am. But I'm going to give Marisa over to the Mancinis and get my ten million. This is actually working out better with your stupid interference. Now that you've killed my partners, even with half the ransom I get a bigger cut. I keep it all."

Jack tried to speak but couldn't. He just shook his head.

"What? Speak up." She sneered. "They won't get me, if that's what you're trying to say. I send Marisa down the ski lift, and the Mancinis send the money up at the same time. Nice, huh? Of course, she'll be dead by the time she reaches the bottom. I'll give her just the thing to make sure of that. That's my present to Severino. And right after they get her body, I'll give them a call. I'll warn them you were in on it and give them the number of our room at the Imperial. I'm sure they'll be real nice to Kiku and Alice."

"Bitch." Jack coughed, and blood sprayed across the ground.

"Yeah. But now I'm a rich bitch. Now I'm the one who gets to disappear and start over."

She stood up.

"If you weren't such a Boy Scout, you might have saved the girl. I'm sure you'd have figured it out. I played Prescott, and he went right along with my idea. Men are so easy. All you have to do is press the right buttons. With Walter, it was hate. You were right: it was revenge. But not for his partner. He couldn't stand that he was going to retire without beating Severino. But you? You're the white knight. The guy at the garage wasn't there to kill me. He was getting instructions *from* me. But you thought I needed rescuing."

Jack spat up more blood.

"You're a good guy, Jack. And the good always die young. They should find your body in a couple days."

Jennifer walked around and got into Prescott's car with Marisa. Jack kept his head down as they drove away.

Damn it. Breathe, Jack. You're lunged. Army Emergency Evac class. Plug the hole.

He felt through his shirt and found the bullet hole. He pushed some of the fabric from his shirt into the wound. If he had any air in his lungs, he'd have been screaming; it felt as though his chest was being torn in two. He coughed, and his mouth filled with blood. He spat it out, but at least he could draw in a little air.

This will probably kill me—plugging the hole this way—but I just need to buy enough time to get to Marisa.

He clawed at the ground and pulled himself to his feet. He could see the Impala through the woods.

Move.

He stumbled forward. He had to force his legs to keep going. More blood seeped from his mouth, and he gritted his teeth.

No time. Faster.

He held the wound on his side. Everything was becoming gray. He knew that with a chest wound the last thing he should do was move, but he had no choice. He staggered as fast as he could. When he finally leaned against the Impala, his bloody hands fumbled for the door handle. The big door swung open.

He fought for air. *Breathe. Made it. Breathe.*

His vision blurred, and he swayed. Air wheezed out of his lungs, and he coughed up another mouthful of blood. His head hung down, and he looked at the door panel.

He grabbed it. This was going to hurt.

He yanked hard, and the panel popped open. The pain felt like a knife in his chest, and he fell forward against the doorframe. But he gritted his teeth and pulled out Paolo's Magnum.

Two shots left.

He dropped the gun on the seat and sat down. His right arm seemed to be cooperating more than the left.

And then he realized: *I have no keys.* Jennifer took them when she went to get help.

His hand shaking uncontrollably, he grabbed the ignition and tried to jiggle the worn-out dial. It didn't turn.

Come on, baby.

He tried again.

Please, girl. Please.

The ignition rotated forward, and the Impala roared to life.

Good girl.

He slammed the car into reverse. Back on the road, he pumped the brakes and spun the wheel. He slumped sideways and spat up more blood.

Groaning, he grabbed the steering wheel tightly and pulled himself back to a sitting position. The transmission clicked into drive, and he jammed the gas pedal to the floor. He struggled with his left hand but managed to pull the seat belt across his chest.

She's headed for the ski lift.

Jack tried to recall the map Replacement had pulled up on her laptop earlier.

She'll have to go all the way down and then cross over to the road. But there's a tiny dirt road that runs straight down. Maybe I can get in front of her.

Jack's feet fumbled with the pedals as he raced furiously down the curving roads. He scanned ahead for the turn onto the dirt road and gritted his teeth when he saw it. Both feet jammed down on the brake, slowing him down just enough to take the hard right.

No one would really call this a road; it was at best a logging path that ran straight down the mountainside. But it was his only chance of getting to Marisa in time. Rocks pinged off the undercarriage, and branches raked the sides of the car. One particularly deep pothole tossed him sideways, and his head slammed into the window. His vision blurred, and he wiped his eyes with the back of his hand. His eyes burned. His hands were covered in blood.

He swerved around another pothole, and then the whole car lurched left as he clipped a tree. The sound of crushing metal filled his ears as the car scraped along the pine trunk. In the rearview mirror, he saw his quarter panel spin off into the woods. He fought the wheel as the front end kicked in the air off a rock, and as the Impala shot forward, he was pushed into the seat belt. Pain exploded in his side.

The shirt came out.

His left hand shook as he reached again for his wound. Gulping for air that would only come in the smallest amounts, and struggling to see through the branches that crashed against the windshield, he grasped the shirt fabric and crammed it back into the hole in his side.

A huge branch broke off the driver's side mirror, and the windshield spider-webbed with a loud crack. The wheel pulled left, which brought the car swinging dangerously toward a tree, and Jack yanked right hard with both hands. The Impala straightened out, and fortunately, so did the road. Jack tried to press himself back into the seat.

Through the woods, down below and to the side, he saw the sedan moving along the main road. He was ahead of it now. If he went a little farther, he could double back. He floored it, and the shocks groaned in protest. The main road approached, and he locked up the brakes and cut the wheel.

He jammed the gas pedal down, and the Impala surged forward. Jennifer's car came around the corner up ahead.

If Jennifer gets away, Marisa's dead. She'll kill Marisa before she'd let her go. But if I hit that car hard enough, Jennifer won't be going anywhere.

Jack rubbed the dashboard. *Sorry, baby. I don't think either of us gets out of this alive today.*

Jack reached over and picked up Paolo's gun, then wedged it between the seats. Everything in the car not nailed down was about to go flying, and if he did manage to survive a head-on crash he might need the Magnum. Then he put both hands on the wheel.

Steady.

Jennifer's car kept coming straight at him.

She'll try to cut right.

He could see Jennifer now, and she looked scared.

Marisa's in the back with a seat belt. She should be safe. Please let her be safe.

Jennifer was firing now, and bullets pinged off the Impala.

Jack made sure he flashed her a bloody grin.

For one split second, everything froze. He saw Marisa in the back seat. Her head rose, and she looked directly at him.

Love. Guilt. Anguish. Anger.

Jack didn't know whether he could actually see all those emotions on her face, or whether he just knew her so intimately he could read her thoughts.

God, please let her live.

Jennifer hit the brakes.

Jack hit the gas.

Tires screeched. Glass shattered. Metal exploded.

Everything went black.

44

FOOL'S BARGAIN

Jack coughed, and blood sprayed all over the dashboard. His head rested against cold glass. Puzzled, he opened his eyes. His vision was blurry, but he could see that the driver-side window somehow hadn't broken.

Everything else had.

The whole front seat was at a strange angle. Twisted metal rods poked through the firewall into the leg section of the passenger seat. Glass was everywhere, and the passenger door was gone.

Prescott's car was fused together with the Impala. Jennifer was slumped over the steering wheel, unmoving. Jack's eyes searched for Marisa, but he could see only a small portion of the sedan's back seat. His breath was ragged, and as he exhaled, he could hear bubbling in his chest.

Smoke rose from the engines of the cars, but Jack could no longer move. His right hand twitched, and his legs were numb. He closed his eyes and listened to a hissing from somewhere in the wreckage.

Metal clinking on the road caused him to open his eyes. Someone stood where the passenger-side door had been. Jack groaned as he tilted his head.

It was Marisa.

Tears ran down her face. She knelt on the front seat, broken glass crunching beneath her.

"It's okay, Angel," Jack wheezed.

"No, not you, baby. Not you…" She touched his hand, but he couldn't feel it. "Listen…"

Crying, she pulled herself closer. She winced and gritted her teeth.

"No regrets," Jack coughed.

Marisa's hand reached out and softly caressed his face.

"No. Please, Jack. I can't lose you, too. Not because of me."

Jack tried to shake his head, but the pain cut off what little air he was getting. "Do me a favor?"

Marisa's tears fell on his shoulder.

"Live."

She sobbed and sat back on her haunches. Her hand went to her mouth. Weeping, she nodded and moved out of the car. "Hang on. I'll get help. I'll get help," she repeated as she stumbled backward.

She has no shoes.

Marisa started to run. At first he thought she was running the wrong way, but then he realized the impact had spun the cars around almost one hundred eighty degrees.

Her hair fanned out as she raced away. She ran down the hill, and Jack smiled as he thought of the little girl in the picture.

She'll be okay.

Jack coughed, and again he felt the cold glass against his face. He watched Marisa disappear in the distance.

The Reaper made a fool's bargain.

He closed his eyes.

***

"Jack! *Jack!*"

Someone was beating on the driver's side window.

Jack's eyes opened slowly. His thoughts were muddled, but he recognized Replacement. She was pulling at the door with all her might. Her eyes were huge, and tears poured down her face.

Jack lifted his head. He coughed, but no blood came out. Replacement ran around the car and crawled onto the seat beside him. Her hands hovered over his broken body.

"Jack, what can I do?"

"Marisa... ran... down."

Replacement looked back. Kiku was standing behind her.

"Kiku? Kiku, tell me what to do!" Replacement begged.

Kiku lowered her eyes.

Replacement's hand touched Jack's head. "I'm going for help. Don't you give up. Damn it, Jack, please don't leave me."

"Alice..." Jack swallowed. "Thanks."

"Please?" Replacement begged.

Jack's eyes started to close again, but he forced them to stay open and drew in a ragged breath. If this was the last time he was going to see her face, he wanted it to last.

Replacement turned and bolted. Her legs were a blur as she raced away. Her arms pumped, her feet kicked up, and he knew she was giving everything she had, trying to save him.

He knew she couldn't.

She never looked back.

"I love you," Jack whispered.

His breathing became shallower. He looked at Kiku. She had Paolo's Magnum in her hand; it shook.

"Are you suffering, Officer?" Tears hung off her long lashes.

She can end this. End me.

He looked over at Jennifer's body. Dead.

I'm not afraid to die. I'm going to. Kiku would make it quick. Painless.

"I'm good." He managed a wink.

"You're in pain."

Pain. I'm suffocating. I can't feel half my body, and the parts I can I wish I couldn't.

"Pain and me," Jack coughed. "We're old friends."

"Shall I tell Alice?"

"If I die."

Kiku nodded.

"Take care… of her…" Jack coughed. "From a distance." He managed a crooked grin.

Kiku started to weep.

Jack Stratton closed his eyes.

45

VERY GOOD HANDS

Jack's eyes fluttered open, but he couldn't see. The light was so bright he had to shut his eyes again to let them adjust. He listened instead, and heard a faint beep from his left. He felt sheets underneath him. The smell of antiseptic and medicines reached his nose, and his stomach churned.

Hospital.

Slowly, he opened one eye. Marisa was asleep in the chair next to the bed. Her hand lay on the bed rail. Her cheeks were much thinner, but…

She's alive.

Jack gave up on thinking. There was a dull pain behind his eyes, and he could only imagine what it would feel like if he wasn't on whatever painkiller they'd used to numb him. He was covered in tubes and wires. When he tried to open his mouth, he realized some tube was even down his throat. The realization brought a quick panic, but his fatigue overrode his pain.

With considerable effort, he slid his hand over to bump Marisa's. Her eyes lifted like a sunrise, and her chest rose. The corners of her lips curled up, and she closed her eyes again and settled back into the chair.

Jack lifted his finger and rubbed it against hers. She gasped and sat bolt upright. He tried to smile, but the movement hurt his throat.

"Jack." Marisa jumped up and leaned down close to him. "Don't move. Don't move. Doctor! Doctor!" She ran out into the hallway. He heard a crash in the corridor and running feet.

"Is he awake? Jack!" Replacement sprinted into the room.

She ran so fast she didn't stop in time, and slammed into his bed. Jack felt a numbed ripple course through his body. If it wasn't for the pain medication, he was certain he'd be crying like a baby.

"Alice," Marisa snapped.

"Get the doctor," Replacement ordered. "Jack. It's okay. You're okay." Her face was right next to his. *"Get the doctor!"* she screamed right into his face.

"Doctor!" Marisa yelled from the doorway. "No one's coming!" She slapped her hand against her leg.

Replacement raced back out of the room. A minute later she returned, herding one orderly, three nurses, and one doctor in front of her. He wondered what she'd said to get them there so fast.

She and Marisa ran to one side of the bed while the doctor approached from the other.

"Officer Stratton." The older man smiled and looked up at Marisa and Replacement. "It would appear you're in very good hands." He winked, and Jack closed his eyes again.

46

MARISA

Marisa stood by the window and looked at the man lying in the bed. *Jack Stratton.* He was covered in tubes and wires. The mask hid his pale face but not his shallow breathing.

She closed her eyes tightly as the separate memories of two gunshots rang in her ears. Her hand went to her mouth, and she fought the urge to run to his side. She turned to the window instead. Everyone had finally left. The parade of people who loved him had been long. Marisa had remained out of sight in the waiting room across the way, but she had watched them.

Alice, Cindy, Mrs. Stevens, Aunt Haddie.

Flowers now filled the room, and Marisa inhaled deeply.

He'd hate it. Hate the attention. But he loves them. He loves this town. Being a policeman.

She closed her eyes and wrapped her arms around herself. A shiver rippled down her body as the realization of what she needed to do sank in.

The sound of heels on the linoleum brought her head up. It wasn't a nurse who stood in the doorway; it was a beautiful Japanese woman. She carried a vase filled with red chrysanthemums. Marisa tilted her head as she tried to remember where she'd seen the woman before. Her eyes rounded.

The cabin.

Kiku set down her vase and walked over to the side of the bed. She placed a hand on the side of Jack's face and bowed her head. After a moment, she straightened up and walked over to Marisa.

"I saw you at the cabin." Marisa's voice was just above a whisper. "I want to thank you."

"That is not necessary." The woman looked back at Jack. "I was merely an accessory."

Marisa watched Jack's chest rise and fall. "I'm sure he wouldn't agree."

"He would give Alice and me all the credit. He is a good man."

Marisa's chest tightened. She walked over to the hospital bed. Jack's monitors beeped and clicked. Marisa pulled up the corner of his blanket so she could cover more of his arm.

"It is no longer safe for you in Darrington," Kiku whispered. "Now that people know where you are, they will be tempted to use you."

I know.

Marisa touched Jack's shoulder.

His skin feels better. Not as hot.

Marisa inhaled deeply. She looked at Kiku and sighed. "Thank you."

"I mean no offense, Ms. Vitagliano." Kiku leaned down, kissed Jack's cheek, and then walked to the door. She didn't look back when she spoke. "But I did it for Jack."

***

Jack looked at the vase of wilting chrysanthemums. Another petal fell down to land on the shelf. He picked the letter back up.

> *Jack,*
>
> *Words could never convey how much you meant to me before this happened. Now...*
>
> *I saw you right before the impact of the car accident. I saw your face. I saw your eyes. You were willing to sacrifice your life for mine. You offered it, my love. I had no choice then. But now, that's something I can't let you do.*
>
> *I have to go. I don't know where right now, but I have to leave Darrington, and I can't ask you to go with me. I know you would, but I can't let you. You have so much here. So many who love you. You have a life.*
>
> *You asked me to live, and I'll try. I ask the same of you.*
>
> Tu sei il bello mio: *You are my beautiful one.*
>
> *Marisa*

At the bottom of the letter was a sketch of the girl in the field. As Jack looked at it now, he was sure the little girl was smiling.

Beneath the picture, Marisa had written: *The original is hanging in your living room.*

Jack let the paper fall from his hand as another chrysanthemum petal floated down to the floor.

47

A DOG IN A SLED

Jack sat propped up against the pillows while two FBI agents and his union delegate stood on either side of his bed. Both of the FBI agents had Marine haircuts and wore dark black suits, white shirts, black shoes, and serious expressions.

The taller one was Dan Haney, but Jack couldn't remember the other guy's name.

Jack's union delegate was Peter Bruff. He was dressed in ski pants and a red shirt screen-printed with a dog in a sled being pulled by six humans. He'd come the second Replacement told him he was needed.

"We're not re-interviewing him," Haney explained again. "We just have two additional questions."

Peter turned to look at Jack, and his snow pants swished squeakily.

Jack tried not to laugh at the odd sound. "Ask away."

"We appreciate your help, Officer Stratton, but we just need you to answer a few—"

"Two," Peter interjected.

"We need you to answer two additional questions. Now, you've stated that your recollection of the events is hazy because of your head injury?"

"We've been over that a thousand times," Peter blurted out. "Anything he says gets a little asterisk next to it saying, 'may not be accurate due to short-term memory loss caused by head trauma.'"

Haney exhaled. "Duly noted. Now, we are wrapping up our investigation and want to confirm you drove Agent Rivers to the cabin. Is that correct?"

Jack opened his mouth, but Peter spoke. "He assumes he did because it's his car, but that statement 'may not be accurate due to short-term memory loss caused by head trauma.'"

"When you were in the cabin, you can't recall who fired the shots or if anyone else was with you and Agent Rivers at the time?"

Jack nodded.

Peter was about to say something, but Haney beat him to the punch. "But that statement 'may not be accurate due to short-term memory loss caused by head trauma.'"

Jack noticed the corner of Haney's mouth turn up.

Haney looked at Jack. "Thank you for your time, Officer."

After they left, Jack turned to Peter. "Thanks for coming."

"It's what I'm here for." Peter smiled. "Listen, Jack. Cindy thinks there's a chance of you getting reinstated, but between you and me, no. If you want to, you can apply in another county."

"Really? How'd you manage that? Are you sure that email isn't going on my record?"

"It won't. You apply someplace else, and your record's clean. Don't thank me. You have to be the luckiest guy in the world. The whole email database crashed, and the only account they can't recover is yours. What are the chances?"

Zero, unless you factor in Replacement.

"Thanks, Peter."

"I've gotta run. Cindy is waiting in the hall to talk to you. Are you good for another visitor?"

"Sure. Send her in."

Peter's snow pants swished as he walked out of the room, and Cindy breezed in. Jack's face lit up. He couldn't help but smile when Cindy was around.

"Hi, Jack." She walked over and kissed his cheek. "How are you feeling?"

"Fine. Cindy, I really appreciate you coming, but you didn't have to come again."

She held her hand up. "I most certainly did. Poor Alice won't leave your side. This is the first day she's away, and that's because she's doing something for you, too."

Jack rolled his eyes.

"I'm not trying to make you feel guilty, but that's how it is. Don't go getting all down. You'll be out of here in another week."

"Why a week? Doesn't someone else need this bed?"

"Oh, right, those doctors must be a bunch of nitwits wanting to keep you here," she said sarcastically. "After you nearly died—oh, did you know that technically you *were* dead when they brought you in? Collapsed lung, shot. What on earth can those doctors be thinking wanting to keep you in a hospital, of all places?"

"You're laying it on a little thick."

"Am I? Jack, if Marisa's brother hadn't been on Big Blue, you wouldn't be here. Even with his help, you—" She stopped as her eyes welled up and her lip quivered.

"Cindy. I'm good now."

"Sorry," she muttered. "It's just... that was horrible."

She dabbed at her eyes, blew her nose, then reached down and pulled a book from her bag.

Jack lifted his hand. "Hold on. Show me the cover."

She frowned and flipped the paperback around so he could see it. On the cover was a shirtless man with six-pack abs holding a beautiful girl in a flowery dress.

Jack's lip curled up.

"You liked the last one," Cindy said with a grin.

"I didn't."

"You did, too. Besides, I promised Alice I'd spend the afternoon with you, and I will."

"I should have known she put you up to this."

Jack slowly drifted off as Cindy began to read to him.

SHE DIDN'T MAKE IT

Replacement wheeled Jack to the hospital's front exit, but when they reached the doors, he stopped the wheelchair. "I can walk from here."

He stood up, and Replacement frowned. "You heard the doctors; you need to take it easy."

"I've been taking it easy for four weeks. I don't want 'easy' anymore."

They walked through the big double doors, and Jack looked for Replacement's Bug. "Where's your car?"

She shrugged. "I parked around the corner. I'll go get it."

"I can walk."

Her eyes narrowed as she looked him up and down. "Okay." She slid her arm around his waist.

"Have you talked to Marisa?"

"Umm... yeah."

That can't be good.

"Can you elaborate?"

"Well, she said she needed to move."

Jack looked at the sidewalk as they walked.

She's gone.

"She might let us know when she gets settled," he said.

Replacement wrinkled her nose and closed one eye. "I sorta already know."

Jack sighed. "If she didn't tell you, I don't want to know."

"But she did." Replacement let out a little whistle. "I kinda took her there."

"Where?"

"Hope Falls."

Jack's mouth fell open. "You took Marisa to Hope Falls? Really?"

"You're not mad?"

Jack stopped to think for a second. "No. No, I think that's a great idea. Maybe we can call Kristine and see if Marisa can stay there until she finds a place."

"I did. Kristine put Marisa up at the inn. She even let her set up an easel in the widow's walk."

Jack could picture Marisa up there at sunset, painting.

She'll be happy.

"Good job."

Replacement beamed. She took his hand.

"I haven't asked yet, but how's my car?" Jack asked.

Replacement stopped.

Damn.

"Did they tow her to Sully's?"

She nodded but didn't look at him.

"What did he say?"

She looked up, and he knew his Impala hadn't made it.

"Sully said everything was gone. Engine, frame, just everything. The driver's side was the only thing that made it. It was the most protected…" She looked away.

He put his hand on her shoulder, and she spun around and hugged him. Jack's eyes rolled back from the pain, but he tried to mask it. He softly touched her hair.

"You were so hurt," she said. "I remembered you told Ilario to go to the drop at the base of Big Blue, so I ran there as fast as I could. Ilario put a tube in your chest, and there was so much blood. I… They took you to the hospital, but you…" She buried her face in his chest and cried.

A couple walking by gave Jack a pitying look, and he awkwardly smiled. He stroked Replacement's back as she tried to get hold of herself.

She straightened up and wiped her eyes. "I'm sorry."

"It's okay. And thanks." Jack smiled.

"Thanks?" Replacement lifted an eyebrow.

"What am I supposed to say? I'm sorry I almost died and freaked you out?"

"That would be better than 'thanks.'"

Jack laughed. He put his arm around her shoulders, and they started to walk again. When they reached the end of the block, he stumbled slightly.

"Are you okay?" Replacement put her hand on his chest.

"I'm fine. I just got distracted." He pointed to the curb, where a jet-black Charger was parked.

Replacement crossed her hands behind her back and raised herself up on her toes. "Do you like it?"

"Like it? It's my favorite…"

His voice trailed off when she held out her hand and let a set of keys dangle from her fingers.

No way.

No WAY.

His mouth fell open, and she squealed. He grabbed her around the waist.

"Don't pick me up. Don't. Don't," she protested.

He picked her up and spun her around anyway. He knew he'd be sore tonight, but he didn't care.

"Thank you." He looked at her with amazement.

She pushed him toward the driver's side. "Get in. Start *her* up."

She ran over to the passenger side while he slid onto the driver's seat. He rolled his fingers around the steering wheel and looked over the dashboard.

"Wait a second. This is… this is *my* Charger. It's my police car. How?"

"Is that okay?" She knelt on the seat, gazed up at him, and held her breath.

His mouth twitched into a smile. "But how?"

Replacement clapped and wiggled in the seat. "I begged Sully to fix the Impala, and when he couldn't, I knew how bummed out you'd be, and I knew you loved *this* car. Well, they sent this one to Sully's after Murphy crashed it. I only had a little money, but Sully called in some markers. He knew a mechanic and a body guy, so we went there and Sully said, 'I never ask for nothing, but I'm askin' for a favor now.'" Replacement laughed as she imitated his voice. "They said it wasn't as bad as it looked, and Sully got the parts from another Charger."

Jack started the car. The engine's roar turned into a purr. He rubbed the dashboard, and Replacement laughed. He closed his eyes as he gripped the steering wheel. "I don't know how to thank you."

"Thank *me*?" Replacement scoffed. "After everything you do for me?"

"You're always doing stuff for me."

He turned to look at her, and she sat down in her seat. She folded her hands, and he could see her pressing her fingernails into them.

He reached over to place his hand on hers.

She looked down as she spoke. "In the emergency room… I was pretty messed up. Did you know they announce it? They say 'code blue.' I didn't know what it meant. A nurse told me. I sorta pushed into the room and… I saw you. Kiku took me away. She wanted me to know what your last words were."

"She told you?"

"She thought you were dead. We all did." Replacement turned to look at him. Her eyes searched his. "Forget every stupid thing I said. I've loved you since I first saw you, and I don't want another second to go by without letting you know that."

Jack smiled.

Replacement looked down for a few moments, then looked up again. "This is the part where you're supposed to say something back."

He chuckled nervously, but as he gazed at her emerald-green eyes, he knew.

"I love you, too, Alice."

EPILOGUE

The shiny two-seater sports car pulled into the parking lot of the Boar's Butt, and Kiku opened her door. The four guys who had just exited the restaurant stopped dead in their tracks. With three-inch heels, a clingy black dress, and long hair streaming down her back, she was every drunk's fantasy come to life.

They watched as she crossed the parking lot and sauntered up the steps. After exchanging looks, they silently agreed they had left a little too early. They jostled one another as they scrambled back toward the bar.

As Kiku stepped inside, she got a similar reaction from the patrons inside the Boar's Butt. The guys' mouths dropped and the women's eyes narrowed. Saying she was dressed to kill would be an understatement, and so would saying she was drop-dead gorgeous. A faint smile played on her lips as she crossed the floor to the bar.

"Whiskey—neat." Her voice was low, and the two men on either side of her leaned in, drawn like metal to a magnet.

She sipped the drink and waited. Man after man tried to summon the courage to approach her. But like knights trying to draw Excalibur from the stone, each was met with failure. Some she cut down with a look, others with a shake of her head, but each left dejected, and one by one the smiles on the men in the room grew fewer.

Finally, the man she'd been waiting for approached.

Ralph Waller was a beefy man in his late twenties. Divorced and recently fired from his job at a car wash for theft, he had a lot of time on his hands, and most of it he now spent doing one of two things: drinking and hunting. Ralph was a bow hunter, and not a very good one. Drunks usually aren't. Ralph had been deer hunting recently, but there were two things wrong with that. One, it wasn't in season. And two, he'd shot a deer and only wounded it. Ralph, being Ralph, had been too lazy and heartless to chase the deer down, so he'd left it to suffer and die in the woods.

Kiku turned to smile at him.

Ralph practically drooled as he offered to buy her another drink, which she gratefully accepted.

It had only taken Kiku one trip to the local sports store to get the name of the man who hunted around Woodlawn Drive with the bright-red, razor-tipped arrows no regular hunter would use. After that, Ralph's reputation and big mouth had made it easy for her to find him.

She decided she would take her time talking to him tonight. She worked the conversation around to hunting, and she let Ralph brag. She would let him ramble and boast until he confessed his sin.

She raised her glass and drained the shot. Her smile broadened until her red lips revealed her pearly white canines. She bit her bottom lip and leaned closer to him; her foot ran up his leg. "How would you like to go hunting?" she asked. Her voice was loud enough that a man two seats over fell off his stool.

Ralph's chest rose and fell rapidly. He licked his lips, swallowed, and nodded.

Kiku left a twenty on the bar and sauntered toward the door.

Ralph excitedly hopped off the barstool and pounded two men next to him on the back. "I'm going hunting, boys. I've gone and bagged me a hot one."

Kiku held the door open for the eager man, and her eyes gleamed as he raced past her and into the night.

Ralph was right about going hunting, but he was wrong about one thing.

He wasn't the hunter; he was the prey.

THE END

THE DETECTIVE JACK STRATTON
MYSTERY-THRILLER SERIES

The Detective Jack Stratton Mystery-Thriller Series, authored by *Wall Street Journal* bestselling writer Christopher Greyson, has over 5,000 five-star reviews and over one million readers and counting. If you'd love to read another page-turning thriller with mystery, humor, and a dash of romance, pick up the next book in the highly acclaimed series today.

AND THEN SHE WAS GONE

A hometown hero with a heart of gold, Jack Stratton was raised in a whorehouse by his prostitute mother. Jack seemed destined to become another statistic, but now his life has taken a turn for the better. Determined to escape his past, he's headed for a career in law enforcement. When his foster mother asks him to look into a girl's disappearance, Jack quickly gets drawn into a baffling mystery. As Jack digs deeper, everyone becomes a suspect—including himself. Caught between the criminals and the cops, can Jack discover the truth in time to save the girl? Or will he become the next victim?

GIRL JACKED

Guilt has driven a wedge between Jack and the family he loves. When Jack, now a police officer, hears the news that his foster sister Michelle is missing, it cuts straight to his core. The police think she just took off, but Jack knows Michelle would never leave her loved ones behind—like he did. Forced to confront the demons from his past, Jack must take action, find Michelle, and bring her home... or die trying.

JACK KNIFED

Constant nightmares have forced Jack to seek answers about his rough childhood and the dark secrets hidden there. The mystery surrounding Jack's birth father leads Jack to investigate the twenty-seven-year-old murder case in Hope Falls.

JACKS ARE WILD

When Jack's sexy old flame disappears, no one thinks it's suspicious except Jack and one unbalanced witness. Jack feels in his gut that something is wrong. He knows that Marisa has a past, and if it ever caught up with her—it would be deadly. The trail leads him into all sorts of trouble—landing him smack in the middle of an all-out mob war between the Italian Mafia and the Japanese Yakuza.

JACK AND THE GIANT KILLER

Rogue hero Jack Stratton is back in another action-packed, thrilling adventure. While recovering from a gunshot wound, Jack gets a seemingly harmless private investigation job—locate the owner of a lost dog—Jack begrudgingly assists. Little does he know it will place him directly in the crosshairs of a merciless serial killer.

DATA JACK

In this digital age of hackers, spyware, and cyber terrorism—data is more valuable than gold. Thieves plan to steal the keys to the digital kingdom and with this much money at stake, they'll kill for it. Can Jack and Alice (aka Replacement) stop the pack of ruthless criminals before they can *Data Jack?*

JACK OF HEARTS

When his mother and the members of her neighborhood book club ask him to catch the "Orange Blossom Cove Bandit," a small-time thief who's stealing garden gnomes and peace of mind from their quiet retirement community, how can Jack refuse? The peculiar mystery proves to be more than it appears, and things take a deadly turn. Now, Jack finds it's up to him to stop a crazed killer, save his parents, and win the hand of the girl he loves—but if he survives, will it be Jack who ends up with a broken heart?

JACK FROST

Jack has a new assignment: to investigate the suspicious death of a soundman on the hit TV show *Planet Survival.* Jack goes undercover as a security agent where the show is filming on nearby Mount Minuit. Soon trapped on the treacherous peak by a blizzard, a mysterious killer continues to stalk the cast and crew of *Planet Survival.* What started out as a game is now a deadly competition for survival. As the temperature drops and the body count rises, what will get them first? The mountain or the killer?

Hear your favorite characters come to life
in audio versions of the
Detective Jack Stratton Mystery-Thriller Series!
Audio Books now available on Audible!

Novels featuring Jack Stratton in order:
AND THEN SHE WAS GONE
GIRL JACKED
JACK KNIFED
JACKS ARE WILD
JACK AND THE GIANT KILLER
DATA JACK
JACK OF HEARTS
JACK FROST

Psychological Thriller
THE GIRL WHO LIVED

Ten years ago, four people were brutally murdered. One girl lived. As the anniversary of the murders approaches, Faith Winters is released from the psychiatric hospital and yanked back to the last spot on earth she wants to be—her hometown where the slayings took place. Wracked by the lingering echoes of survivor's guilt, Faith spirals into a black hole of alcoholism and wanton self-destruction. Finding no solace at the bottom of a bottle, Faith decides to track down her sister's killer—and then discovers that she's the one being hunted.

Epic Fantasy
PURE OF HEART

Orphaned and alone, rogue-teen Dean Walker has learned how to take care of himself on the rough city streets. Unjustly wanted by the police, he takes refuge within the shadows of the city. When Dean stumbles upon an old man being mugged, he tries to help—only to discover that the victim is anything but helpless and far more than he appears. Together with three friends, he sets out on an epic quest where only the pure of heart will prevail.

INTRODUCING
THE ADVENTURES OF FINN AND ANNIE

A SPECIAL COLLECTION OF MYSTERIES EXCLUSIVELY FOR CHRISTOPHER GREYSON'S LOYAL READERS

Finnian Church chased his boyhood dream of following in his father's law-enforcing footsteps by way of the United States Armed Forces. As soon as he finished his tour of duty, Finn planned to report to the police academy. But the winds of war have a way of changing a man's plans. Finn returned home a decorated war hero, but without a leg. Disillusioned but undaunted, it wasn't long before he discovered a way to keep his ambitions alive and earn a living as an insurance investigator.

Finn finds himself in need of a videographer to document the accident scenes. Into his orderly business and simple life walks Annie Summers. A lovely free spirit and single mother of two, Annie has a physical challenge of her own—she's been completely deaf since childhood.

Finn and Annie find themselves tested and growing in ways they never imagined. Join this unlikely duo as they investigate their way through murder, arson, theft, embezzlement, and maybe even love, seeking to distinguish between truth and lies, scammers and victims.

This FREE special collection of mysteries by *Wall Street Journal* bestselling author CHRISTOPHER GREYSON is available EXCLUSIVELY to loyal readers. Get your FREE first installment ONLY at ChristopherGreyson.com. Become a Preferred Reader to enjoy additional FREE *Adventures of Finn and Annie*, advanced notifications of book releases, and more.

Don't miss out, visit ChristopherGreyson.com and JOIN TODAY!

You could win a brand new
HD KINDLE FIRE TABLET
when you go to
ChristopherGreyson.com
Enter as many times as you'd like.
No purchase necessary.
It's just my way of thanking my loyal readers.

Looking for a mystery series mixed with romantic suspense?
Be sure to check out Katherine Greyson's bestselling series:
EVERYONE KEEPS SECRETS

ACKNOWLEDGMENTS

I would like to thank all the wonderful readers out there. It is you who make the literary world what it is today—a place of dreams filled with tales of adventure! To all of you who have taken Jack and Replacement under your wings and spread the word via social media and who have taken the time to go back and write a great review, I say THANK YOU! Your efforts keep the characters alive and give me the encouragement and time to keep writing. I can't thank YOU enough.

Word of mouth is crucial for any author to succeed. If you enjoyed the series, please consider leaving a review at Amazon, even if it is only a line or two; it would make all the difference and I would appreciate it very much.

I would also like to thank my wife. She's the best wife, mother, and partner in crime any man could have. She is an invaluable content editor and I could not do this without her! My thanks also go out to: my two awesome kids, my dear mother, my family, my fantastic editors—David Gatewood of Lone Trout Editing, Faith Williams of The Atwater Group, and Karen Lawson and Janet Hitchcock of The Proof is in the Reading. My fabulous proofreader—Charlie Wilson of Landmark Editorial. My fabulous consultant Dianne Jones, Kay Bloomberg, the unbelievably helpful beta readers, including Megan Mason and Michael Muir, and the two best kids in the world.

ABOUT THE AUTHOR

My name is Christopher Greyson, and I am a storyteller.

Since I was a little boy, I have dreamt of what mystery was around the next corner, or what quest lay over the hill. If I couldn't find an adventure, one usually found me, and now I weave those tales into my stories. I am blessed to have written the bestselling Detective Jack Stratton Mystery-Thriller Series. The collection includes *And Then She Was GONE, Girl Jacked, Jack Knifed, Jacks Are Wild, Jack and the Giant Killer, Data Jack, Jack of Hearts, Jack Frost,* with *Jack of Diamonds* due later this year. I have also penned the bestselling psychological thriller, *The Girl Who Lived* and a special collection of mysteries, *The Adventures of Finn and Annie.*

My background is an eclectic mix of degrees in theatre, communications, and computer science. Currently I reside in Massachusetts with my lovely wife and two fantastic children. My wife, Katherine Greyson, who is my chief content editor, is an author of her own romance series, *Everyone Keeps Secrets.*

My love for tales of mystery and adventure began with my grandfather, a decorated World War I hero. I will never forget being introduced to his friend, a WWI pilot who flew across the skies at the same time as the feared, legendary Red Baron. My love of reading and storytelling eventually led me to write *Pure of Heart,* a young adult fantasy that I released in 2014.

I love to hear from my readers. Please visit ChristopherGreyson.com, where you can become a preferred reader and enjoy additional FREE *Adventures of Finn and Annie,* advanced notifications of book releases and more! Thank you for reading my novels. I hope my stories have brightened your day.

Sincerely,